Table of Co

The Firstborn of Death

Stories and Poems
Naomi Libicki

Copyright Page

This is a work of fiction. Similarities to real people, places, or events are entirely coincidental.

THE FIRSTBORN OF DEATH: STORIES AND POEMS

Dedication

For Alter, my necessity.

The Firstborn of Death

Elias looked up from his books at the sound of the door, which stuck and scraped against the concrete floor as Saleh opened it. "Welcome," she said, head bowed, eyes modestly downcast.

The social worker, Miss Shkedy, twisted her painted mouth in annoyance for a moment before remembering to smile, a wide grin filled with white teeth, and say, "Good morning."

Saleh spoke Iraqi—or, as Miss Shkedy would have it, Arabic, considering it no different than the language of the local Arabs. Miss Shkedy spoke Hebrew. Miss Shkedy may have been working with the residents of Shabtai for nearly ten years, but she wouldn't learn Iraqi; Saleh, equally stubborn, had raised five children in Israel without picking up more than a few phrases of Hebrew. But Elias knew that they understood each others' basic greetings even as they looked past each other in feigned incomprehension. He wasn't sure if Miss Shkedy knew that it had become by this point a battle of wills.

"She thinks I'm stupid, that woman," Saleh would say after Miss Shkedy's visits were over, scattering chicken feathers or corn husks, or slamming a ball of dough forcefully down into a bowl.

And Elias would hum in agreement, lining up his inks and parchment to scribe an amulet for a neighbor with a sick baby. Saleh had certainly never made any effort to convince Miss Shkedy otherwise. And why should she? Didn't she have enough to do with looking after the children, and keeping the house, and visiting the women of the neighborhood to discover what their problems were, and taking care of them when she could? It was no part of Saleh's duties to make herself understood by Miss Shkedy, but it was part of Miss Shkedy's profession to try to understand Saleh, and as far as Elias could tell, she hadn't.

And also, Elias had not had twenty-five years of happy marriage by arguing with his wife.

"She comes in here with her sandals and her mosquito-bitten legs and thinks I'm useless," Saleh would go on. "I'd like to see her cross the desert hidden in the back of a truck with three children."

The offending sandals, with Miss Shkedy's toenails painted to match her lips, were in evidence today, tracking dirt from outside onto Saleh's carpet. Later, Saleh would take the carpet out back and beat it angrily, but for now she silently fetched the kettle from the kitchen corner and poured tea for Elias and for Miss Shkedy, who sat down without invitation in the chair opposite, where Elias's petitioners would usually sit.

"And a bright morning to you, Miss Shkedy," said Elias. "What can I do for you?"

"I've asked you to call me Ruti." She took a sip of tea and called out, "Thank you, Saleh!" which Saleh pretended not to hear.

"And I've asked you to call me Rabbi Alafi."

"There's no need to be so formal. We've known each other for years," said Miss Shkedy. "Anyway, you don't have your certification."

Anger will cause a sage to lose his wisdom, Elias reminded himself. "I received ordination from the hands of Rabbi Yaakov Mufatzi. I don't need certification from some young Lithuanian flower-of-Torah."

"You do if you want a job with the Rabbinate," Miss Shkedy said with a shrug. "If you don't look for a job, you're going to lose your unemployment benefits."

"Thank God, we get by. Our David works in construction now, and our Gila, of course, gets her salary from the army—"

"And your other children sleep on the floor," Miss Shkedy interrupted. "With a Rabbinate job you could get a three-room in PetachTikvah, leave this slum behind."

"And leave my people behind too?" Elias's voice began to rise despite himself, and Miss Shkedy rocked back in her chair, frowning. "The government promised to build us homes here. Instead, it's nine years, and still no electricity, no sewer... I had a beautiful house in Baghdad, you know, with a lemon tree in the courtyard."

Miss Shkedy pushed her teacup away in disgust and stood. "To hear them tell it, every barefoot beggar had a lemon tree in the courtyard in Baghdad. My family had a townhouse in Budapest too, right on the Danube. If it wasn't destroyed in the war, no doubt some Party official is living there now." She slapped down a pamphlet bound in cheap yellow paper on the table. "There's a rabbinical examination next month, on the 15th of June. I got you the test materials."

After she left, Saleh grimly took up the carpet and carried it out back. Elias examined the yellow pamphlet with distaste. It contained holy texts, so would have to be taken to geniza, rather than simply thrown on the trash heap.

One of the girls had lost her gun on Friday morning, so they all had to stay on base and search until it was found. Then the bus broke down in the middle of the desert, and Gila ended up sitting on her duffel bag, with her gun across her knees, everyone fighting over the few scraps of shade the bus cast by the side of the road. Of course, when the replacement bus got there an hour later, it was already full, so the people who'd been on the first bus had to stand, clinging to the seats for dear life as the bus rattled along the road to Shabtai. After all that, wouldn't it have been too bad if Gila had gotten home after sunset, too late to help with the Shabbat preparations?

No such luck.

The sun was still high in the sky, glaring down at her as the bus spit her out at the edge of town. Gila adjusted her gun and duffel bag and strode down the unpaved paths between shacks, ignoring running, shrieking children, stray cats, and the catcalls of a group of young men clustered outside one of the shacks, smoking cigarettes or nargilas. When she got to her own house, she found her brother Yossi crouched by a circle drawn in the dust with a handful of other schoolboys.

"Lazy donkey, what are you doing playing marbles on Friday afternoon?" said Gila.

Yossi looked up and wrinkled his nose at her. "Mama told me to mind Etti, so there."

And so was little Etti in the circle too, hair in her face, drawing figures in the dust and looking bored.

"Some babysitter. Don't let her eat the marbles."

Etti leapt to her feet, and with a cry of "Gila!" attached herself to Gila's leg like a burr. Gila tried not to hit her with the duffel or the gun as she made her way to the house. The door stuck as usual, and as Gila kicked off her shoes she was hit in the face with a cloud of savory steam, chicken and cinnamon and mint, that reminded her that she hadn't eaten since breakfast at the base.

"Where have you been?" Gila's mother called from the kitchen corner. "I've had no help all day."

"The bus broke down. Yossi doesn't seem very busy." Gila sat on the floor, started to disassemble her gun, and smacked Etti's reaching hand away. Her brother Moshe was sitting at their father's work table, bent over a stack of books. "And Moshe's just reading."

"Moshe's matriculation exams are only a month and a half away. You know that."

Gila's mother bent over to take a tray of stuffed tomatoes out of the oven. Moshe's ears went red and he buried himself deeper into the book he was reading, trying to pretend the argument wasn't happening. Etti grabbed the barrel sleeve of Gila's gun, and Gila smacked her again and grabbed it back.

"Leave it, little flea! It's dangerous," Gila said, and then, to her mother again, "So? Let Moshe go to work when he's finished with school like David and I did. Where is David anyway?"

"He took an extra shift at the building site," Gila's mother said, pressing her lips together in satisfaction as if to say: see, someone is providing for this family.

Someone was trying to get out of housework, more like. Cups with coffee sludge on the bottom littered the floor near the couch where Moshe slept, and some of them were filled with cigarette butts. David had had his friends over again, and who was going to have to clean up after them?

Gila's mother went on, "You're filthy. Go to the washhouse, then you can clean up in here." Of course! "And take Etti."

Gila stowed the pieces of her gun in the clothes chest, and took out a blouse, a flared flower-print skirt, and stockings; a smock in the same flower print for Etti, and a cake of soap from by the sink. She snagged a stuffed tomato from the tray at the same time, and scalded her fingers and the roof of her mouth on it on the way to the women's showers.

When they got there, just Gila's luck, Shoshana Alzem was coming out with dripping hair in a cloud of rose-scented steam. "You used up all the water in the tank again, didn't you," Gila said sourly.

"Shabbat shalom, Gila! How nice to see you! I'm pretty sure there's some left."

Shoshana Alzem had been a filthy liar when she and Gila had been in school together, too.

The water was a trickle, and cold. Etti howled and bit Gila's arm when she washed her hair, but finally Gila managed to get her washed, dressed, and her hair braided. "Go find Yossi, he's supposed to be looking after you," she said afterwards.

The kid was just going to get dirty again, but Gila didn't want her hanging around when she was showering. You knew it was bad when you missed the privacy and luxurious amounts of water of the army showers.

A few minutes to dress, put up her hair and put some color on her lips, and then it was: pick up the mess. Wash the dishes, including the disgusting coffee cups. Collect the week's washing to take to the laundry, which meant going into David's room, one of the two bedrooms that had been built onto the shack in the last few years, and picking up his clothes from every corner where he'd tossed them. They stank of tobacco, and the floor was a minefield of more coffee cups, and a couple of greasy nargilas that also needed to be emptied and washed.

Take the washing to the laundry. "Don't let Mrs. Shama refuse to take the money, her husband hasn't been able to work since that accident with the tractor." And so, a horribly embarrassing argument with Mrs. Shama at the laundry, while Gila awkwardly held out a handful of lira, and Mrs. Shama clutched the amulet that hung around her neck and started crying and telling a rambling anecdote about Gila's father.

Take up the carpet. Beat the carpet. Scrub the floor. Back to the laundry to haul back the sacks of wet washing and hang it out to dry. Meanwhile, in the house, Gila's mother had been cooking steadily the whole time, and there was a new stack of dishes to wash. At some point while Gila was out, Moshe had gone to the showers with Yossi, but he hadn't put away his books, and who had to do that? Oh, guess.

Finally, with the food all cooked and the house as clean as it was going to get and sunset on the way, Gila's mother lit the oil lamps and Gila sank down onto the couch, exhausted.

"Grab the other end of the couch, Julia—"

"Gila," Gila sighed. She'd been Gila since she'd started kindergarten when she was six, and if her mother hadn't gotten it in the past twelve years she was never going to, but Gila kept trying.

"—and help me move it into the corner. Then go ask the Pelechs for their table; we're having company tonight."

Before the afternoon prayer, the men in the synagogue recited the order of the composition of incense: balm, onycha, galbanum, and frankincense—by weight, seventy maneh of each; myrrh, cassia, spikenard and saffron—by weight, sixteen maneh of each; twelve maneh of costus, three maneh of aromatic bark, and nine maneh of cinnamon.

Elias's lips formed the words automatically, but his eyes kept drifting to the door. Moshe stood beside him, eyes half-closed, seemingly lost in prayer. David was late.

It wasn't, God knew, the first time. Elias knew what people said: Rabbi Alafi, a learned man, a pious man, certainly, the best person to ask for a legal opinion or an exorcism; what a shame he was too unworldly to keep his children in line. And maybe he was. A man who took a firmer hand with his son would probably not find himself hoping that he was simply desecrating Shabbat by smoking with his no-good friends.

A few minutes later, with the afternoon prayer concluded and Elias's head bent to the words of the Song of Songs, the corrugated steel door swung open. David, silhouetted against the banded orange sky, slouched in. His hair was full of grease and he'd thrown a white shirt on over his work clothes.

"What?" he muttered under his breath, sliding onto the bench next to Elias. "I'm here."

Elias slid his narrowed eyes over at David and passed him a prayerbook without pausing in his recitation. David flipped through the book, his legs sprawled in front of the bench as if he was sitting on the step and smoking.

As if Elias hadn't been picturing his flayed corpse lying in a sewage ditch, only to be discovered when someone noticed the gathering clouds of flies.

The first such body had been found a month ago, the state of it ensuring that no one knew who it had been when it was alive. The second one, found a week and a half ago, had been identified only because no one had seen Tzvi Shmuel for several days. Terrorists, said the police. A mad killer, maybe. They could spare few men and little time for a nameless vagrant and a man with no family or prospects, who'd spent his days drinking and playing backgammon before they were suddenly cut short.

And so, as the prayers drew to a close, as men kissed their prayerbooks and replaced them in the dented metal cabinet, they turned to Elias. And so, Saleh had been cooking all day for the crowds she knew would gather in their small house and spill out onto their patch of dirt.

Almost half the men followed Elias home from the synagogue, and there were more squeezed into the house, along with their wives and children. Elias said kiddush, blessed the wine and bread, and the people of Shabtai sat in borrowed chairs at borrowed tables while Saleh and Gila handed out borrowed bowls filled with kubbeh soup.

"Rabbi, I need an amulet for Ezra," Toya Bakshi said humbly, as she accepted her torn-off piece of bread. "He travels for work, and every day I'm frightened—"

"Ask me after Shabbat," Elias said. "I'll write for anyone who needs one." According to the law, Elias needed certification from the Rabbinate to scribe amulets, but if the police couldn't be bothered to investigate killings, they certainly wouldn't waste their time with someone who scribed amulets and didn't even accept money in payment, only the occasional chicken or sack of flour.

"It's the Firstborn of Death," Toya's old father put in, slurping soup noisily. "My grandfather told me he heard him once, chasing a man through the streets. Noon time, with the fever-wind blowing, and the sound of running feet, of tearing flesh. He tried to peek through the curtains, he said, but his mother slapped his hand away."

Yosef Hai snorted, tilting his chair back on two legs. He was only here because his mother had dragged him along. "What, you think it's some thing from back in Iraq? And we dragged it all the way across the desert with us?

And it's been living quietly among us all this time, and only now decided to kill?"

"Don't speak so lightly," said Elias. "The ways of demons are strange. Your elders understand these things."

"It's immodesty in women that gives demons sway over the community," Yosef's mother Varda added, narrowing her eyes at Gila as she came around with more soup. "A woman should not carry a man's weapon."

Gila slammed a bowl down in front of Varda, pressed her lips together, and turned away, angry footfalls muffled by the dirt of the yard. Elias watched her until she disappeared into the house.

"I will write amulets for anyone who needs them," he repeated with a sigh. "I have been studying this thing, and I will see what can be done."

The next afternoon, when Gila's father and David and Moshe were at afternoon prayers, Gila's mother went out to visit friends. She tried to get Gila to come with her, but it was obvious that those old gossips didn't want to see Gila anyway.

"Why should I go out?" Gila said, and added, quoting scripture with a curled lip, "All the honor of the king's daughter is within."

For a second she thought her mother was going to slap her, but in the end she just pressed her lips together and said, "Impudent. Keep an eye on Yossi and Etti."

By which Gila understood that her mother knew what her friends thought of Gila as well as Gila did. What was the point of pretending otherwise?

So Gila kept an eye on Yossi and Etti. Along with a gang of Yossi's friends, they pelted from one neighbor's patch of dirt to another, playing some make-believe game, partisans or something. Gila watched them, sitting in one of the borrowed chairs outside that hadn't been returned yet, bored out of her mind.

And when Shoshana Alzem came by with all the old crowd, Leah and Miriam and Tikki and Carmela, of course Gila invited them in. The little fleas were looking after themselves anyway. Gila handed around cups of mud coffee and whatever was left of the cardamom cookies. Tikki turned on the radio.

"Turn that down, do you want the whole neighborhood to hear?" Gila snapped, lunging over with her hands still full of coffee cups to adjust the volume. "Aren't you the one who has an exemption from the army because you're religious?"

"Pfff, are you the military police or the modesty police?" Tikki waved away this objection to her Shabbat-breaking and sang along with the radio, nonsense words in English: "I'll see my girl soon in King-ston town!"

"Forget it, Gila, dance with me," Shoshana said. She stood in the middle of the carpet, shaking her shoulders and hips.

Gila snorted a laugh. "Is that supposed to be a samba?" But she set down her coffee cup and gave an experimental wiggle to the rhythm.

She twirled Shoshana, and Leah caught her. Shoshana twirled Leah and flung her in Carmela's direction, who missed the catch, and Leah landed on the couch. A cup shattered. Miriam dragged Tikki into the dance and in another minute they were all collapsed on the couch, breathless, and Harry Belafonte was replaced with a snooty announcer-voice saying, "The Voice of Israel from Jerusalem, here is the news."

"Ugh," said Tikki, reaching over to shut off the radio.

Gila slapped her hand away. "No, I want to hear it."

The Egyptians were stopping ships in the Suez Canal again. A hiker had been killed by terrorists. "...and in the continuing investigation of the murders in the town of Shabtai in Hevel Lakhish, police are asking anyone with information to contact—"

This time, when Tikki lunged over Gila to turn off the radio, Gila didn't stop her, and she spun the dial with a decisive click, silencing the snooty voice. "Why do you listen to that shit? They don't know anything."

"Here," said Shoshana, pressing something into Gila's hand.

Gila opened her hand to look at it, a palm-sized picture frame, cheap metal and cheaper plastic, stamped into curves and swirls that imitated filigree. Inside the frame, Gila recognized the first few words of Psalm 91. Curiously, she extracted the paper with a fingernail—thin paper, folded and refolded. Printed, not scribed, and the paper that hadn't been visible through the frame was simply blank.

"It's an amulet," Shoshana said reproachfully. "I worry, you know, always taking the bus back and forth to base all by yourself."

"By myself, if only. Then maybe I could get a seat," Gila muttered. But Shoshana was looking at her with big eyes and a pouting lower lip, and she had meant well. Gila sighed and tried to fold the paper back up and shove it into the frame. "Yeah. Thanks."

Gila held the amulet, uncomfortably aware of the sweat of her palm and the edges of the metal, while Carmela talked about how Yosef Hai had a car that he'd bought off a guy he'd known in the army and he was going to take her to the cinema in Kiryat Gat. Leah and Miriam argued about politics, because Leah was going to vote for the Freedom party, and Miriam was going to vote for the Union of North African Immigrants, which, as Leah pointed out, was stupid, because everyone knew they weren't going to get any seats, and anyway Miriam was Iraqi and not North African? Shoshana tried again to teach Gila the steps to the samba, not discouraged by the fact that she herself didn't know them.

Then children started shrieking and howling outside, and Gila said, "O God, I've got to check on my brother and sister."

Gila waded into the cluster of brats and pried apart Yossi and Benny Shamsi, who were rolling around in the dirt pummeling each other. It was harder to loosen Etti's teeth from Eli Bakshi's arm, or his fist from her hair.

"Go on home! Shoo! Animals!" Gila shouted, and neighborhood children scattered in all directions. She ushered Yossi and Etti inside, only pausing to drop Shoshana's amulet in the pocket of her army blazer, hanging on the lines with the rest of the laundry. Yossi's nose dripped blood, and Etti, red-eyed and scowling, wiped away a furious tear. Leah and Miriam and Carmela were already gone by the time they came in, and Shoshana and Tikki quickly made themselves scarce too. Gila handed Yossi a handkerchief, then dragged the old battered backgammon set out of the bookcase and tried to teach Etti the rules until it was too dark to see the pieces.

After Shabbat, before Elias had even finished saying havdalah to mark the beginning of the new work week, the first petitioners arrived. Toya Bakshi, and young Effi Hai with the baby, and more people pushing inside as Elias lit a candle for his work table, got out his parchment and inks. Saleh and Gila, side-by-side, worked through the pile of dishes from Shabbat by the light of more candles in the kitchen corner.

Elias scribed: names of angels and verses of Psalms and invocations in Aramaic, arranged in sacred geometries, each letter tiny and precise. Small enough to be rolled up and tied with a bit of red string and kept in a pocket or amulet case. He wrote each amulet, tied it off, whispered a blessing and kissed it, passed it into the outstretched hand before him, started on the next one. In the background, throughout, the sounds of conversation and the trickle of water.

The crowd thinned. David came in, loud and swaggering, with a couple of his friends, stepping over Yossi and Etti where they'd passed out on the floor. Moshe tucked himself up in the very corner of the couch, holding a book in front of his face like a shield.

"Your father will make amulets for anyone who asks." Once the other noise died down, Elias could hear Saleh's quiet but insistent voice. "You should ask."

"I have an amulet," Gila muttered. "Shoshana Alzem gave it to me."

"Oh, is Shoshana Alzem a trained scribe now? Does she have a mystical knowledge of names?"

Gila snickered, her habitual belligerence swallowed in amusement. Elias handed a completed amulet to Varda Hai, who took it and left with perfunctory thanks, leaving the Alafi family alone for once.

"She didn't scribe it, she bought it," said Gila.

Elias set down his pen, his hands shaking, a growing headache behind his eyes. Anger will cause a sage to lose his wisdom, he reminded himself. "Of course. Only certified, qualified rabbis may sell amulets."

"O God, Abba!" Gila turned away from the sink, throwing up her hands, Elias looked up from his desk, and they met each others' eyes, equally stubborn. Her blouse was wet at the armpits, and her hair likewise soaked with sweat and falling out of its twist, dark circles like thumbprints beneath her eyes. "I know, the Rabbinate disrespects you. The State disrespects you. I know! I hear it every week! What about everyone here? What about the people who push into our house, and eat the food that Imma cooks, and insult your family, why should you spend all night scribing amulets in exchange for what, a bag of tomatoes and a free load of laundry that Imma won't even let me accept? And I should ask you for one too, I'd be ashamed—"

The door opened with the sound of scraping concrete, and Sasson Katan, broad-faced and genial, smelling of the week's first smoke, looked with undisguised interest between Gila and Elias. "I came to ask for an amulet, Rabbi Alafi. Is it a bad time?"

"Knock!" Gila snapped, and pushed through the door behind him.

Elias sighed. "Of course not. Come in, sit, it will be done in a few minutes."

"Abba." Moshe looked over the edge of his book, his eyes wide. "Is it true, what Yosef Hai said? Did we really drag this thing across the desert with us?"

Moshe had only been a baby then. Saleh had fretted so much about keeping him quiet, and he had been quiet ever since, so quiet you forgot he was listening.

"If we did, we will deal with it. Just study, Moshe." And Elias bent his head again to scribe for Sasson Katan, trying to ignore his headache.

Before the amulet was finished, Gila came slinking back. Moshe stood to let her take a mattress from the couch, and she set it on the floor next to Etti's, curled up and slept, or pretended to. It was another hour until the petitioners finally stopped arriving, and longer than that before Elias blew out his candle and went to bed.

Sunday morning. Sunlight fell through the thin curtains, sharp as shrapnel, and Gila threw her arm across her eyes and groaned. Still half asleep, she dragged herself out to the clotheslines, retrieved her uniforms, threw open the clothes-chest, reassembled her gun. Yossi and Etti lay sprawled out on their mattress, skinny arms and legs slack with sleep. No one else was around. Her father and Moshe, presumably, were at prayers. David was likely sleeping in his own room. Her mother—who knew? Visiting neighbors, gathering fenugreek, something. Gila pulled on one uniform, the hard little box of Shoshana's amulet resting against her breast, and shoved the other uniforms into her duffel bag. Shouldered her duffel bag. Stuffed a heel of bread into her mouth, her feet into her shoes.

This early, the streets of Shabtai were deserted. The wind carried an old newspaper past her feet, along with other garbage left uncollected over Shabbat, a cloud of stinking dust, and the heavy clanking sounds of construction vehicles. Gila frowned. At the edge of town, a plume of dust rose into the air. Since when was the government building in Shabtai? It was a temporary accommodation only, they always said, there was no need...

She quickened her pace, gun bouncing against her shoulder at every step, though she couldn't have said what she was apprehensive about. The sounds grew louder, the air thicker, and before she reached the main road with the bus stop, her feet stopped at the edge of a newly-flattened ribbon of earth, curving in a familiar sacred geometry, letters freshly incised into the dirt as the dust settled. She raised her head from the inscription to the plume of dust moving off into the distance, the growling road roller kicking it up.

"David!" she shouted, breaking into a run. "David, what in the hell!"

She was winded, her shoulder feeling bruised, when she caught up with the slow-moving vehicle. It rolled to a stop, and David rested one hairy forearm along the window-well and leaned out towards her. "What?"

"What what?" she retorted, rising up on her toes in a futile attempt to put herself at the same height. "Where did you get a field scriber, that's army ordnance—"

"Are you the military police now? People walk off from bases with stuff all the time, don't be a goody-two-shoes."

"Donkey! You didn't forget you had your scriber in your pocket when you went home for Shabbat!" She kicked the vehicle's retrofitted back cylinder for emphasis. Where a civilian road-roller would have had a smooth cylinder, this one was covered in a grid of lines resembling pen-strokes; the operator could control which ones lay flat against the cylinder and which ones protruded, to spell out different words and names. It wasn't quite as tall as Gila, and weighed easily four times as much. "O God, you're as bad as the old people, like we're back in Iraq, always trying to stay one step ahead of the authorities and find some way around the rules—it's army stuff for a reason! You wore this uniform too! It's us, protecting us."

"And what do you think I'm doing, simpleton?" David wasn't even yelling, that was the infuriating part. He leaned back in the driver's seat, relaxed as if he was smoking a nargila and idly arguing about politics with his friends. "Protecting us. There's this demon, maybe you heard? Flaying people alive?"

"Of course I—" Gila dropped to her haunches, looking at the letters, the curve of the lines. She'd watched her father scribe his amulets over and over again the night before, his eyes dark, his hand only shaking in the moments he set down his pen. "Simpleton yourself! You're doing it backwards—this will keep the demon in, not out."

"Yeah." David's voice was still calm, but it took on a serious edge that Gila seldom heard. "Abba said—we brought it with us, when we came here. It's ours. We can't let it escape."

"The Firstborn of Death. Menahem Bakshi said his grandfather heard it. With the fever-wind blowing, and the sound of running feet—" The wind kicked up a cloud of dust. Gila sat back on her heels and quoted: "He eats the tissues of his flesh; he eats his tissues—the Firstborn of Death. He is torn out of his tent, his safe place; he marches him to the King of Terrors."

David leaned out of the cab of the vehicle, frowning.

"What?" said Gila. "I learned Tanakh in school, just because Abba never taught me Talmud doesn't mean—"

"He'd have taught you! If you'd asked."

"Should I have asked? Does a good daughter—"

"Does a good daughter enlist in the army?" They stared at each other for a few seconds, then David went on with a shrug, "He did try to teach me. It didn't take. Moshe is the one who—Gila. Where's Moshe?"

"What do you mean? He went to synagogue with Abba."

"No, he—"

David turned the key of the road-roller. The engine's idling growl went quiet. And in the distance—the sound of running feet.

He jumped down from the cab and sprinted back along the lines he'd just carved into the earth. Gila, with shorter legs, encumbered with her duffel bag and gun, couldn't keep up; it was all she could do to keep him in sight. The sacred words circled Shabtai like a flower, and it was at the junction of two of the lines that they saw a figure with loose, dust-colored skin, long arms and legs ending in twisted claws, a hanging jaw dripping some liquid that hissed as it hit the dirt. Huge wings with draggled gray feathers grew from its back. Over its bony shoulder it carried a body, Moshe's body, wide eyes staring beneath sleep-cowlicked hair. The air was thick with the smell of sickness, poison, and blood.

The creature turned one way and then another at the junction of the lines. David screamed. Gila couldn't get the breath to. Her legs burned with the strain as she kept running, as David barreled into the thing. Moshe hit the ground with a sickening thud, and it dropped to its haunches, teeth snapping, the sound of tearing flesh loud in the morning quiet. Gila felt a searing pain on her breast, and she reached for her uniform pocket, burning her hand on the ruined amulet, bubbling plastic and corroded metal, thin paper already ash.

She threw it away from her. Unslung her gun, held it steady. One shot at the thing's head. Recoil hit her hard in the chest, but the thing was flung backwards, flames crackling around its head, and she took two more shots at the center of its torso, each one accompanied by a deafening crack, a burst of radiance, the smell of of gunpowder, balm, onycha, galbanum, and frankincense.

The barrel of her gun glowed with curving lines, holy names. The Firstborn of Death wailed, burned, and was consumed, flames licking it to ashes that blew away on the wind.

She jogged the last few steps, fell to her knees beside her brothers. David's face was sliced open, a single cut baring flesh and bone. He shivered in the heat, clutching Moshe to him. Moshe's eyes were open without seeing, breath coming shallowly, strips of torn skin hanging from every part of his body.

"O God, O God." Her stomach churned and she set her gun on the ground with shaking hands. "What do I do?"

David looked at her, and his mouth moved, and nothing she understood came out. But behind his shoulder, a car was pulling over, one of the few cars in Shabtai, the social worker Ruti Shkedy's little buff-colored Studebaker.

Ruti strode out, slamming the driver's door behind her. "What happened? I heard—" she came closer, and she saw, and for a second her face looked like Gila felt: drained, sick, helpless. Then her mouth set in a firm line. "Help me get them into the car. I'll take you to the hospital."

Sasson Katan owned the general store, and the general store had Shabtai's only phone, so it was Sasson Katan who came to tell Elias and Saleh that their three oldest children were in the hospital in Rehovot. Yosef Hai had a car he'd bought off a man he'd known in the army, and Elias and Saleh held onto its rickety, bouncing seats on the drive through the desert to the city. When they arrived at the hospital, Miss Shkedy was there to meet them, to fill out forms and yell at the receptionists at the front desk until they let Elias and Saleh through.

"Thank you," said Elias stiffly. And, after a pause, even more stiffly: "Ruti."

She pursed her painted lips. "No need to thank me. It's my job." An equally long and awkward pause. "Rabbi Alafi."

And so it was. Filling out forms and bullying receptionists on behalf of new immigrants whose grasp of Hebrew was shaky, who were unfamiliar with the customs of the country in which they now lived. Elias might not have needed it, but he was glad not to have to do it himself just now.

A bandage, stained an ugly red, adorned David's face. His speech was slurred, but otherwise he seemed well enough, giving his report to a young policeman with expansive gestures and, Elias was sure, unnecessary flourishes on the truth. Moshe lay in the bed beside him, bandaged from head to foot. The doctors were uncertain how well he would recover, but he would live, which was more than any of the Firstborn of Death's other victims had done. For now, he slept peacefully. Elias left Saleh with the boys and went to find Gila.

She, the doctors said, had been unhurt, except for shock. He found her huddled on a chair in the corridor, her uniform rumpled and blackened at the breast pocket, her gun across her knees, her face streaked with tears. He laid a hand on her head, and she turned her face up to him.

"Abba. I didn't ask you for an amulet."

"I wrote you one anyway."

Her grip tightened on her gun. The holy names he'd incised on its barrel were still faintly visible. "But—" she said, her mouth twisting unhappily. "Isn't it written, a woman should not carry a man's weapon?"

"Have you been listening to Varda Hai? I never do." Elias sat down on the chair next to her. "It's also written, answer not a fool according to his folly. And, God will deliver Sisera into the hands of a woman. Many things are written, Gila, my love."

She sighed and rested her head on his shoulder. "You sound like someone who could pass a rabbinical exam, if he wanted," she said.

"Well." Of course he could. That wasn't the issue. And yet... "Maybe so."

Another One's Treasure

In a land of infinite plenty, you'd be amazed at what people throw out.

I mean, check out these boots. Go on, touch them—feel that? That's genuine leather. I've been wearing them for the last seven years, and except for a couple of scuffs, they're as good as new. Soles, too. I found them, hand to God, just sitting on a bench in a park. Why'd someone throw them out? They weren't the latest fashion, maybe. The people who live there, they don't think like you and me.

There was a fad around that time—they called it "decluttering". It was amazing. Clothes, books, fancy kitchen equipment. Heaps of it piled up outside every building. Well, I didn't have much use for the fancy kitchen stuff, did I? You need a kitchen. But I helped myself to four coats, each bigger than the last, because it gets chilly at night in Paradise, even if it's never quite too cold to sleep out. And I'd sit under a streetlamp, wrapped up in my four coats, and read.

The words they left by the wayside! Stories and histories, cookbooks and travel books and gardening books. How to Fix Your Car's Engine. Fifteen Thinking Exercises to Build Your Brain Power. Good and Evil: How to Recognize Them.

Well, it didn't last. Security caught up with me eventually, and I got the bum's rush to the other side of the gate, flaming revolving sword blocking the way and all.

But even though I left as empty-handed as I came, I still know how to fix an engine. All the maps in the travel books I read are still in my head, and I've been to a fair few of those places since. A wanderer on the face of the earth, same as I ever was.

And maybe I never found the Tree of Life, but I've still got these boots.

Myth

In the riot of Spring's flowers
    Grow the seeds of Spring's destruction
    In the blistering heat
    Of the glance she shares with Summer
    On a lonely forest path

Because brightly colored flowers
    Are Springtime's greatest hustle
    Seducing pollinators
    In a feast of sex and death

And when flowers fall and wither
    Under Summer's scorching fingers
    Like phantom fairy wealth

Then fruit begins to swell
    The seeds hidden underneath

Spring laughs last with her last breath

The Rush of the Rock-Staked Seas

The cranes called in the evening. Bhertis collected fallen feathers. At night, she took crane-shape, spreading her wings and flying along the sky-river. Here and there, the hazel trees on Boar Island showed leaves of yellow or flame-red. The young pigs would be fat, and soon there would be salmon in the stream.

The morning was silent. Chill mist crept in at the doorway. "The cranes have gone," Bhertis told the people.

Gwemdis nodded. For several days, the foragers had been ranging further for oysters, and finding fewer of them. She sealed up her basket of acorn meal while her daughter Melit packed seaweed from the drying-rack, leaving any that was still too wet to travel. Her son Dakru wasn't in their hut.

Bhertis found him with Bhug, shaping spear points. He had grown in the summer like a reed, sharp eyes, quick feet, quick hands. No wonder Bhug wanted him for the hunt.

Bhug grinned when Bhertis told him. His feet were already feeling forest trails, his mouth already tasting meat.

The people struck camp, stretched hides over coracle frames, then packed reed mats and house-poles and storage baskets into them. Each coracle held two adults with paddles, and the children, summer-fat and summer-brown, sat on the bundles. By noon they reached the shallows and disembarked, pulling the coracles through the reeds and up onto shore, to their winter camp beneath the birches. It was a long pull. The shallows had risen to wash the bases of the trees of last fall's campground. They had to make this year's further inland.

The children trampled the summer's growth at the camp while the hunters turned coracle-frames back into roofs and foragers cut bundles of reeds for thatch. Bhertis went down to the river to gather yellow pigment-stones. The spring floods had brought fewer of them this year, but there were enough. She ground the stones, collected her urine in a bowl, mixed the pigment, and marked the white birches of the campsite with her hand-prints, showing any who might approach that this was the place of Bhertis' people.

As she worked, she felt herself watched from between the trees and among the undergrowth, but when she turned she was too slow to catch the watcher. This continued as she ringed the camp, until rustling leaves betrayed a position. She shied a stone at it and out of the leaves tumbled Dakru.

Bhertis made her face grim. "Shirker, go back to your work."

He scampered off, grinning as if he saw the lie in her face. Sharp eyes, quick feet. She had spied on the mysteries too as a girl.

The evening's meal was acorn cakes with seaweed. Tomorrow would be soon enough for hunting. By smoke and twilight, Bhertis called the names of the boar people and their mothers' names, spoke their beginning and their end.

The next morning Bhug led the hunters out, Dakru clutching his new-carved spear. Gwemdis and the other foragers took the meandering forest ways, up the hill or down the stream, to gather acorns and hazelnuts, blackberries and mushrooms. Bhertis mixed red pigment from her stores and painted strength on Melit's breasts and thighs, protection on her belly, for the growing baby. And Dakru came running back from the forest, unbloodied spear in his hand, and said, "Come see."

He led her from the sun-dappled shade of the birches to the deeper cool under oak and hazel. The hunters clustered around the broken growth of a boar-trail. The smell of blood and viscera still hung in the air, perhaps a day stale. Black flies buzzed around the scraps. There had been a hunt here indeed, but not of Bhertis' people.

Bhertis knelt, touched the blood-soaked dirt, brought it to her mouth to taste. Fall after fall, the boar people had given themselves to Bhertis' people. Who else knew their names, and their mothers' names?

Whoever it was had left little behind. Bloody dirt and guts and the snapped-off bone point of a spear. The strangers' hunting party had left a trail where they'd carried their kill away, and Bhertis and the hunters followed it until it crossed another boar-track.

They found no boar that day. Dakru brought down a moorhen with a slung stone, and Rughis brought down another, and Bhug speared a catfish. Even with hazelnuts and blackberries, it was thin eating for Bhertis' people.

There would be no more acorn meal until a month in the river had leached the bitterness from the nuts that Gwemdis and Melit had gathered that day.

Bhertis ate the birds' livers, for wisdom. She collected their feathers, for flight.

In the night, she took moorhen-shape, and stalked with broad feet through the shallows, swam up towards the source of the river, seeking the boar people or the strangers who had called and killed them. On the riverbank she spotted an enormous sow, with a flame-colored crest of fur on her head, running down in a mane of stiff bristles between her shoulders.

Before Bhertis could call to her, the sow charged, churning up the mud of the river. Bhertis backed up, beating her wings, but there was no time to take to the air before the sow's tusks pierced her breast, and she fell awake in her hut with aching ribs.

"Any sign?" Bhug asked her in the morning.

"Bad," Bhertis answered.

Bhug shrugged and led the hunters out. If the signs were good, or if the signs were bad, Bhertis' people needed to eat in the winter.

Bhertis joined Gwemdis and Melit and the other foragers. They chatted as they left the camp, but even the children grew quiet and drew closer to their parents when they passed the circle of trees Bhertis had marked.

Weyho had a taste for mushrooms, and an eye for them. Bhertis followed him. He brushed leaves aside from the shy brown caps of boletes, and pretended not to see a patch of yellow chanterelles so his small daughter could discover them. Bhertis found a single amanita the size of her palm, a few white flecks clinging to its red cap. She tucked it into the folds of her cape, to be kept warm next to her heart.

When the hunters returned to camp, Rughis carried a young tusker slung across her shoulders, and Dakru and Tetko carried Bhug between them. Dakru, on Bhug's right side, was splashed with the blood that flowed from his armpit and ribs.

Weyho and Melit went to help the other hunters with the butchering and cooking, and Dakru and Tetko laid Bhug in his hut while Bhertis made a plaster of mud and ash and red pigment. Dakru hovered by Bhertis' shoulder, and she shooed him away with, "Go wash."

When he returned, clean, Bhertis let him help apply the mixture to Bhug's wounded side. Bhug gripped Bhertis' hand and said, "Bad luck."

Bhertis nodded, tight-lipped.

When the boar was cooked, Weyho offered the first slice to Bhug. He turned his face away. Rughis had to eat it. She looked like it might choke her.

Twilight and smoke. Bhertis said to Dakru, "Find me the strangers' trail."

Quick feet, sharp eyes, and Bhertis was growing old. Dakru led the way through the boar-tracks, under the oaks, up a rocky hill where the trees thinned out. The wind carried smoke from a strange camp, the smell of roast boar, and the sound of a strange call. Like a bird's call, like a woman singing, but not.

As they got closer, they crawled on bellies and elbows until they came to a place where they could see the strangers' camp, and not be seen.

Bhertis counted. Twenty of them, perhaps. Fewer than Bhertis' people. Not much fewer. And perhaps more she hadn't seen. Broad shoulders, broad bodies, thick brows, short arms and legs. Heavy-foot people. One of them, a woman with hair the color of a flame, sat cross-legged on a flat stone a little away from the fire, playing a flute.

Bhertis touched Dakru on the arm, and they crept back the way they'd come.

Under the dark of the oaks, Dakru said, "We will come back with our spears, and we will fight them."

"Stupid," said Bhertis. "Their hunters will die, and our hunters will die, and neither people will live through the winter."

"Then what?" said Dakru.

"I will fight. I and the flame-haired wise woman. We have already begun."

Bhertis and Dakru returned to camp. The sky-river spilled bright across the sky.

Bhertis had the lore from Nisdos. Nisdos had the lore from Speks. Speks had the lore from Wodr. Wodr had the lore from Wehitis. Wehitis had the lore from Helem. Helem had the lore from Lokus. Lokus had the lore from Medhu. Medhu had the lore from Doru. Doru had the lore from Hesth. Hesth had the lore from Kleyteh. Kleyteh had the lore from Dehtis. Dehtis had the lore from Mori. Mori had the lore from Hekmo. Hekmo had the lore from Waylos.

When Waylos spoke for the people, the islands had been hills, the shallows broad plains, and the deep channels rivers running through them. Waylos' people had followed the deer, season after season across the grasslands. If Waylos had met a wise woman of the heavy-foot people in those days, they might have traded, red pigment for a bone flute.

The sea had rushed in, season after season. Bhertis had seen deer as a girl. Not for years now. There could be no trade, nor each people skirting past the other, each making its own way. Bhertis had claimed these woods, and she would keep them.

She took the mushroom out of the folds of her cape, warm from her skin. Bit, chewed, spat. Swallowed bitter saliva, and sat watching the stars until her vision lurched like a coracle on choppy waters. The sky-river flowed and churned.

She took mushroom shape. Far beneath the earth, countless fingers fine as hairs. Touching all, calling all, speaking the name of every tree on Boar Island. Waiting for the fall rains to burst forth from the soil, succulent, irresistible, poisoned.

A sow, her crest flame-red, came snuffling through the undergrowth. Devoured, Bhertis was victorious.

She woke late in the morning with a throbbing head. Bhug, clear-eyed and grumbling, sat in his hut working a new spear-point. His right hand had strength to grip, but his arm wouldn't move far and the work tired him quickly.

Mist and drizzle settled over the camp. Rughis led a few of the hunters out to try and spear fish or birds. Gwemdis and Weyho and the children went out to forage while Melit and the others worked on preparing what was left of the boar, nuts, and mushrooms. After checking on Bhug and painting fresh strength on Melit, Bhertis took her headache along the forest trail Dakru had shown her the night before, to see what her night's work had done.

There was little activity in the strangers' camp. Most of them seemed to be under shelter. But Bhertis smelled foulness and sick even from her hiding place above the camp.

Well. Good.

The flame-haired wise woman ducked out from under a roof and peered up through the rain as though she knew Bhertis was there. Perhaps she did, even if she couldn't see her. Bhertis backed away slowly and returned to her own camp.

That night, in mushroom shape, Bhertis sent her fingers questing through the soil, asking the trees for news. The forest was oddly silent. There was no sign of the other wise woman.

The earth slid and shifted, severing Bhertis' fingers. She gasped in pain, a useless scattering of spores. Blinded, sundered, diminished with every shift of the soil—the other wise woman was the earth itself. Unable to speak with the trees or feed from them, Bhertis' caps dried out, rotted and ran.

The next day, Weyho returned to camp white-faced and red-eyed. He had found Gwemdis' body in the river. He could not raise her alone.

Bhertis went with the others to help. Rughis stayed behind and held Melit as she wept. Dakru could not be prevented from coming along.

Gwemdis had, it seemed, been going to check on her baskets of acorns in the river when the earth of the bank gave way beneath her. If she had not died instantly, she had been unable to extricate herself from the rocks and roots where she fell. If she had called for help, no one had heard.

They retrieved her body and carried her body back to camp in silence. Bhertis mixed red pigment and painted Gwemdis' body while the others dug a grave. Away from the soggy ground of the shallows, not too close to the camp, but still within the circle of Bhertis' hand prints. Even Bhug helped dig, though his side was still stiff.

They lowered her into the grave. Melit put her shell-bead necklace on her mother's chest, and Bhertis added the long moorhen feathers she'd saved, so that Gewmdis might fly to the sky river. Dakru placed his new spear in the grave.

"You will need that," Bhertis said sharply.

Dakru's eyes burned like embers in the ashes. "No. I will not."

"Bhug is injured," said Bhretis, "And Rughis leads the hunt now, and—"

"And my mother is dead, and there is no one else with forage wisdom to match hers, and how will we feed our people in the winter?" Dakru finished for her. "And if you die in this fight with the wise woman of the heavy-foot people? Whose people will we be then?"

Bhertis dipped her head in acknowledgment. "Dakru's. You will be Dakru's people. I will give you the lore." Then she beckoned Dakru to follow. "Let the others cover Gwemdis over. You and I have work."

She led him to the edge of the shallows, where she shed her cape, and, after a moment, he did as well. As she waded through the reeds, she said: "I had the lore from Nisdos. Nisdos had the lore from Speks. Speks had the lore from Wodr. Wodr had the lore from Wehitis. Wehitis had the lore from Helem. Helem had the lore from Lokus. Lokus had the lore from Medhu. Medhu had the lore from Doru. Doru had the lore from Hesth. Hesth had the lore from Kleyteh. Kleyteh had the lore from Dehtis. Dehtis had the lore from Mori. Mori had the lore from Hekmo. Hekmo had the lore from Waylos. Now I give the lore to you. Say it."

It took Dakru several repetitions before he had the sequence of names. By that time, the open water lapped the tops of Bhertis' thighs, and Dakru's waist. He didn't yet have his full growth.

If Bhertis fell in battle with the flame-haired wise woman—they had so little time.

Bhertis said, "The names of water: sea, river, wave, shallows, channel, aquifer, rain. The mothers' names of water: cloud, snow, ice, spring. Call them."

Dakru called, and ripples broke against Bhertis' skin. "Listen to the water," she said. "Taste its spray in the air, its salt on your tongue. Move with it. You have a man's spirit, and a man's shape. To change your shape, you must release your hold on the one you have."

He didn't have the knowing of it yet. There was only so much she could give him, so fast. She left him behind as she dissolved into water-shape.

Bhertis, in water-shape, touched the other wise woman, in earth-shape. She lapped her shores, seeped into her cracks, sunk into her surface. If the other wise woman was solid and enduring, Bhertis was formless, shifting, patient. Season after season, the sea rushed in, making shallows out of plains, islands out of hills. Time after time, Bhertis rushed in and then retreated, wearing the other's banks away until they crumbled.

Bhertis' sleeping mat was soaked when she woke, her hair wet and matted, her lips caked with salt. Dakru—who must have led her woman-shape back to her hut—sat on his heels, watching her with wide eyes.

"Did you win?" he said.

"Come," Bhertis answered. "We'll see."

The rest of the people still slept. The morning star burned through the mist, and Bhertis and Dakru climbed the hill that overlooked the camp of the heavy-foot people.

The camp was struck. The people carried children on their shoulders and hips, bundles on their backs. The flame-haired wise woman walked in front, into the shallows. Her people followed her.

They had no boats. But they must have come to Boar Island somehow. Did they know a secret way through the shallows? Could they swim? They walked, and the water rose higher around them, and the mist swallowed them from view.

Bhertis dug her fingers into the soil, tiny pebbles biting beneath the nails. Dakru let out a victorious whoop.

"Be silent," Bhertis chided him. "Have respect. And learn this: nothing is ever over."

By the time they returned to camp, it was empty. Bhertis showed Dakru the place in the river where the yellow pigment rocks washed up, and renewed the handprints that had washed off in the rain. She taught him the names and mothers' names of many things. She told him of the days of Nisdos, of Helem, of Dehtis, of Waylos. She drew him a deer in the earth. He had never seen one.

Rhugis and the hunters returned with a full-grown tusker. Bhug, though still stiff, helped carry it. Weyho had a basket full of mushrooms and Melit had found honey. The people feasted and had left over, to store up for the winter.

Evening fell. The days were growing shorter. Moorhens called and Bhertis gathered feathers. She took flight along the sky-river.

Islands spread out below her, breaking through water like new growth through frost. Beyond the islands, open sea. Nowhere could she find track or trail of the other wise woman, or her people.

Beyond the open sea, land. Land such as Waylos might have known, wide, endless, heaped up in great cliffs at the edge of the water.

The flame-haired wise woman, in rock-shape, fell into the sea.

She fell, and fell, and fell, and the force of it knocked Bhertis backwards through the sky. And the water rose up, and up, and up.

The name of water: wave. The mother's name of wave: rock-fall.

And the force of it knocked Bhertis awake in her hut, and she grabbed Dakru's arm and she said, "The coracles—"

She had time to stagger out of her hut. The shallows, by moonlight, were broad plains, such as Waylos might have known. The air was filled with a roar. And down by the deeper channel, the water heaped up in a great cliff, driving closer.

When the wave hit, it dragged Bhertis under. She reached for Dakru, for Melit, for Bhug, for her people, but the water swept them away. Her bones snapped. Her sight went dark.

The islands were washed clean.

Girls' Night

"Cinderella," said her stepmother, "you *shall* go to the ball!"

"Oh, goody," Cinderella grumbled.

"Now, don't be like that," said her stepmother. "We can't all expect to catch the prince, but I'm sure there will be some nice marquises and baronets who'd look your way—if only you'd smile a bit more."

"What are you wearing? Do you want to borrow something of mine?" said her first stepsister, tearing through the wardrobe with an alarming glint in her eye. "The purple one would probably fit you, I guess... or, oh! There's this blue one! It's kind of boob-tastic, but at least no one will notice your butt, am I right?"

"What's wrong with my..." Cinderella started, but her first stepsister had already dashed off, leaving Cinderella with a double armful of frothy ballgowns.

"Oh lord! You can't do your hair like that!" Her second stepsister shoved her into a chair in front of the vanity table, and started taking a bewildering variety of instruments from the drawers. Smoke was coming out of one of them. "If only you'd used that avocado mask like I told you to—but we'll do what we can."

"Ow!" said Cinderella, as her second stepsister jabbed at her head with a pin.

"Don't be a baby," said her second stepsister. "And do me a favor and dance with Count Robert, won't you? Maybe if you step on his feet hard enough he'll have to go home, and he won't be trying to grope me all night." From somewhere in her décolletage, a synthesized voice began to sing that partying was fun, and that everyone was looking forward to the weekend. "I've got to take this—don't you dare move for the next ten minutes, or it won't set up right."

Her second stepsister swept out of the room in a cloud of cellphone chatter, and Cinderella stared at herself in the mirror glumly, wondering if she could get all those pins out by herself. In a corner of the room, the air shimmered and sparkled and chimed with the sound of tiny silver bells. Cinderella leapt up and got a scorch from the curling iron.

"What's wrong, love?" said her fairy godmother.

Cinderella scrubbed at her face and tried not to sniffle. "I don't... I don't want to go to the ball."

"Is that all," said her fairy godmother. She marched to the door and called out into the hallway, "Cinderella can't come! She has swine flu! And E. coli!"

"Oh, but..." her stepmother's voice protested.

"You don't want the Health Police in here, do you?" said her fairy godmother. The sounds of bustling and excited preparations continued for a few minutes, and then the household descended into unaccustomed quiet.

"There," said her fairy godmother. She waved her magic wand, and Cinderella was dressed in pajamas, with her hair down from its elaborate style. There was a bowl of popcorn and two mugs of hot chocolate on the bedside table, and the mirror on the vanity had been replaced with a 65-inch flatscreen monitor. "I happen to know of a site where they've leaked some scenes from next season's *Game of Thrones*." She grabbed the bowl of popcorn and sat down on the bed.

Cinderella sat down next to her. "Awesome," she said, and took a long sip of her hot chocolate. On the screen, Peter Dinklage was running someone through with a longsword. It was going to be a good night.

The Treasures Beneath the Earth

Soft as summer rain, sweet as burnt sugar, harsh as the last breath I ever took, a trickle of rum touches my lips. Rum, and blood, and saltwater tears.

I died with a pick in my hands and a shackle on my leg, in a chain of men down underneath the earth when the mine fell in. Now I take my pick and dig my way up, following the taste of rum and the smell of blood through the rocks and dirt like we used to follow veins of coal, and the shackle on my leg jerks as the men on the other side of me do the same.

The earth gives way before us, and we stand on the hillside in the dawn light and the free air. Ten dead men, picks in hand, legs chained together. No stone or monument to mark our resting place. Just a woman, arms and bare legs caked with dirt. A kitchen knife and a bottle of rum in the pockets of her apron, and her eyes red with tears.

Larsi, I want to say, but my lungs were crushed in the cave-in, and I can't shape air into words anymore.

"Syrem?" It's as if she's echoing my thought, the way we used to say what the other one was thinking when I was alive, the way she'd answer a question before I asked it aloud.

But now her eyes travel over me, looking from one dead man to another. We all look alike now, and I can't speak to tell her who I am, or step out of the line with my leg in shackles. After one last searching look, she turns away, dabs her lower lip with mud and whatever else is on her hand, and spreads her arms out, palms down, in supplication to the gods below.

"Thank you for accepting what I've paid, and what I will pay. Thank you for what you've given me." Her voice is rough with tears, and dull, with none of the strained hope it held when she said my name. What does she have to hope for? She's paid in rum and tears and blood, and now she has ten dead men, and a pile of debt to the gods below that she'll never dig her way out of alive. Softly, she finishes her prayer: "Your will be done."

We stride forward in step, picks shouldered, chains clanking. It's through no will of mine, but I know where we're going: it's the same weary walk we used to make every night, from the mine entrance to the holding pens, behind the stakewall, in the shadow of the courthouse. Larsi walks behind us. I can't turn my head to see her, but I hear her footfalls, soft against earth and stone.

We come within sight of the stakewall. The guard at the gate shouts, fires at us. More guards come running, more bullets fly. I take one in the gut, one in the shoulder. The only thing I feel is a bit of force, pushing me backwards. Not enough to slow our advance.

Our picks, made for chipping away at stone, tear through wood easily. Flesh is even easier. We step over the wreckage of the stakewall and guards alike. One guard flees, and whatever force is drawing us onward doesn't care, but Larsi won't let him escape—I hear her full-throated scream, the sucking sound of a knife in flesh, of breath driven from lungs, and then a thud as one more body hits the earth.

We break the locks on the holding pens as we go. The men within run from us, chains clanking, and no one stops them, not Larsi, not the slaughtered guards. It's hard to feel anything with dead flesh, when a bullet is no more than a gentle shove, but I think I'm glad.

The courthouse looms ahead, tall and imposing above the holding pens and the wreckage of the stakewall. Where I was once dragged before the magistrate, where the priest condemned me to hard labor in the name of the gods below, where the mine foreman counted the profits that flowed like rum, like tears or blood, while I and my fellow-prisoners worked beneath the earth.

Slate roof. Fresh paint. Stout wooden doors and guards with braid on their jackets—we break them all with the picks in our hands, and pass inside. We come to the courtroom, its desk piled high with ledgers, because it's also the mine foreman's office. Behind the desk, a shrine with the statue of the deep goddess, the queen beneath the earth. This is also her temple. In the doorway, the magistrate, the mine foreman, the priest—the man who is all three at once—seeing his guards cut down, he empties his own gun, then lets it fall, spent, and tries to hide behind his desk. Larsi shouts, grabs him by the shirtfront. Her knife flashes, falls, as he tries to wrench himself from her grasp. Blood splashes the statue of the deep goddess.

The floorboards buckle and twist. The floor splits, and a woman rises from the earth, black as the veins of coal, with a weight to her that's more than human.

"Goddess!" the foreman calls. "Destroy them!"

No stirring of air, but only silence, when the goddess speaks. I feel the shape of her words in my dead bones. **Are you my servant?** she asks the foreman. **Or am I yours?**

He opens his mouth, and his lips move, but no sound comes out.

You cannot speak lies in my presence. Have you nothing else to say?

Nothing. Only a scowl of wordless fury at Larsi, at the goddess, at the men he condemned to work and to die. Only the wrath of a man who took whatever he wanted, did whatever he liked, now caught in the grip of a will greater than his own.

The goddess sits herself on his desk, the shadows gathering around her. **This is my house,** she says. **You handed down false judgments in my name, and took my treasures, which were not yours to take. But you are mine, and now you return to me.**

She reaches out to the foreman, and he makes one convulsive movement, as if he could escape her, before his flesh dries on his bones, and his bones crumble to black coal dust, falling softly to the floor.

Then the goddess turns to Larsi. **I have given you my treasures, as you asked,** she says. **Now return me my due.**

Larsi kneels at the goddess's feet. Fresh tears mix with dried earth, with rum and blood, as she bows her head and says, "Your will be done."

I want to throw myself between them, but my body doesn't answer my will. The most I can do is rattle a chain. The goddess reaches for me, touches my lower lip with her fingertips, coal dust and mud on dead flesh, and my dead lungs fill with air.

Speak, she tells me.

"The man who used to sit there," I say, my voice weak and reedy. "He handed down false judgments, and took what wasn't his to take. Will you do the same?"

Anger gathers around her like shadows, and her eyes glow with coal fires. **What is not mine to take?** she asks. **What is not mine?**

I can't speak lies in her presence. "Nothing. I'm yours, and so is Larsi, and the guards and the prisoners and all. The beams of this house, and the coal dug out of the ground—it burns, and then it's gone, and it comes back to you. Everything comes back to you in time. So what did Larsi take, that she's got to pay you for? What can anyone take?"

You yourself said it, she answers. **What is taken is time. What is taken is mine.**

"Then... I did my time, down under the earth. When he handed down judgment in your name, when the air was crushed from my lungs, it was taken from me. Can't we call it even?"

Larsi rushes over, throws her arms around my cold, torn flesh. "Don't, Syrem. I knew the price," she whispers in my ear. "I never meant to go on without you. I don't want to."

I hold her, looking over her shoulder to the goddess.

We are not even, the goddess says. **You are mine. And I will collect my due. In time.**

"Yes," I say. I drop my head and tuck it into Larsi's shoulder. She smells like sweat, like freshly turned earth, like the sun-warmed peaches we used to share before the magistrate's men rounded me up.

I don't see the goddess return to earth, but she has a weight to her that's more than human, and I know when she's gone. On either side of me, I feel the pull of chains, hear the rattle of men taking their first breath in years. And I hold onto Larsi, warm and living, and I don't mean to let go for whatever time we've got left.

The Waxing Moon and the Waning Moon

In the old, old days, when the world was still wet with the waters of the flood as a newborn child is wet with the waters of the womb—before men left their footprints upon it—the earth bore the sky two daughters: Nilu, the waxing moon, and Linami, the waning moon. Their mother gave them each two mantles, one of light and one of darkness, so that they might wear one while they washed the other, and their father gave them each two weeks of every month to rule the night sky.

In those days Nilu and Linami played together in their mother's garden, splashing each other while they beat their mantles clean against the rocks of the stream, climbing trees and eating their fruit, combing each others' hair and piling it up in braids and curls.

But as month followed month, the feeling between them soured. At full moon, Nilu would say to herself: "Why should I give way to my sister?" And she would grow red with rage.

And at moon-dark, Linami would say to herself: "Why should I give way to my sister?" And she would hide her face in her mantle of darkness and weep.

Then came the days of men, the children of flint and fire. They danced and beat drums for the moon's waxing and left bright stems of hollyhock on Nilu's altars, and snake-speakers would tell their petitioners: "Begin a journey while the moon is waxing, and it will surely prosper, but if you begin it while the moon wanes, it will fail."

And Linami said to herself in bitterness: "The men love Nilu best."

But when the moon waned, the men played soft music on flutes and left garlands of poppies and lilies on Linami's altars, and the snake-speakers told their petitioners: "Broach your amphora of wine while the moon is waning, and it will taste sweet, but if you broach it while the moon is waxing it will surely be sour."

And Nilu said to herself in bitterness: "The men love Linami best." So the love that had been between them turned to hatred.

In those later days, when the paths between the world of men and the world of gods were already beginning to be overgrown with disuse, a shepherd lived in the dark wild hills. The milk of his ewes was the richest, and their wool the thickest, and the meat of his lambs the sweetest, and every year his flock increased. And soon he had in trade not only grain and wine to see his family through the winter, but silver as well: first a little, and then much.

This shepherd had a son, whose name was Sulesh. Sulesh had followed his father's flocks from the time he could walk until he was a youth almost grown—and a handsome youth, with long, strong arms and legs browned by the sun, and dark hair tumbling over his shoulders as a caper bush tumbles over a wall. He loved wandering the hills with the sun on his face and the wind at his back, and a cup of wine from a new-broached amphora, and the company of young men and women, but best of all he loved to sing. His voice was sweet and clear, and when he sat by his father's flocks and accompanied himself on his lyre, anyone who passed would lay down their burdens and stop to hear him.

Sulesh's father, seeing this, and having some silver, said to himself: "Why should I not send my son to the city, that he might learn to be a poet? Then I will have not only the finest flocks, and the best woolen embroidery, and wine and grain and silver beside, but also a name that will be heard from the hills to the farthest islands."

So he gave Sulesh some of his silver, and sent him down to the city to learn to be a poet.

But in the city, Sulesh still loved a cup of wine from a new-broached amphora and the company of young men and women, and he learned to enjoy dice as well, but trying to memorize epic poems made his head hurt. And soon enough he returned to the hills with his father's money spent, and nothing to show for it but a few new drinking songs he'd learned.

His father was angry, but it was not Sulesh's way to quarrel, and it was not his father's way to let his son go hungry, whatever he had done. So Sulesh returned to following the flocks. And in his short time in the city, he had grown yet more handsome, and his voice had grown deep and rich, so that it was not just the young men and women who stopped to listen and to look, but even the waxing moon, Nilu, and the waning moon, Linami.

And one evening, after the sun had set but before full dark, as the new moon was rising over the hills, Nilu herself came to the grove where Sulesh was singing and playing his lyre.

Three nights they lay together in the grove, and Nilu loved Sulesh as only a goddess can love. Her hands and mouth were hot, and her hair was flames, and she drew him into her as one draws a partner into a wild dance. And on the third night Nilu said to Sulesh: "Tell me, O man, whom do you love best?"

Sulesh said: "You." And Nilu was well pleased.

Some weeks later, while Sulesh was singing and playing his lyre in the grove, and the gibbous moon was rising over the hills, Linami herself came to listen to him, to look and to love. Her touch was like the cool breeze off the sea, and the taste of her skin was like wine. Three nights they lay together in the grove, and on the third night Linami said: "O child of flint and fire, whom do you love best?"

Sulseh said: "You." Linami was well pleased, and Sulesh, too, was happy.

But his happiness could not last, for some months later, as the full moon was rising over the hills, Linami set out in search of her sister, for it was time for Nilu to give way in the night sky. And she found her lying in the grove with Sulesh, and she hid her face in her mantle of light and wept.

Nilu, seeing her sister's tears and understanding the reason for them, grew red with rage, and she said: "O greedy man, you said you loved me best!"

Sulesh said: "I do. Your mouth and hands are hot, and your hair is fire; how could I love anyone any better?"

Linami wept all the more, and between her sobs she said: "Faithless child of flint and fire! You said you loved me best!"

And Sulesh said: "I do. Your touch is like the breeze off the ocean, and how could I love anyone better?"

Nilu stood, and shook out her flaming hair, and wrapped her mantle of light around herself, saying: "O Sulesh, from the day man first set his footprints upon the world until today, I have never known any as foolhardy as you. How dare you trifle with the affections of two goddesses, who could crush you beneath their heels as you would crush a grasshopper?"

And Sulesh said: "It has never been my way to refuse the blessings of the gods when they are given, but to accept them with an open hand and a grateful heart."

Linami dried her eyes on the corner of her mantle, saying: "And never to count the consequences?"

Sulesh bowed his head and said nothing, for it was true.

Nilu, red with rage, said: "Then hear my judgment: for the deceitful flatteries your tongue has spoken, let it never speak again, but be still as stone."

And Linami, white with grief, said: "And for the tears you have caused me, let your own tears flow unceasingly."

And for once the sisters were united, not in play as they had once been in their mother's garden long ago, but in bitterness against their lover who had proven false. And Nilu gave way, and Linami took her place as ruler of the night sky, but of Sulesh there was nothing left but a tumble of stones on the hillside by the grove, and a spring pouring unceasingly through them.

Now Sulesh could not go wandering through the hills, or drink wine, or spend time in the company of young men and women. Nor could he sing, and his lyre lay useless, broken among the stones and being worn away by the water. His father found it one day, as he went searching the hills for Sulesh, and he sat by the spring and wept, and regretted that his last words to his son had been words of anger.

And Sulesh could not embrace his father, and tell him that he, too, was sorry that he had squandered his father's money and hopes, and that he loved him and always had. As often as Sulesh's father came to the grove, Sulesh tried to speak words of comfort to him, but his tongue was still, and his only voice the tumble of water over stones.

Month followed month, and year followed year, and Sulesh's father came no more to the grove, for he walked the dark paths of the underworld instead. And that was a mystery Sulesh would never learn, as he had failed to learn the epic poems when he had gone to the city. So the first songs he sang with his new voice were songs of grief and regret.

But his sorrow could not last, for he still felt the sun and the wind in the hills he had loved as a youth, and he loved them still. And what he should have regretted most of all he found he could not: the movements of Nilu, that were like a dance, and the taste of Linami, that was like wine. Indeed, as he sang of them, it seemed he felt them again.

And so he did, because the beauty of his song drew them to him as it had before. Linami heard, and remembered the days when she and her sister had played together in their mother's garden, and how Nilu could climb the highest trees and bring back the sweetest figs, and pomegranates bursting with jeweled seeds. And Nilu heard, and remembered Linami's gentle way with a comb, and the sleepy pleasure of her sister's deft fingers weaving her hair.

And each of them began to think that while Sulesh had been greedy and foolish, he had been no more greedy and foolish than themselves, and yet he had not been false; rather, they had been false to each other when they had let their love turn to hatred, though they had each been born to be the other's second half.

So one moondark, Nilu said to Linami: "Sister, it is your time to give way to me, and my time to rule the night sky, but give way to me willingly, and I will give way to you willingly at full moon, for I miss the days when the world was still wet with the waters of the flood, and we were friends."

But Linami, who had always been slower to consider than her sister, said: "I will wait and see how it is at full moon."

And at full moon, Linami said to Nilu: "Now will you give way to me willingly? For I, too, miss the days when we played in our mother's garden, and were friends."

Nilu said: "The night sky is yours." And she embraced her sister, and Linami wept, not for sorrow, but for joy.

That all happened long ago. In these days, the gods no longer walk in the world of men. But still, the shepherds who follow their flocks in the dark wild hills say that there is a grove where, at full moon and moon dark, Nilu gives way to Linami and Linami gives way to Nilu with kisses and handclasps. They play together as they once played in their mother's garden when the world was still wet with the waters of the flood, and Sulesh pours forth songs to his loves.

I'm Your One-Way Street

It's the smell of blood that draws me to you. Salt like the ocean, and iron. Not cold iron, but flaming with life.

Who am I? Never mind.

You've stumbled out the back door of the nightclub, stinking drunk, followed by the sounds of violins and blaring horns, to lean against the railing and empty your stomach into the canal. My canal. It's as acceptable an offering to me as carelessly secured laundry blown in on the wind, or the corpses of sparrows that wash down in a summer storm.

Oh, but you: One stocking laddered, and your fox-fur wrap hanging askew, the hair that was carefully crimped and tamed earlier this evening become a wild halo around your face, and the berry-red of your lipstick smeared with too many kisses and too much wine. Under your red sequined dress the belt meant to hold your pad in place has gone crooked with dancing, and a smear of blood marks the top of your thigh.

You stare down into the canal as your stomach settles, gripping the railing to steady the swaying of the world, and you catch bits of your reflection in the spill of light from windows onto the water. You don't guess that there is one looking back. But the ground seems to tilt beneath you, and your hands can no longer find purchase, and you feel yourself plunging headlong into the water. You wonder if you're dreaming.

You are. And your dream gives me shape, hands to rid you of your fox-fur wrap and linger on the back of your neck, slim clever fingers to feel the gooseflesh that I've raised there. Knees to push yours apart, rucking up your skirt as I pull you to me, the press of damp underthings against my leg. A mouth to lick my way down your throat, and teeth to bite, breasts to press against your own and a full lush behind for your hands to grip and your nails to mark as you groan and shudder.

You dream me, and I dream you, with a sharp smell of wine and cigarette smoke. The hands that knead my flesh are strong and calloused, a factory girl's hands, a fact you can't quite hide with bright polish on the blunt-cut nails. The mouth that tickles my navel is hot and avid. Dark eyes in a dark face catch on my eyes and hold while you kneel for me like you should for a goddess, though I'm a very minor one in the scheme of things.

You drink me like a butterfly drinks a flower, with a small darting tongue and more thirst than finesse, like I am the sweetest thing you've tasted in your bright, fragile life. My fingers twist in your corkscrew curls, pulling you closer. Joy comes in ripples, then in a flood that spills over the banks of my body with a roar. You are still clinging to me when it ebbs away.

We lie in my bed, a bed of pebbles and mud and the forgotten detritus of ages. It's my rhythms I am teaching you now, the rise and fall of tides and the heartbeat of cities. My hair streams over your bare shoulder, and I can feel the heat building inside you when the rising intensity brings you to the brink of completion and hear the barely-voiced whine you make when I walk you back from the brink. By the end, the space between each drawing-in of breath and each noisy exhale stretches like a shining, sharp eternity. You cling to my arm and your mouth spills its incoherent moans into my shoulder. I cradle you in my lap and lick your blood off my fingers, savoring the taste of you, stroking your hair as your eyelids grow heavy.

You drowse for half a minute, no more than that. Then your eyes snap open, dark and aware. You're charming like this, a facet of you I haven't yet seen, intelligence in your look to match the strength in your hands. Taking everything in, from the pebbled surface of my bed to the dark glimmer of waves in the sky above, to me, with doubt and avid curiosity and not a little fear.

"I know I got hammered. But I don't think there's a big enough hammer in the world to make me come up with this. It must be real, innit?" Your voice is unsteady, but your smile is brilliant. "You sure as hell pinched me, and I didn't wake up."

"Real as breath," I say.

You push up off my lap. It feels emptier without you already. But that's the way with me: whatever washes up, the currents carry away again. I watch the way your back moves as you adjust your clothing, and in my heart I am bidding you goodbye.

"But where's this place?" you ask. "What're you?"

"A place forgotten between sleeping and waking. Where things meet and come apart and leave no trace, a nowhere on the way from one somewhere to another. As for where we are, it's the Tailor's Bridge Canal."

"Huh." A dry chuckle, down in my realm where nothing is dry. "Been saving that one up, innit? Or do you trot it out for a new girl or boy every night?"

I cannot fathom your anger. "It's what I am."

"Or is it what I am? A good-time girl, good enough for a dance until the wine runs dry, good enough for a tumble until dawn breaks. After that, high-town swell or magic faerie water-spirit, you're all the same, aren't you? Don't want to see my face come morning light."

You're crying. I'm entirely unprepared to deal with this.

"Sorry," you say, trying to swallow your tears. "Sorry. It's just—I want to see you again. Want to feel all the stuff you made me feel—your hands, your mouth. Want to duck out at lunch break and meet you in some cafe, eating cheap sandwiches and watching the world go by—but I can't, can I? I'll wake up in my bed and this'll all have been a dream, and if I take another tumble into Tailor's Bridge Canal I'll get nothing but drowned."

It's all true. I shake my head and grab your hand, though holding on isn't in my nature. "There is a way. The tide will show you. If you remember when you wake, if you still want to. But you'll need my name. And if you forget it—worse things can happen in the borderlands than drowning."

"Tell me your name. I won't forget." You turn your face towards mine, eyes shining with hope and tears, and I lean down and whisper in your ear. You repeat it softly, catching your bottom lip in your teeth like a shy virgin for the first syllable—Vi—and letting your breath out in a sigh for the second—aaah. "I'm Josephine," you add. "Friends call me Jos."

You rest your head in my lap again. "Sleep, Jos," I say. You do. As your breathing grows slow and even, the currents carry you far away from me. I don't think I will ever see you again.

A stick raps against a still-dark window; the knocker-up is doing her rounds, waking the factory girls for another day at work. All around you, girls are groaning and cursing, finding yesterday's clothes by touch and pulling them on, fighting for a turn in the boarding house's only bathroom. You linger in bed, chasing the fragments of a dream as it slips away from you.

Your hand rests on your belly, and you are half-tempted to move it lower, and never mind who notices—that sort of dream. But if you're late again the foreman will dock your pay, so you swing your legs over the edge of the bed and shove your feet into your clogs and take your place in the line for the bathroom. By the time you're on the assembly line, winding one copper coil after another under the hot lights, you've forgotten it.

The lunch bell rings. You have half an hour before you have to be at your station again. Most of the girls open box lunches and eat where they're sitting, or gather in groups to gossip, shouting to be heard over the thud of machinery. You need to get away, to breathe fresh air and fix your eyes on something further away than the end of your nose, even if the time spent walking to and from the corner cafe and ordering the same cheap ham sandwich you could have gotten boxed means that you only have five minutes left to scarf it down.

The cafe overlooks the Green River, and as you eat your sandwich you watch a garbage barge make its way downstream. A couple of sparrows are fighting over some offal that's fallen off the back. Something stirs in you, not quite a memory, and you leave your sandwich half-eaten on the table and go down to the water. You can hear factory bells ringing the end of lunch hour all along the street, but the tide is going out, and you are following it.

The river makes its way through the manufacturing district and an outdoor market, past tenement houses and under a railroad bridge. Following the tug in your gut, you turn away from the bustle of the docks towards the shallow side of the bay where the city gives way to tin-and-scrap-wood shanties. You step out of your clogs and strip off your stockings, wading in among the mudlarks looking for treasures left behind by the retreating waters. The tide is still going out. No one else seems to see the path it reveals, smooth and pebbled, only a few centimeters underwater, lit up in the setting sun. At the end of it—a gateway, an island, a curtain that shimmers like the surface of water seen from beneath.

Each step you take out is harder. The water tugs at your ankles and then swirls around your knees. By the time you reach the gate it's waist-high, and you have to struggle not to be pulled off the path. There's a figure standing on the island, a long sword unsheathed in its hand, wearing overlapping plates of armor that remind you of the odd creatures that fishermen sometimes pull up from the deep sea.

"Child of Man, stranger and no friend," the armored one rasps. "By what right do you walk the borderlands?"

There's a thing you should say. It's at the tip of your tongue. You bite your lip nervously, and slowly release your breath, but no sound comes out. Your feet slip on the slick pebbles. The water pulls you under. It's a long, dark way down.

You're so close to me now, here where salt water meets fresh in a wild churn. I reach out for you, but you twist desperately, trying to throw off my hands—you can't tell them from a hundred other chilly hands wrapping around your legs, dragging at your clothes and your flesh. I call to you, but my voice is lost in a froth of bubbles. There's nothing to give me shape; you don't know me. Once again, you're borne away from me to a place I can't follow, as the cold and dark and wet gives way to searing light.

When we lay together in my bed, spent from our lovemaking—I should have let you rage and weep, and kept my silence. I meant only to offer a moment's comfort before it and I were forgotten altogether. I never dreamed you'd come. But you have, and the everyday world will never take you back any more than the foreman would give you back your job. You are here, lost and beyond my help. I can only watch you plummet, land hard on your hands and knees on a surface of glowing coals. I feel hurt for your hurt, and fear for your fear, and something else when you stagger to your feet, your hands red and blistered, your clothes torn away leaving you nothing but a shredded and singed slip. If these things hadn't happened to you, I would never have known how tough you are, how brave.

You've found the path again, where the cinders are hottest, and you keep walking though you can see no end of it now, though every step burns. Your skin bakes in the heat, your lips crack and bleed, and you lick them with a tongue gone harsh as sandpaper.

The taste of blood recalls me to you. You stagger and nearly fall in the flood of memories, as if in this burning borderland you can feel my cool arms around you, holding you close.

"Love," you say. It hurts to force words from your parched throat, but you keep talking. "I'm no stranger—I was invited, innit? I came to look for my love."

A figure appears before you in answer to your challenge, sword drawn, burnished armor crested like a flamebird. "Have you? Find your love, then."

The armored one stabs downward, and I let loose a scream you can't hear—but the sword passes you by, embedding itself point-first in the ground. The light of the path is extinguished, its heat dimmed. You stand in a twilight forest now. Mist drifts low to the ground, and in the distance, unfamiliar birds call to each other. This would be a pleasant place to rest, if you could rest, now that you remember why you're here.

The armored one is nowhere in sight, though you can hear its rasping, mocking laughter in your mind. Its sword has become a tree, branches hung with overripe fruit that drip onto the forest floor. The smell of blood overwhelms you, and you understand—the fruits are hearts.

Disgusted but compelled, you reach up to touch one. It's Maria—you haven't thought of her in years, but you went to grammar school together, and you kissed her in the coatroom during recess. Later, after she sat at lunch with another girl, you came back with a pair of scissors and cut her coat to shreds.

On the branch above is Conrad, who used to read you poetry and buy you cheap brandy with borrowed money. The first time you had sex, he left you bleeding and unsatisfied on a mattress in a garret room. You drop his heart with a shudder and keep looking.

There's Paula, who was ticklish below her ears, dead in the flu epidemic three years ago. Carl, whose wife took him back in the end. Others, faces long forgotten and names never known, a kiss in a stairwell or a tumble in the alley or a beautiful way of walking that brought a flutter to your heart from across the street. But my heart is nowhere to be found.

You're growing desperate now, heedless of the half-dried blood that coats your hands and the scratches scoring your arms. A branch snaps as you scramble to reach a heart just above your head; sap flows forth, and with it my voice.

"Jos!" I call. And you stop mid-motion, your eyes wide and your lips parted, almost as if you have heard me. A name has power, a woman's name as well as a spirit's.

"Via?" you whisper. Your hand is touching the broken branch. Sap flows down your fingers. Slowly, as in a drunken dream, you touch your fingers to your mouth and taste—along with blood of the more ordinary sort—what you have only tasted once before, when you knelt for me. You know you will never find my heart if you hunt for a hundred years, for I have no heart to keep my love in, as a woman has or a man. I am only a place forgotten between sleeping and waking, a nowhere on the way from one somewhere to another—and I love you no less for that.

"Here she is," you say. "I've found my love."

And your words give me shape, arms to draw you two me, legs to wrap around your waist, lips to speak against your ear. "Jos, my champion, my wonderful human girl."

You laugh; I can feel your belly ripple against mine. "Via," you say, and that's all, all that needs to be said. You let your hands speak for you instead, tangling in my hair and pulling my mouth around to yours.

The twilight forest fades, and you look around when you come up from the kiss, pulling back a little but not letting go. "Where will we go now?" you wonder. "Will you come watch the birds and the barges on the Green River with me, sitting at a sidewalk cafe?"

"Anywhere you like," I say. "Everywhere and nowhere. Anywhere but back."

You flash a wicked grin. "Dunno, I'd like to see you on your back. Bet you'd look fine like that." I pinch you for the pleasure of seeing you jump. You yelp, but your grin just gets wider. "Must be real, innit?"

"Bed first," I say. "Everywhere later."

For You Are Their Creator, and You Know Their Nature (or: To His Koi Mistress)

(cento after children's rhymes collected by Iona and Peter Opie, To His Coy Mistress by Andrew Marvell, and Unetanneh Tokef attributed to Rabbi Amnon of Mainz)

Ladybird, Ladybird, fly away home
    Now; like an amorous bird of prey
    Like dust floats; like a dream flies

Who by water? And who by fire?
    Turning to ashes all my lust
    Your house is on fire; your children all gone

Seagull, Seagull, sit on the sand
    By the Indian Ganges' side
    Your seat established in mercy; sit on it in truth

You wait for me until the day of my death
    Your skin like morning dew
    It's never good weather when you're inland

Crow, Crow, get out of my sight
    For no one is justified in your eyes, in judgment
    And at my back I always hear

A still, silent voice
  The last age should show your heart
  Or else I'll have your liver and light

The Story of Lily, Lark, and Loaf

This is the story of the man who cut a branch from the wrong tree.

There was a man named Benta, and his father was Gervasia, and his father was Senna, and his father was Joa, and his father was Foolish Benta, and his father was Calixta, and his father's fathers came from the land of the Getamee. Now, Benta was a woodcutter, and when he was young and strong and the trees were plentiful, he was able to put aside some money. So he built himself a house, and took himself a wife, and lived very happily. And in time, she bore him a daughter, who was as beautiful as a white flower among brown bracken, so they called her Lily. The next year, she bore another daughter, who was as beautiful as birdsong at dawn, so they called her Lark. And then she bore a third daughter, who was as beautiful as fresh bread after a hard day's work, so they called her Loaf. And then Benta's wife died.

As the years went by, Benta's daughters grew taller and more beautiful, but he himself grew older and weaker, until he did not know how he would feed them all. Then, one morning, Lily came to him, and said, "'Father, last night I dreamed of a great ram, with curling yellow horns and a coat like fine flour."

Benta knew that it was a very lucky thing to dream of an animal, and he said to himself, now she is sure to make her fortune. But to Lily he only said, "And what did he say to you?"

"Only that when I go out to seek my fortune, I should be sure to take the wooden bucket which we use to bring water from the well," she said.

So that same day, Lily embraced her father and her sisters, and, taking nothing with her but a flask of water, a slice of bread, and the wooden bucket, set out to seek her fortune. She had not gone more than five miles when she heard sheep bleating. She followed the sound, climbing up hills and down into clefts until she found a flock of sheep, lost and stranded on a ledge, and thirsty. The wooden bucket was heavy on her arm, and when she looked, she saw it was full of water. So she poured it out, and the more she poured, the more it filled, until there was a stream running down the side of the hillside.

When the sheep had drunk their fill, they followed Lily out of the cleft. And after that Lily lived in the hills, and tended her sheep, but one ewe she sent home to her father and sisters.

For a while Benta, Lark, and Loaf lived contentedly, for the ewe gave milk, and they had cheese and butter to eat. And when her milk stopped, Benta slaughtered the ewe, and sold her hide for flour, and they ate bread and mutton. But presently the bread and mutton ran out, and then Benta did not know how he would feed them all.

Then Lark came and said to him, "Father, last night I dreamed of a great gander, with a sharp red beak and wings like storm clouds."

Knowing the luck that Lily had had, Benta was doubly cheered, and he said to himself, this time Lark is sure to make her fortune. But to Lark he only said, "And what did he say to you?"

"Only that when I go out to seek my fortune, I should be sure to take the stalk of mint that grows outside our door," she said.

So that same day, Lark embraced her father and sister, and, taking nothing with her but a flask of water, a slice of bread, and the stalk of mint, set out to seek her fortune. She had walked for ten miles, and was sitting down by the shore of a lake to eat her supper, when she saw dark green flashes against the light green grass. She crept closer, and saw a nest of goslings hidden in the reeds, and five vipers attacking the young birds. So she threw the stalk of mint that she had in her hand, and each leaf became an arrow, and each arrow pierced a viper in the eye, and killed it. When the older geese returned from browsing in the meadow, Lark shared out her bread among them, and they all agreed that she made a fine companion. And after that Lark lived by the lake, and tended her geese, but one goose she sent home to her father and sister.

For a while Benta and Loaf lived contentedly, for they had eggs to eat. And when the goose stopped laying, Benta slaughtered her, and sold her feathers for beans, and they ate pottage and goose. But presently the pottage and goose ran out, and then Benta did not know how he would feed himself and his daughter.

Then Loaf came and said to him, "Father, last night I dreamed of my mother."

THE FIRSTBORN OF DEATH

Benta knew that it was a very unlucky thing to dream of someone who had died, and he said to himself, before the year is up she is sure to die herself.

But to Loaf he only said, "And what did she say to you?"

"Only that when I go out to seek my fortune, I should be sure to take a staff cut from the tree with the red heart that grows in the center of the forest," she said.

So that same day, Benta embraced his daughter with a heavy heart, and, taking nothing with him but a flask of water, a slice of bread, and his ax, set out for the forest to find the tree with the red heart.

Benta walked fifteen miles, until he could no longer see the sun through the trees, but he still had not reached the center of the forest. So he ate his bread, and drank his water, and slept. And the next day, he walked again until the sun was beginning to set, and at last he stood in the center of the forest, where the tree with the red heart grew.

But when Benta saw the great tree in the middle of its clearing—for not even mushrooms grew in the ground that its gnarled roots touched—when he smelled the rust-and-saltwater scent of its sap, and heard the slow beating of its heart, his nerve failed him. Then he said to himself, why shouldn't I cut a staff from a different tree instead? And how would Loaf know if I did? And after all, he added, beginning to warm up to this idea, perhaps this way I can save her life, for if a tree ever brought bad luck, it was surely this one. So he chose another tree nearby, a straight, sturdy one, and cut off one of its lower branches.

No sooner had he done so, than the Mother of us all spoke to him. "Did you think to cheat Me, Benta Gervasia?" She said. "Then you are a fool; for all return to Me in time, but now it will go hard with you."

Then Benta knew that it was not his dead wife who had spoken to Loaf in her dream, but Herself. And he was afraid, and would have cut a staff from the tree with the red heart after all, but when he turned around he could no longer see it. And as much as he searched for it, the less he found it, until there was nothing for him to do but go home with the staff he had cut.

But he had not walked a mile before the sun set completely, and he could go no further; so he lay down and slept.

He woke in darkness, to the sound of something moving in the forest. He couldn't see it, but he heard its heavy breath near the spot where he lay, and he said to himself, it is a wolf come to eat me up, but it will not find me such easy meat as that. So he reached for his ax, but his hand fell on the staff he had cut instead. Snatching it up, he swung it towards the sound, and felt it hit solidly. The creature cried out—not a wolflike snarl, but a human cry—and thereafter was silent, and presently Benta slept again.

When he awoke, he saw neither body nor blood, neither wolf nor man, but only a few short pieces of wood, and two copper bands that might have once held them together. Well, he said to himself, that is strange. Then he picked up his ax and the staff, and continued on his way home. But though he walked all day, until he could no longer see the sun through the trees, he still did not reach his house; so once more he lay down on the forest floor and slept.

He woke in darkness, to the sound of something moving in the forest. He couldn't see it, but he heard its soft slither through the undergrowth where he lay, and he said to himself, it is a viper come to bite me, but it will not find me such easy meat as that. So he reached for his ax, but his hand fell on the staff he had cut instead. Snatching it up, he drove it down it towards the sound, and felt it crush flesh and bone. The creature cried out—not a serpentlike hiss, but a human cry—and thereafter was silent, and presently Benta slept again.

When he awoke, he saw neither body nor blood, neither viper nor man, but only a trampled patch of mint. Well, he said to himself, that is strange. Then he picked up his ax and the staff, and continued on his way; and he had not gone five miles before he reached his house.

Loaf ran out to meet him and embraced him. She was glad of his return, and gladder of the staff he had brought her. She would have taken it and set out to seek her fortune at once, but Benta said, "It's too late today; stay one more night and leave tomorrow morning." And Loaf agreed.

Then Loaf said to Benta, 'The first day you were gone, my sister Lily came to visit me, and the next morning she left. Did you meet her on the way?'

Benta's heart turned over in his chest, and he knew that it was not a wolf he had killed in the forest, but his daughter. But he only said, "I never saw her."

Then Loaf said, "The second day you were gone, my sister Lark came to visit me, and the next morning she left. Did you meet her on the way?"

Benta's heart turned over in his chest once more, and he knew that it was not a viper he had killed in the forest, but his daughter. But he only said, "I never saw her."

So Benta and Loaf passed the rest of that day in their house by the edge of the forest, as they had many other days before, and when the night fell they slept.

Benta woke in darkness, to the sound of something moving in the house. He couldn't see it, but he heard its tread like the tread of a bear, and smelled its musk like the musk of a hunting cat, and he reached for his ax.

Then he remembered what he had done the previous night, and the night before, and he was heartsick. He let his hand fall, and he spoke instead: "Who are you: man or beast or spirit? And what do you do in my house? Answer quickly, before I chop you up!" But there was no answer.

Again he reached for his ax, but again he hesitated, and he said to himself, first let me see what I am about. So he grabbed a bundle of twigs instead, and thrust them into the last embers of the fire.

All at once, a gust of wind blew through the house, and the bundle of twigs that Benta held blazed so fiercely that it burned his hand, and set fire to his shirt. He shouted and flung the bundle away, and burning twigs landed in every corner of the house.

Then Loaf awoke and saw that her father was on fire, so she snatched off her kirtle, and threw it over him. This smothered the flames, and the two of them stood, Benta gasping in pain, Loaf dressed only in a shirt and clutching her staff, while the house burned around them.

Loaf made for the door, but the fire was there, and Benta took her arm and they climbed onto the table, where the smoke was thinner. He took Loaf's staff and thrust it at the roof again and again, until he had opened a gap in the thatch wide enough to climb out. He scrambled onto the roof, and Loaf scrambled after. But being shorter than her father, she stuck halfway, and could not pull herself out.

By that time, the fire had caught her, and when Benta saw her twisted, burning fingers reaching for his own, his nerve failed him, and he pushed her away, back through the roof. She grabbed the staff, but it snapped in two, and she fell. Benta leapt from the roof and ran, leaving staff, house, and daughter to burn together.

Soon Benta could not run any longer. But although his steps slowed, he did not stop to rest for the rest of the night, nor the day after, until he came to the center of the forest, where the tree with the red heart grew.

He did not have any difficulty finding it. It stood in the middle of a wide clearing, for not even mushrooms grew in the ground that its gnarled roots touched. He smelled the rust-and-saltwater scent of its sap, and heard the slow beating of its heart, and he took his belt, and hanged himself from its lowest branch.

And that is the story of Lily, Lark, and Loaf, whose father was Benta, who cut a branch from the wrong tree.

The Duty of a Ruler

"What is the duty of a ruler?" Gabren said.

Maya scuffed her sandal in the dust. She wished Gabren hadn't asked that question.

She knew Gabren taught her because her father had hired him to. She also knew that she might rule Koloma in her own right one day, though it wasn't likely—if none of her father's wives managed to produce a son, her father would probably find her a husband. But when she sat with Gabren amidst the bustle and smells of the market, she liked to pretend that she was just another student who had come to Gabren as any of them had, seeking wisdom.

She should have expected his question, or one like it. Gabren didn't approve of pretending that things were other than what they were. "The duty of a ruler," said Maya, "is to protect the people of his city—protect them from foreign enemies, from violence and robbery by their fellow-citizens, from drought, starvation and fire. He settles disputes between families, he maintains the roads and the walls and the public buildings, he defends the poor and the fatherless, he commands the army, he appeases the anger of the Bright Gods."

"And how does he protect his people from violence and robbery?" said Gabren.

"He establishes courts," said Maya. "If anyone steals from his fellow-citizen, the judges make him pay back what he took, and have him flogged. Anyone who kills his fellow-citizen is put to death."

"Flogging and executions, are they not violence?"

Maya hesitated. "Well—they are—"

"Then a ruler who permits these things to happen, does he not fail in his duty?" said Gabren.

"They're criminals, that's different—" Maya tried to think about Gabren's questions, not the crowd they were attracting. A boy with a wide straw hat leaned against his oxcart and grinned at her perplexity. The wizened man on the mat on their other side had stopped shouting that he would tell your fortune and change your luck, and sat listening quietly. A few idlers, their cloaks drawn over their heads against the sun, watched at a cautious distance.

"Well then," said Gabren, "how does a ruler protect his people from foreign enemies?"

"If they try to invade, he leads the army, and fights them," said Maya.

"The army—is it made up of criminals?"

"Of course not!" Maya looked over her shoulder, at her pair of guards, but they didn't seem to have taken offense at Gabren's words. Their tattooed faces continued scanning the market. Desert dwellers, her father's soldiers were called, and in whispers, when he couldn't hear—carrion birds. When they spoke Koloman, it was slow and halting. Probably they hadn't been following the dialogue at all.

"Soldiers die in battle, and are injured," said Gabren. "Is a king who orders his soldiers into battle derelict in his duty to protect them?"

"No," said Maya. "Not when it's necessary. Maybe... the duty of a ruler is something else."

"The duty of a ruler," one of the idlers spoke up, "is to uphold the laws and traditions of the city."

Though the cloak that shadowed his face was dusty and cheap, the upper-city tones of his voice gave the lie to his appearance as a New Market rat. But Maya already knew who he was, and that his interest in her conversation with Gabren went beyond passing curiosity. It was Gabren's other students' turn to be held to the fire.

"What are these laws and traditions?" said Gabren.

"They are too many to enumerate now, and they are different for every city," said Jerrel Talyon—that was the idler's name, though no one had told it to Maya. She had discovered it herself, through observation and deduction.

"Then how shall a ruler know what they are, that he may uphold them?"

"He must study history, and know what was done by kings before him," said Jerrel. "He must be familiar with the codes of law that are accepted by the courts. He must observe the customs and behaviors of the kings who came before him, and not deviate from them."

"That is difficult," said Gabren. "Do rulers never shirk it, then?"

"Sometimes," said Jerrel, "they do."

"Are later rulers then bound to emulate them?"

Jerrel made an impatient chopping motion with his hand. "I did not mean that a king should imitate the tyrants of history, or the failures. If he cannot tell which of his predecessors' example is worth following, he must be guided by the courts, and the ancient families, and the Assembly."

"And when the courts hear a case on which the codes of law are silent, or when the Assembly cannot speak with one voice, whom do they consult?"

"The king."

"And how shall he answer them?" said Gabren. "When the ancient families disagree, and customs vary, how shall he decide between them?"

"I cannot tell," Jerrel admitted, covering his confusion with a bow.

The street was now full enough that Maya's guards were visibly nervous. A goatherd had given up trying to drive his flock through the crowd and had joined it instead, and a coffee girl working its edges was doing brisk business. The next man to speak was one of these late arrivals. He also had his face hidden beneath his cloak, but the cloak was finer, and a few oiled ringlets escaped from it. Udo Loyon shouldn't have been there either, but he had less reason to fear discovery than Jerrel did, and he was reckless by nature.

"Why then," said Udo, "the duty of a ruler is the same as that of any man: to please himself."

"Indeed?" said Gabren. "And when a ruler destroys the houses and fields of his people to build himself a pleasure garden, or plunders the jewels of the treasury to make ornaments for himself or his favorite wife, does he do his duty?"

"I say he does." The crowd, which had been quiet, laughed at that.

"Destroying fields is likely to lead to famine," said Gabren, "and extravagance is likely to lead to war, and all of these are likely to lead to civil strife. Are these things pleasant?"

Udo joined in the laughter against himself just as readily as he'd laughed at his own joke. "Well... no."

He made no further argument, and Gabren turned to Maya. "Little Highness, it's time we left."

The crowd began to disperse; Gabren, Maya and the guards left without the farewell or conclusion that a public speaker might ordinarily make. Gabren hadn't been teaching—that was the pretense. He wasn't supposed to take students other than Maya, or to teach a public school except once every month. But her father knew what they did on their walks through the city; even if he didn't have the guards' reports, dozens of people always stopped to listen. Nor would the king care that Udo came faithfully to learn from Gabren, though he'd been banned from speaking in schools or the Assembly, and testifying in court.

That Jerrel Talyon was back in Koloma, though the Assembly had never lifted the order of ostracism against his family—that might have interested Maya's father. But she didn't want to get Gabren in trouble, and she didn't want to be cooped up in the women's quarters in the palace for the rest of her days. Also, Jerrel's family and hers might have been enemies, but she admired his sharp mind and his clear, bold way of speaking. And she liked Udo. He always had a smile for her, and when they spoke, he took her—if not entirely seriously, at least as seriously as he took anything else.

When they returned to the palace, Gabren and the guards left Maya at the entrance to the women's quarters. Maya slipped through the heavy embroidered curtain to find that her mother was waiting.

So was Janna, her father's most junior wife. Maya's mother didn't like to have witnesses when Maya returned home with dust on her sandals and legs, her hair expanded into a lopsided halo—but Janna's pretty nose was as keen as a ferret's for gossip.

"You needn't glare at me like that, Maya," Janna giggled. "Arnya's asked me to help with your bath."

Maya transferred her astonished look to Arnya, who nodded confirmation as she hustled Maya along the corridor. "Your father wants to see you. Oh dear."

She hadn't been quick enough. Talle, the king's first wife and Arnya's ill luck, was lounging in a doorway. "Janna, come with me. I want you to arrange my hair this evening."

"Talle, I need her," Arnya protested. "Why doesn't Berye do it, as she usually does?"

"Oh, she's clearing out a rat's nest in the courtyard." Though Talle usually held her personal maids above such menial tasks. "Why does the child need a bath in the middle of the afternoon? If she had a bath every time she was filthy, there would be no water left in Koloma."

"The king has summoned her to court," said Janna with a sugary smirk. She knew perfectly well that the news would upset Talle, and her telling of it would upset Arnya.

Talle pressed her lips together. "Why?"

"I wasn't told," said Arnya.

"I don't suppose you would be. How long has it been since you saw the king?"

"I don't know. I haven't kept count," said Arnya. Maya knew it had been more than a month.

"Have you been called to court, too, Talle?" said Maya.

Talle looked at Maya like she was one of the rats in the courtyard. "Haven't you taught your child not to ask impertinent questions, Arnya? You had better do so quickly. The king has less patience for them than I do. Anyway, I can't spare Janna."

"I will help you myself. After Maya's bath," said Arnya.

"What use would you be?" Janna laughed. "You're hopeless with oil and hair-irons."

"But you may be of some use in clearing out rats," said Talle. "If you are thorough about it. You know how rats are. If they are not killed, they breed."

Arnya looked Maya over again, taking in her disheveled state despairingly. "All right. But I must have a minute with Maya."

Talle took her time answering, clearly weighing the advantages of thwarting Arnya against the possibility of getting interesting news out of Janna afterwards. "A minute," she agreed. She didn't move from the doorway.

"Will you excuse us, please?" said Arnya.

"Highness," prompted Talle.

"Highness," said Arnya, and Talle laughed and drifted off towards her room.

They came to the baths, and Arnya undressed Maya and plunged her into the water. Between the two of them, Arnya and Janna scrubbed her, oiled and dressed her hair, and pleated her best embroidered drape. Arnya clicked her tongue as Janna started to fasten the clasps.

"These won't do for court," she said. "Will you bring my clasps with the blue glass?"

"Of course." Janna left readily enough, her footsteps slapping against the wet tiles, but not fading down the hallway beyond.

"Your father has called that tutor of yours in, too," hissed Arnya, too low for any eavesdropper to hear. "Have the two of you been getting up to anything?"

"What on earth would we have been getting up to?" said Maya. But she whispered too.

"You tell me." Arnya was clever enough to realize Maya's question hadn't been a denial. "Blasphemy? Drunkenness? Sex?"

Maya burst into laughter. "Bright Gods, Arnya! My father probably just wants to see how my lessons are coming along." Actually, Maya couldn't think of a subject that was likely to interest him less, but she didn't want to worry Arnya—which was like not wanting to get the sea wet.

"Well... do you know your lessons?"

"Hah," said Maya. "I can handle a few questions from my father."

Janna's returned then—either she had finally gone to get the clasps, or she'd sent a maid to get them for her. "Talle says the rats won't wait. I'll finish getting Maya ready."

Arnya had said everything she'd meant to say—at least, there was nothing more she'd say in front of Janna. She gave Maya one last worried look and left. Jana bent over Maya to fasten the clasps, and whispered against her ear, "Why have you been called to court, really?"

"I don't know. Honestly, Janna." It was what Maya would have said anyway, so she was glad it happened to be true.

"At least tell me what your mother wanted to talk to you about," Janna coaxed. "I wouldn't tell Talle. Not if we were friends. Did you know my father sent me a box of sesame sweets and I haven't shared them with anyone?"

Maya didn't answer. Did Janna think she was three years old? Or would that bribe actually have tempted Janna?

"Fine, then," said Janna, fixing the second clasp with a spiteful jab at Maya's shoulder. "I bet you don't know anything interesting anyway." And they walked to the entrance of the women's quarters in silence, where a pair of guards were waiting to take her to her father.

The guards stepped aside as Maya came into the throne room and went down on her knees. All around her, courtiers hummed like flies at midday.

"Get up, Maya," said the king. He looked much the same as he always did, sitting on his ornate wooden throne and making it seem comfortable. He had the cheerful expression of someone who knew that nobody wanted to risk making him unhappy. "I was just saying to Gabren," he went on, nodding at Gabren where he stood across the audience floor from Maya, "that it's been some time since I took an interest in your education."

"That's true, Majesty," said Maya. Her father hadn't taken an interest in her education since he'd appointed Gabren her tutor, four years ago.

"And, Gabren," said the king, "how is my daughter's education going?"

"Well, I think, Majesty," said Gabren. "Her Highness is clever."

Maya's face glowed. It had been the politic thing to say, but Gabren wouldn't have said it if he hadn't meant it. Clever!

"You give school down by the New Market every full moon, don't you?" said the king.

"Yes, Majesty," said Gabren.

"Maya's never been to one, has she?" said the king.

"No, Majesty," said Gabren.

"She should," said the king. "Maybe I should, as well. We could all use a little more wisdom, eh?"

There was a subdued hum among the courtiers. One agreed with the king, of course. But it wouldn't do to agree too enthusiastically to that particular statement. Gabren inclined his head. "Majesty."

"Attal!" said the king. "When is next full moon?"

Attal Jabian, in the High Priest's apron, sat with the other officials of the city on a low dais beneath the king's throne. His handsome face was strikingly similar to that of his sister, the queen, and the expression of masked hostility on it was identical. "In four days, Majesty."

"Excellent," said the king. "Maya, you will accompany me to Gabren's next school, in four days' time. Make arrangements, Klyed."

"Majesty," Klyed Anytus rumbled. The Chief General of Koloma, Klyed was taller and broader by two handspans than any other man in the room, and he had blue-black, curving tattoos on his face, souvenirs of his long exile among the desert dwellers. Men with elaborate hairstyles and gold-fringed cloaks hovered around the other officials, and around the king, but no one wanted to stand close to Klyed. It was a matter of record that he had once disemboweled a messenger who had brought him unwelcome orders.

Deven Devenyon, the bejeweled and bored Steward of the Granaries, made a remark that Maya couldn't hear. The courtiers hovering near him buzzed, and one of them—Iy Argus, old Goff Argus' nephew—frowned.

"Maya, Gabren, you may go now," said the king. They bowed and went, followed by the guards. When they reached the corridor that led to the women's quarters, Maya felt safe enough to meet Gabren's eye and speak.

"Gabren," she said, "do you know what that was about?"

"The king said his purpose was to inform himself about your education," said Gabren. "Is that not enough to account for the interview?"

"Well, it's strange," said Maya. "He's never shown the slightest interest before."

"And did he show any interest today?"

"Um," said Maya. "No. I see what you're getting at. No, if he were interested in my education, he would have asked me about it, or you. He didn't. The only thing he did do was invite himself to your next school. That must have been the point."

"Himself and you," said Gabren. "But if he wanted to attend my school, he could simply have come. No, he wanted it to be known that you and he were going to my school. Either by me, or you, or someone else present, or someone whom someone present was likely to tell. It's worth considering not only the king's words, but the reactions of the others. Do you recall them?"

Attal Jabian had been annoyed at being used as a calendar, but that was just her father tweaking his pride. Then she remembered Deven Devenyon's whispered remark, and Iy Argus' flash of anger. If that was injured pride, it was a deeper wound.

Maya chose her next words carefully. There were lattices in the walls, and a careless word in the palace could echo and re-echo in ears and throats. "When my father told Klyed to make arrangements—the king's safety in the city isn't the Chief General's responsibility. Maybe Klyed doing the Defender of the Palace's job upset some people." Iy Argus, and probably a half a dozen others, who thought that the position should be theirs. But there'd been no Defender of the Palace since old Goff Argus had died the year before. "Is that... was that the whole reason for this?"

Gabren looked troubled. "Perhaps. Or perhaps not. We may have to apply patience to the problem, in place of logic."

"Gabren?" said Maya.

They had reached the entrance to the women's quarters. "I suspect we'll find out in time," said Gabren. "Good night, little Highness, and be good."

Arnya met Maya on the other side of the curtain, alone this time, and they walked together to the bedroom they shared. "Well, I was right," said Maya, more cheerfully than she felt. "My father was only taking an interest in my education. He wants me to see what one of Gabren's famous schools is like, and he's curious himself. So we'll be attending the next one together."

"Really," said Arnya, undoing Maya's blue-glass clasps. "That must be interesting."

Maya was startled to hear Arnya speak for once without an edge of wariness. The glimpse she caught of Arnya's face, before she ducked her head to unwind Maya's drape, was wistful.

"Would you like to go to a school, sometime? Really?" Maya asked.

"Oh, yes," said Arnya.

Maya climbed into her bed. "Then if I'm ever queen, I'll have Gabren give a school in the palace, and I'll invite all the women. See if I don't." And with this happy thought, she fell asleep.

"Well," said Maya, climbing into her bed, "if I'm ever queen, I'll have Gabren give a school in the palace, and I'll invite all the women. See if I don't." And with this happy thought, she fell asleep.

Four days later, Maya and her father walked down to the New Market to hear Gabren's school. Her hair had been heavily oiled, and she had to remember to keep her head at a certain angle not to muss it, which made her neck hurt. She had also been given a gold-fringed cloak. It was too warm, and she was sure it made her look like a puppet.

In place of her usual two guards, there were six. Three walked in front, and three behind.

Leaving the palace, they passed the houses of the ancient families, from the Argus's old and sprawling compound to the bright new buildings of the Devenyons. The Devenyons were an ancient family by courtesy, not chronology. It was only eight years since the Talyons' complex had stood on that spot; it had been destroyed at the same time the entire family was ostracized, during the year of fire.

Crowds had been gathering along their route since they left the palace. By the time they got to the port road, the guards were shoving people to clear a path. The soldiers on the wall did a flourish with their spears as Maya and her father passed, and Maya's father waved. The hubbub grew louder.

The New Market was usually sparsely populated at noon; when Gabren and Maya had their conversations there, they might draw a few dozen people, and clog a single street. Now the entire central square was full. Shaven-headed port workers jostled elbows with courtiers, who trod on the toes of farmers up from their fields. Gabren had a fine voice, but Maya doubted he could make himself heard to all the people who had gathered today.

The guards shoved, the crowd parted, and Maya, her father, and their six tall shadows made their way to the front. Gabren made a gesture, and silence spread out in waves from where he stood.

"Is it possible," Gabren began, "That a man should harm another, and thereby profit himself? Let us consider this.

"You may say to me, 'Gabren, you are asking a foolish question. Surely men rob one another every day.'

"Then I would ask you, 'What is robbery? Is it a good thing, or evil?'

"If you told me that robbery was evil, I would ask you, 'What is it that we call evil? Is it not that which harms us? How then can robbery profit anyone?'

"And if you told me that robbery was good, I would ask you, 'What is it that we call good? Is it not that which benefits us? How then can robbery harm anyone? For it is surely true that nothing can be both a thing, and its opposite.'"

The people might have turned out to see the king, but Gabren had their full attention. No one spoke as Maya let her eyes wander over the crowd, and no one even seemed to move. Before she knew what she was hearing, Maya heard a pair of arrows whistle through the air. Before she knew what she was seeing, one struck her father in the back, and the other struck the guard to her left in the neck. The guard fell, but her father didn't.

One of the guards who was still standing gathered Maya in his arms and started to run. Another ran ahead and two more behind, clearing a path with feet and elbows and swords. She could see her father, his own sword drawn, cutting and hacking as men with daggers and clubs swarmed around him. Six guards minus one dead minus the four who had Maya should have equaled one, but Maya counted at least five fighting alongside her father, and more scattered through the crowd, trying to reach him, or fighting where they stood.

The arrow still stuck out of her father's back, but it wasn't slowing him down, and just before the crowd and the growing distance between them hid him from view, Maya saw why. Facts clicked into place like beads on an abacus.

Her father was wearing boiled leather under his robe and cloak—and she had thought she was hot and uncomfortable! He had left the palace with only a few guards, but many more had been waiting, secretly, in the market. This was what he had been planning for, when he'd announced in court that the two of them would be at Gabren's school.

Once they were clear of the New Market, the crowds got thinner, but only just. There was confusion and panic; people ran in all directions, and several fights seemed to have sprung up independently. Then the guard holding Maya staggered and went down on his knees. She tumbled out of his arms as a cloaked man drew back his knife to strike again. But her guard, balanced on knees and one hand, struck first, and opened the assassin from groin to ribcage. A spray of blood covered Maya and the two men fell in a heap together.

"Highness!" called the guards who had been running behind her. Something had delayed them—no doubt the same sort of something that lay before her in the street—and now they slowed further, looking around desperately. They couldn't see her. Maya took a breath to call out and nearly choked on the stench of it.

"Maya!" cried another voice, one she knew. "Help!" She staggered upright and saw, through a shifting screen of legs and feet, Udo being set upon alone by three large men with sticks.

Maya launched herself across the street, landing next to Udo. "Stop," she said, and Udo's attackers stopped, if only in surprise at having a girl intrude suddenly on their beating. They had wrapped cloaks around their heads, but they couldn't hide the shapes of their bodies, the way they stood, the ties on their sandals. "Addan Devenyon. Yuhil Devenyon. Derjen Noyon. I know you."

She knew them, and they knew her. There weren't many girls in the streets with gold-fringed cloaks. One of them took a step toward her, raising his stick. They wouldn't dare—or maybe they would—she knew them, would anyone else? But another one grabbed him by the sleeve, pointed, pulled him away. All three of Udo's attackers fled, pushing their way through the crowds.

"You came," said Udo, struggling to his knees.

It must have been her guards that had made the men run, but Maya couldn't see them. There were too many people, and she was too short.

"I called, and you came," said Udo. "I can't believe it."

"That's because you're a fool," said a familiar voice. Maya saw the look on Udo's face turn to horror, felt an arm pin her own to her sides.

"A fool," repeated Jerrel. "Superstitious, vain. How can anyone love truth and virtue if he loves perfumed hair oil as much? You deserve to be beaten to death by a mob, and someday you will be. Maya was your luck today, but she's mine now."

"I need a messenger," he went on. "You'll do, Udo. Go and tell the king that I have his heir. And that I am willing to leave Koloma, if I may do so alive."

Maya was lifted up and flung over Jerrel's shoulder, and he broke into a run. "Help!" she yelled. "Help, guards!"

Jerrel didn't even bother to silence her. She couldn't make herself heard over the noise in the street. Upside down, head jolting in time to Jerrel's strides, she couldn't even see where he was taking her. At some point, she passed out.

Maya was awakened by somebody slapping her face, and became aware of pain and a horrible stiffness in her back and shoulders. She couldn't feel her arms at all. She was lying on a bare earth floor with her hands and elbows lashed together behind her back, Jerrel squatting in front of her. "My apologies. You have been sleeping half the day. I was afraid that I or that idiot Udo had damaged you."

She licked her lips, and tested what muscles she could. "No, I'm... healthy," she said. *Fine* didn't cover her situation.

He helped her sit, and held a bowl to her lips. "You require water. Drink."

Finishing the water, Maya realized that she was hungrier than she had ever been. "Is there food?" she asked.

Jerrel laughed shortly. "If there were, I would have eaten it myself," he said. It was just as well. He clearly wasn't taking chances, and Maya hated the thought of being fed by hand.

"You might as well know," she said, "I'm no use to you. My father won't let you leave Koloma alive."

"I believe you're right," said Jerrel. "He would be foolish to do so, and he is not. But let us both hope that he acts foolishly for once. I don't intend to let you outlive me."

There was silence, and a dull ache along the side of her face and her neck, where she had been battered against Jerrel's shoulders. Maya thought about food. Great piles of fluffy white couscous, topped with strips of beef in a sauce of sweet cane juice, with fried yam on the side and coffee to finish. She tried to imagine a peaceful resolution to her situation, Jerrel perhaps being allowed to walk far enough along the road out of Koloma to avoid pursuit, then Maya being allowed to walk back and return to her much-relieved father... it was too implausible for even a momentary distraction. The rescue fantasies that she began all ended with her as a bloody corpse, which reminded her—"Jerrel," she said, "why were those Devenyons trying to kill Udo?"

Jerrel grinned nastily. "He slandered Yuhil Devenyon's wife. Didn't you know? The Assembly found no truth in Udo's words, but they wouldn't give the Devenyons his life. So they tried to take it themselves. If they weren't a pack of upstarts, one could almost respect them. Perhaps it is not surprising, what I am reduced to, when only the merchants remember what it is to be free men."

"'Perhaps it is not surprising?'" Maya echoed. "You're not a fool, Jerrel. You didn't really expect that you would stab the king and shout 'Down with tyrants!' and the whole city would fall in line." As soon as she said it, she knew it was true. And something else. "You didn't take the walk out of

Koloma eight years ago carrying enough gold in your hands to raise an army. You had a sponsor. Who?"

Jerrel didn't answer. He sat against the opposite wall and toyed with his knife.

"Whoever he is—or they are—they've betrayed you." That was a guess. But the look on Jerrel's face told Maya it was probably an accurate one. "Why choose them over me? We learned together with Gabren for two years and I never betrayed you."

"Didn't you?" Jerrel said. "Perhaps not knowingly. Were you never told that you and I were betrothed, at one time? That was broken, along with much else, when we were ostracized from Koloma."

"That—I was two years old. I never knew. I didn't betray you, even so—I mean, I haven't married anyone else in the meantime."

Jerrel laughed. "If you are offering to uphold your half of the bargain, it is simultaneously too late and too early for that."

Maya couldn't think of a single thing to say. There was no further conversation, and though Maya had slept her fill and more, her head hurt and her vision was blurred. Soon she dozed off again.

It was dark when she woke, roused by a new smell. "Fire," she said muzzily. She could hear it too, and see dim flickers among the straw of the roof.

"Well," said Jerrel. "I would seem to have my answer."

Maya filled her lungs with air—it was still good, thank what little luck she had—and screamed, as Jerrel took a firmer grip on his knife and a step towards her.

A figure came smashing through the door. As Jerrel drew back his hand to strike, the man drove his long spear into the roof, and it fell in.

Caught off balance, Jerrel's blow fell across the front of Maya's body, glancing off her ribs. She rolled away. Bright Gods, she was dizzy. Too weak to cough and clear her lungs of smoke, and she could feel her life coming out of her chest. Jerrel's hair had caught fire, and it made a flaming halo around his face as the knife fell again.

It didn't reach Maya. The figure stepped between them, and in the light of the burning roof she could make out the inhumanly large frame of the Chief General of Koloma, Klyed Anytus. She didn't see what happened after that, but when it was over, Klyed was still standing, and Jerrel wasn't. She had a brief impression of being wrapped in a damp cloak and lifted up, and then nothing at all.

Maya woke up in the physician's room in the palace. The cut across her chest had been sewn up, and ointments had been applied to her scrapes and burns, but it all still hurt. Patches of her hair had burned off as well. Two of her father's guards, desert dwellers with tattooed faces, stood by the head of her bed. Two soldiers of the regular army, with bright spears and neckguards, stood by the foot. "What are you..." Maya said.

"The king and queen have been concerned about you, Highness," said one of the soldiers. "Obviously the previous arrangements made for your safety were insufficient."

The king... and queen? Talle would have been better pleased if Jerrel's knife had found its target, unless Maya was very much mistaken. Janna had once told her that someone had told her that Talle had tried to kill Maya with her own hands, when she was a baby.

"Can you walk, Highness?" said the other soldier. Maya swung her legs over the edge of the bed. She could. "We'll take you to the women's quarters."

When they got there, Talle was waiting. "Maya," she said. "I thank the Bright Gods you're well."

Hearing Talle speak politely made Maya's eyes cross. "Talle? Where's Arnya?"

"Ostracized," said Talle. "For her involvement in Jerrel Talyon's conspiracy."

"What?" Maya wanted to run to her room, find Arnya there, show Talle that it wasn't true. "Arnya never conspired with anyone!"

"Pardon me, but how would you know?" said Talle. "You have been running wild so much, and in your proper place so seldom. Were you ever informed of your former engagement to Jerrel Talyon, for instance?"

It was on the tip of Maya's tongue to answer *yes*, but she bit it back, and she wasn't sure why.

"That was at Arnya's instigation," Talle went on. "Her family and the Talyons were very close. It was a great blow to her when they were ostracized. You know what her position here has been since. Do you think she would have scrupled at anything to gain herself a little more security?"

"Yes!" said Maya.

"The Assembly did not," said Talle. "Unanimously did not. Arnya took the walk yesterday morning, and I officially adopted you as soon as you were restored. It's a pity you weren't well enough to attend the ceremony. It was quite nice."

They passed into an open courtyard where Janna sat chatting with a couple of maids. The maids were working on intricate beadwork. Janna was eating dates.

"Maya!" Janna called. "You look like a rag doll that's been dragged through an ash heap! I'm glad you're back. There's been no one to clear the rats out of the walls since Arnya left. Would you like a date?"

The blue-glass clasps that Arnya had lent to Maya a few days before glinted at Janna's shoulders. Maya was too choked with outrage to speak.

"Thank you, Janna," said Talle smoothly. "Maya is tired. Please excuse us." She swept past Janna, and Maya followed her, for once, willingly.

Once they'd left the courtyard, Talle sighed. "I know you have no love for me, but if you cannot regard me as a mother, will you regard me as an ally? Like it or not, you're mine now, Maya. And I will go to great lengths to protect what is mine."

"Is that why the extra guards?" said Maya.

"Klyed's men are desert dwellers, strangers. But Iyyan and Meled are family. Our family. They will not fail you." At the curtain of Maya and Arnya's room—Maya's room—Talle paused. "Would you like to rest? I'll send along some food to you presently. After that you will have a bath, and some fresh clothing," she looked at Maya doubtfully, "and a haircut. Your father the king wishes you to be at the banquet tonight, and I will have you presentable."

There was only one bed in the room. All of Arnya's things had been cleared out. As much as she could carry by herself, according to the ancient law of Koloma. Everything else had already found its way to Janna's hands, or those of the upper maids. Not that there was much. Arnya hadn't had many possessions of her own. Maya lay on her bed and cried until the tears stopped coming. After that, she just shook.

She had to sit up and compose herself when a maid came in with a tray of food. The fluffy white couscous she'd dreamed about was there, although without the beef and yams, etcetera. It tasted like paste. Maya gave up after half a plate.

Though the banquet wouldn't be for another two hours, Maya went to the entrance of the women's quarters after her bath. She found both sets of guards waiting there, glowering at each other. "I want to see my tutor," she announced, hiding—she hoped—the fear curled in her stomach. If Gabren was gone, too...

But one of the soldiers said, "He's in the library, Highness," and they led her there.

Gabren put aside his scroll and stood when he saw Maya come in. Her guards trailed her as she walked towards him. "Do you have to hover?" she said. "There's only one entrance to this room. Guard that."

"Highness," said the taller of the two desert dwellers, and they started to withdraw.

The soldiers stayed close. "We cannot leave you, Highness," said one of them. "The king has entrusted us with your safety."

"He would have done better to have entrusted you with digging latrines," said Maya, "since the Bright Gods seem to have entrusted you with all the sense of gophers."

The soldier didn't answer, nor did he move. The guards, seeing this interplay, came to stand near Maya as well. She snarled and turned her back.

"Little Highness," said Gabren, "when you lose your temper you lose what no one else can take from you, and you gain nothing."

Maya sat, resting her elbows on the table and her head in her hands. "I know. I'm sorry, Gabren."

"Well," said Gabren, resuming his seat, "I am not the one whom you treated rudely. You can gain no advantage by offending people whose duty it is to protect you. They cannot disobey their orders, and they know what happened to the two men who lost track of you on the way to the palace, even if you don't."

Maya raised her head. "Gabren, what's happened?"

"After the fighting started," said Gabren, "I made my own way back to the palace. The king and his men had already returned by the time I got there, and another complement of guards arrived shortly thereafter, along with the two who had been responsible for you. The Chief General ordered their execution, which was carried out immediately. The king then called for an emergency meeting of the Assembly, to be held an hour before sunset, to discuss the appointment of a new Defender of the Palace. The Chief General, meanwhile, was supervising the search for you, when Udo Loyon was brought in with a message from Jerrel Talyon."

Something about the way Gabren said this clicked another bead into place inside Maya's head. She felt sick. "Jerrel was wrong, then."

Gabren tilted his head and raised his eyebrows.

"He said that Udo deserved to be beaten to death by a mob and that someday he would be. But he wasn't," said Maya, looking firmly at the table. "Was he?"

"No."

"Klyed killed him."

"Yes."

"Two cuts to the belly." Maya drew them on her own belly with a finger. "Then left to die as his guts spilled out. Just like the messenger my grandfather sent him, ordering him to surrender."

"Yes."

Maya swallowed. Without lifting her eyes, she said, "Go on."

"The king had opened the Assembly to all the men of the city who wished to attend, so I was there, though of course I could not speak. The king began by speaking about the unrest in the city, and the conspiracy of Jerrel Talyon. Then the High Priest accused Arnya of involvement in the conspiracy, and called for her ostracism."

Talle hadn't told Maya that it was her brother Attal who'd introduced the measure to ostracize Arnya. But Maya wasn't surprised. "On what evidence?"

"On the evidence of Arnya's well-known, if long-ago, association with the Talyon family. He argued that she must have helped deliver you into Jerrel Talyon's hands, to fulfill the engagement with him that she had contracted for you when you were young. He also claimed more recent intelligence, obtained from his sister the queen, of Arnya's secret communications with several of the conspirators."

"Talle told me that the Assembly was unanimous," said Maya. "No one spoke for her. Not her uncle or brothers?"

"I believe," said Gabren, "they were simply glad it was not them."

"Not my father?"

"Technically, the king has no vote in the Assembly," said Gabren. "And he needed the support of the Jabian family for the next measure he proposed, to appoint the Chief General's man Chakkan as Defender of the Palace. Many members of the ancient families did not like it."

Maya gave a dry, painful laugh. "I should say. A desert dweller, given the ancient post of the Argus family! But... the measure went through, didn't it. My father carried it."

"Yes."

"And then?"

"There was more talk, but nothing of substance," said Gabren. "The Assembly broke up at full dark. Some hours later, the Chief General returned to the Palace, with you and Jerrel Talyon, both gravely injured. You lived. Jerrel did not. At dawn, Arnya took the walk out of Koloma, and the queen officially adopted you. After that, I believe you know as much as I do."

Maya ran her fingers along the grain of the table in silence; she must have breathed more smoke than she thought, because her throat hurt from talking. She had what she had come for, an account of what had happened from a source she trusted. "Gabren," she said, "did I do wrong?"

She went on quickly, before he could reply. "You said, 'What is it that we call evil? Is it not that which harms us?' Well, when I saw Udo being attacked by three men with sticks, fallen, bleeding, and they meant to keep hitting him until he died, and he called for my help, I helped him.

"The consequences of that action have been," Maya counted off on her fingers, "my two guards were killed, Arnya was ostracized, I was kidnapped, stabbed, burnt, and nearly died, and Udo would have been better off if I'd left him. Are we then to conclude, that when someone asks for your help, and will die if you don't give it, helping him is evil?"

Gabren didn't answer right away. Maya looked up finally, to see his face drawn tight in exhaustion or pain. "You make a convincing argument that it can be. However... let us consider this matter further. You have described Arnya's ostracism as a consequence of your actions, but is this justified?"

"If I hadn't gone missing, Talle and her brother wouldn't have had any excuse to go after her," said Maya.

Gabren shrugged. "The king needed a favor from their family. Do you think they couldn't have found another excuse?"

"No," said Maya. "I suppose they could have."

"Well," said Gabren. "You say that Udo would have been better off if you had left him. Is this justified?"

Maya stared at him in disbelief. "To die like that—it's horrible. Anything's better."

"I do not believe that being beaten to death by sticks is pleasant." Gabren gave a bitter twist to the last word. Maybe he was remembering their last conversation with Udo, how he'd laughed when Gabren demolished his argument. "In any case, you didn't volunteer your help. He asked for it."

"He didn't know," said Maya. "He couldn't know what would happen to him."

"Did you?"

"No! But—"

Gabren held up a hand. "Either ignorance of the consequences of an action absolves one of the responsibility for those consequences, or it does not. If it does, then you are not responsible for the manner of Udo's death, being necessarily ignorant of it at the time. If, on the other hand, it does not, then it was Udo who chose the manner of his death, not you. You merely saved him from a death he did not choose.

"As for your own injuries," Gabren went on, "surely the worst harm one can do to oneself is to do evil. Therefore. If your action was evil, you have harmed yourself, but if it was good, you can only have benefited yourself."

Gabren had cleared Maya of all the charges she had leveled against herself except one. "And the guards?" said Maya.

Gabren spread his hands. "Well, Little Highness, what did you think would to happen to them if they lost you?"

"I didn't," said Maya. "Think." Gabren had often observed that acting without thought was the primary source of evil. This time he was silent. "Gabren, some people call you the wisest man alive."

Now it was Gabren who would not look at her. "All that proves is that some people say foolish things."

"It also proves that people respect you," said Maya. "You have friends, and influence, and not just in Koloma. I don't. Arnya's own family voted for her ostracism. Even if they wanted to, they'd be afraid to help her. Gabren, will you see that she's taken care of? That she has something to eat, somewhere to sleep, someone to look after her interests and protect her? Will you make sure that she knows that I'm all right, and that I'm sorry?"

Gabren touched Maya—which he had never done before—on the side of her face, where new skin was beginning to come up in red bumps. "Highness, this influence you speak of—do you remember how I used to recruit students, when we walked in the city?"

Maya blinked. "You never did."

"Someone once asked my teacher, Lykon, why people called him the wisest man on earth," said Gabren. "Lykon answered that he was not especially wise, but the man persisted in his question. Finally Lykon said, 'I have no more wisdom than any other man. Perhaps people think me wise, because when anyone comes to me seeking wisdom, I do not turn him away.' I have tried to live by that. I believe I have succeeded. But it is not a course of action that has worked out well for my students."

"Gabren?"

"Concerning Arnya," said Gabren, "it will be done. But answer me this: what is the duty of a ruler?"

When they'd discussed the question in the market, they hadn't found a satisfactory answer. But Maya had thought about it, in the days before events had swept other thoughts from her mind, and she saw where they'd gone wrong. Udo, Jerrel, herself—they had all proposed that a ruler should rule in a certain way, but circumstances might arise which made that way of ruling inappropriate, or impossible. There was only one duty no circumstance could excuse a ruler from, if he would remain a ruler. "To rule," said Maya.

"And what must a ruler do, before he begins to rule?"

Surely a ruler should learn wisdom, and virtue, and gain the support of his people before he began to rule, but there had been many rulers in history who'd done none of these things. Anyone could be a ruler, it seemed, as long as the blood beat in his veins. "He—" Maya began. But Gabren had already risen to leave.

Maya sat for a few minutes longer. She touched the scar on her chest through the fine fabric of her drape. An inch deeper, and she could never have hoped to rule at all. Before a ruler could rule, he had to survive to see his coronation.

"Iyyan Jabian," she said, "I apologize for my words earlier. Will you take me back to the women's quarters, please?"

There was just enough time left to dress before the banquet. Maya wore the same embroidered drape she had worn to court five days before, but her clasps shone with lapis, not glass, and her arms were weighed down with gold bracelets. It seemed there were advantages to being Talle's daughter, rather than Arnya's.

At the banquet, she sat at her father's right, and Talle sat at his left. Gabren sat at one of the lower tables. Maya didn't look at him. Despite his warning, she didn't think her life was in immediate danger. Even Jerrel hadn't tried to kill her until he was backed into a corner. If Maya was quiet, and caused no trouble, she could hope to live for several years yet. So could Gabren.

If she was not quiet... it was true that Gabren had a wider influence than she did. But he wasn't valuable in the same way. She might act, and fail, and survive. He would die.

But his questions had shown her what she could do. And if acting without thinking was evil, surely thinking without acting was as bad.

Maya's stomach turned at the smell of the meats in rich sauces, and the sticky-sweet barley cakes. She picked at her roasted pigeon and couscous, and watched the entertainers. There was a juggler with a monkey, and she even laughed when the monkey ran between the juggler's legs and made him drop his sticks. And she waited.

She had worked out how Gabren recruited students without seeming to. He only spoke, at a time and place where he would be heard. That was where his influence came from—and if he could do it, so could she.

When the jugglers were replaced by singers and flute girls, and the meat and cakes by water and wine, women usually excused themselves. Talle gave Maya a well-bred frown, clearly expecting her to do the usual thing.

She turned to her father instead. "Majesty, may I ask a question?"

"Ask," he said.

"Can you tell me," said Maya, "who was the instigator behind the recent rebellion in the city?"

"You met him briefly, I believe," said the king. "Jerrel Talyon."

"I met him. But I didn't realize at the time how very strong he must have been."

"What do you mean?" said the king. He was growing irritated, Maya saw, but he wasn't ready to dismiss her yet.

"How else could he have carried away enough gold from Koloma to raise up a rebel army?"

The king laughed, and there were chuckles from along the table as well. Good. He wasn't taking her seriously, but he was interested.

"No, it wasn't the Talyons alone who paid for the troops and weapons," said the king. "When you are older, you will find that there are always those who think they would benefit by installing a new king."

"Indeed, there were many in positions of power and influence who sympathized with the Talyons," Attal Jabian put in blandly. "Arnya the king's former wife was one."

No one would be entertained by a small girl crying for her mother. Maya couldn't stop her hands from clenching, or her mouth from tightening, but she kept the quaver out of her voice. "But this is terrible. None of the maids in the women's quarters will consent to work anymore, now that such a treasure has been divided between them."

That drew laughs from all the tables, louder than the joke deserved. Not all the feasters had diluted their wine as much as the king, nor drunk as moderately.

Chakkan frowned. He had been appointed Defender of the Palace only yesterday; he had never sat at the high table before, and it was clear he didn't approve of this style of humor. "The source of all this gold, this planning—we have not found. But we have found their cutthroats, their safe houses. We ask questions, they cannot hide for long."

"Will they wait patiently to be found?" asked Maya. "Or will they flee, and leave their schemes and their fortunes to scratch out their livings in foreign lands?"

"Some may," said the king. "Most will act."

"Then their first act must me to kill you, and me, as well," said Maya. "To clear their path to the throne."

"Little Maya, haven't you been paying attention?" said the king. "What do you suppose Jerrel Talyon wanted you for? You were to be his path to the throne."

"Then the true instigator of these events," said Maya, "must be someone who also seeks to secure such a path."

The king's laughter this time was uproarious, but strangely enough none of the courtiers joined in. "Someone who has asked me for your hand in marriage, you mean? I thought of that, too, and in fact I have been keeping a little list. Haven't I, Deven?"

"Majesty—" the Steward of the Granaries began to stammer. The king kept talking over him.

"But why are you blushing, Klyed, Chakkan? It doesn't become your tattoos. I think you have swallowed your wine the wrong way, Attal. You see, Maya," he said, laughing again, "it is useless. There is no one at this table who hasn't."

"Well," said Maya, "perhaps I misspoke. You are clearly on your guard on this path. But someone who could never hope to use this path might think of securing another. Might have already done so."

"'Someone who could never hope to use this path?'" said the king. "The Bright Gods forbid marriage between first-order relatives, of course. But I am the only one of those you have, and I am already king. Beyond that, any man could hope to marry you."

"Yes," Maya agreed. "Any man."

The attention of the room was no longer focused on Maya. Everyone turned to stare at the queen.

"Majesty," she said, "this is nonsense. It is her tutor who has been filling her head with it. Everyone knows he used to teach Jerrel Talyon before he was ostracized, now we are starting to hear that he continued to do so after he returned. He told Maya that Arnya was ostracized because of my family's ambitions, that she should use her recent ordeal to benefit herself, that she should begin to be a ruler."

It was not ostracism that Talle was preparing for Gabren—he had no ancient lineage. It was the headsman's hurdle. And now Maya had no more need to hide her fury. She rounded on Talle. "These are words you have from your cousins, who were assigned to be my guards. Why should the king need to hear them from you? If there are armed men in the palace who answer to another authority than the king's, that is treason."

Talle slapped her, stingingly. "Be silent!" she hissed. "I ought to have rid myself of you when you were born. I would have, if Arnya had not woken up despite the poppy juice she'd taken—if she had not screamed like a madwoman—by the Bright Gods I will not fail a second time!"

"Talle Jabian," said the king, "you have confessed in this court to the attempted murder of my heir."

Talle started to turn, to speak, but the king was faster. His sword was out of its sheath, and it swung back and bit deep into her neck. There was a sickening wet sound, and two thumps, one after the other, as the queen's body and head hit the floor. The high table and everyone sitting at it was spattered with blood.

There was a choked-off shriek from one of the flute-girls, and retching from many of the heavier drinkers. No one spoke. The king wiped off his sword, re-sheathed it, and turned to Maya. "Well, daughter," he said. "Have you any more questions?"

"Majesty," said Maya shakily, "I am satisfied." She had known that people would die, if she spoke. She had hoped it would be Talle, rather than herself, or Gabren, or even her father. But she had not been expecting this.

"Adeks, Yeb," said Chakkan to Maya's guards, "take her Highness to the barracks. Keep her safe. Tonight we have work."

Maya let herself be led away quietly. She was glad of one thing—her father seemed in no hurry to marry her off. It was good. She would live, and she would rule. When she did, there would be changes.

Kuemo of the Masks

This is the story of Akemuz, corn-mother, grave-mother
This is the story of her grief and her fury
Of her wanderings, on the earth and below the earth
The year turns, we wait for the rains

O Akemuz!
Hear your story, dwell in us
Feed us, sustain us, preserve us

So. You want a story.

Would you like to hear the old legends of the gods told anew, or see fresh tales performed for wondering eyes? That's my trade, though I'm not the player my mother was.

When my mother sang, it was like a touch that lingered even after the sound was gone. When my mother danced, she turned the plain boards of a players' cart into the primeval forest, or the palace of a king, or the home of the gods. When my mother put on a mask, she became the role.

I grew up hearing stories of her brilliance and her fire. Every member of my father's troupe had a particular play they remembered, or a song they could never thereafter hear, no matter who sang it, without a chill running through them.

My own memories of her are few. I only distinctly recall the day she left.

I'd been crying. I remember how hot and puffy my face felt, how cool her fingers against my skin. "It's the way of things, Garuz, my daughter," she said. "It's time."

She was already carrying her things on her back. Even for a player, she had very little: a change of clothes, a sturdy cloak, a bedroll, a cooking pot and a knife. A string of coral beads my father had given her. Everything else, the masks and the costumes, the carts and tents and furniture, belonged to the troupe. There was one more thing she owned, and she placed it in front of me: a heavy wooden chest with iron fittings.

"Your father will carry this for you until you're strong enough," she said, "but I mean it for you. Your legacy."

I tried to lift the chest. She was right; it was too heavy. I swallowed back my tears and asked, "What's inside?"

I don't know what I was hoping for—something that would make what was happening into a mistake, or a joke, or a story. I didn't understand. What way of things? Why was she leaving? What had I done wrong?

"Masks," she said, "and a script. They're very old, very dangerous."

I waited for her to say that I must never open it, never put on the masks, never read the script. Though I was very young, I'd already seen more plays than I could count, and I knew how they went. But she didn't say anything else.

Maybe she trusted my good sense, my native caution, my cowardice—whatever you like to call it. The plain fact is as the years passed, I did grow strong enough to carry the chest myself, but I never did open it.

The players of my father's troupe, when they spoke of her, spoke as if she'd gone away with another troupe or group of wanderers, as anyone might. They certainly never suggested she might be dead, nor do I think that it was only to spare my feelings, or my father's. But we never saw her again, never got word of her from other travelers or from the people of towns and cities. It was as if when she left us, she left the earth altogether.

I can see that you're startled that I speak so casually of her leaving, that I say anyone might do it. I've heard that in the towns and cities, priests join men and women together with strong and fearsome vows, and which require strong reasons or large bribes to unwind.

Among the players and travelers, however, the leader of each troupe is a priest. They leave honey and cakes at wayside shrines and know the incantations to ward against demons. They are the ones to invite the dead to feast with the living at springtime, to speak the turning of the year in autumn, and to return their people to the earth at last. But they don't join men and women in marriage—rather, each one loves as almighty Abrekudo inspires them, and comes and goes as they like.

It's a custom, I admit, that sometimes results in uncared-for children—beaten, starved, sold for evil purposes, abandoned by the wayside or on the doorstep of those same priests of towns and cities. And since that's what they see of players' children, it might be no surprise that they think our ways are wicked, and preach the virtues of hearth, home, and fidelity.

But that never happened in my father's troupe. There were a fair handful of us children, it's true, and we might have gone undisciplined, unschooled, and even—in lean times, when anyone might—unfed, but we never went unloved.

Foyez: Swear that you won't beget children.

Ubeyez: Shall I give my oath by the point of the sword, or shall I give my oath by its hilt?

Now, what story shall I tell? I know one about a king so desperate to avoid his prophesied fate that he killed or drove away all his family—no? Not that one?

Another story from my childhood, then? Or from later, after I had grown strong enough to carry the chest, and my mother was little more than a legend to me? I think I know which story you want. It began with a sword.

The sword, when its wielder pulled it out of my father's chest, made a horrible grating sound. Blood followed. At first it hardly seemed real. It looked just like the bit of staging we did with a pig's bladder, but there was more of it, and more, so much, the smell of it hanging thick in the air—he staggered backwards. I ran to catch him and was knocked to my knees by the force of his fall. I held him, blood soaking my dress, his back against my chest as I felt his last rattling breaths. His head jerked up, his arms spasmed, and then he fell limp.

For a moment, I met the eyes of his murderer. They were wide and wild, and he looked, I think, surprised by the turn events had taken. Then there was no time to think.

Kounua and Beyix, twins who had grown up alongside me in our troupe, rushed forward, howling, their swords drawn. They were real swords—we didn't go entirely defenseless against the dangers of the road—but I knew that the closest they'd come to a real fight was the time we'd done a production of *The Tyrant of Orodrua*. The twins knew how to look frightening, anyway. If we were facing a rowdy, drunken crowd—if first blood hadn't already been spilled—it might have been enough. Against the robbers who'd surrounded our carts and their comrades pouring out of the forest around, it was hopeless. Beyix hadn't taken two strides before an arrow skewered him in the thigh, and he fell.

I left my father's body where it lay and tried to drag Beyix towards the carts. If we managed to break free of the robbers and run, we couldn't leave him behind. He was heavy, and the ground was rough, and in between wracking sobs, he cursed me at every stone and thistle I dragged him over. In the meantime, the rest of the troupe grabbed whatever weapons came to hand. Daggers, eating knives, the legs of folding camp stools. One or two of the donkeys tried to run, but, finding themselves still encumbered with the carts, dug in their heels, kicked out randomly, and screamed. Amtrez, who was just old enough at the time to remember the lines of the page in a few plays, perched on top of one of the carts, lobbing stones.

It was all over before I succeeded in lifting Beyix into the bed of the cart. Kounua was down, her sword knocked out of reach, snarling defiance at her attackers through a disordered fringe of auburn curls. Iazem, one of our older actors, lay unmoving with a cudgel still clutched in his gnarled hand. Everyone who had taken up arms had either been felled, disarmed, incapacitated, or retreated behind the carts.

"Stand down!" the robber chief—the one who'd stabbed my father—bellowed at his men. Then he addressed us. "Travelers: surrender, hand over your money and your goods, and you may collect your dead and your injured and be on your way. Refuse, and we'll collect the loot from your corpses."

In response, Amtrez let fly with another stone, which whistled past the chief's head and struck one of the men behind him in the shoulder, to little effect. I scrambled to the top of the cart, where the little fool with his milk-white skin was a prime target, and pulled him down; at the same time, the chief knocked aside the bow of an archer who had begun to take aim.

For the space of several long breaths, no one spoke. Our leader was dead, killed in a hasty exchange of tempers with the robber chief, and we'd had no time to choose a new one. At the moment, there was no one who had the authority to answer for all of us. We were all frightened, confused, and angry—but I was the one who found myself at a vantage point where I could speak and be heard, and I knew what our answer must be. I stood up on the roof of the cart and cried, "We surrender!"

Then I climbed back down into the cart, took up the boards where the troupe's common cash-box was kept, and lifted it out. Beyix was no longer cursing. He lay with his eyes closed, his breath ragged and uneven. My heart clenched to see it, but I was already doing the only thing I could for him. Kounua glared when I came down from the cart and approached the chief; still, she didn't argue with me, and I didn't acknowledge her.

"This is the troupe's money," I said, holding out the box to the chief. "It isn't much, and we'll go hungry until we perform again, but here it is; take it. I'll go around to the other members of the troupe and collect their personal cash and their jewelry. Only leave us our donkeys and our carts, our costumes and sets and props. They'd be little use to you, but they're life to us, so don't compound your blasphemy against Kuemo of the Masks by touching sacred things to which you have no right."

I didn't think the warning against blasphemy would count for much with a robber and a murderer, but to my surprise, he drew back, not touching the box I offered him. "You're *players*."

There were mutters of consternation among the other robbers too. Maybe some of them still clung to old superstitions; more likely they were annoyed to discover that we'd hardly been worth the trouble of attacking. I saw, once I was among them, that not all the casualties had been on our side, and several of the robbers were bloodied or mazed as well. One of them said to his fellow in a whisper that belonged on a stage: "I said a merchant caravan would have more guards."

The chief could read the mood of his band at least as well as I could, so it was his turn to be wrong-footed and have to think quickly. Whatever the man's faults, hesitation wasn't one of them, not when he'd stabbed my father and not then. He swept me a bow. "Please forgive the mistake. We only resorted to arms to defend ourselves, but we wouldn't dare send you out onto the road to starve, or deprive you of the jewels that so well become you." As I was wearing only a set of hoops in my ears and a few plain bronze bracelets, this was a ridiculous piece of flattery. I wondered where he had learned it. "My men and I live far from civilization, but we haven't completely forgotten all its proprieties—though it's been long since any of us has done something so civilized as see a play. You must have pity on us, wasting away in boredom, and accompany us back to our camp and perform for us. You'll be rewarded, I assure you." His teeth flashed white in his thick black beard, bandit fierceness and courtly manners combining in one grin. "I insist."

And I could hardly refuse. "If we do this," I said, "we are your guests, and you are bound to feed us, shelter us, defend us, and send us safely on our way. We must bury our dead, properly with all the rites, and tend to our injured—if you have anyone among you skilled in healing, send them to us. If you harm us in any way, it's an affront not just to Kuemo of the Masks but to Foyez Hospitable as well."

"Agreed!" His grin flashed again, delighted, as if the last few terrifying, deadly minutes had never happened. As if Beyix wasn't dying in the largest of the carts at my back, as if my dress weren't soaked in his blood and my father's. The chief unscrewed an earring from his ear, a golden teardrop with a fulgent red jewel at the end, and dropped it into my hand in token of our agreement. I closed my fist around it, silently vowing to Foyez that if the troupe got out of this alive and whole—as whole as we were—I would dedicate it to him at the next shrine we passed. It wasn't entirely pious on my part. I wanted to get the damned thing out of my hands as soon as I decently could.

This is the song of the dead
This is the song of love and remembered deeds

Of duty fulfilled, on the earth and below the earth
The year turns, the dead ground brings forth new life

O ancestors!
Hear your song, feast with us
Be recalled, be honored, be at peace

We came to the robbers' camp blindfolded. It was about an hour's journey—we weren't force-marched like soldiers, but neither were we allowed to slow or rest, and anyone who couldn't keep up was loaded into the carts. The old, the children, the injured, the dead. The robber chief tied a thick rag around my eyes himself, talking all the while in that odd, cultivated accent of his: "I apologize for the necessity, but you must understand that we can't have you leading the king's men to our camp once you reach the city..."

As if it mattered what I understood and what I didn't. Or as if I were a maiden of Akemuz, to wash away his sins with my tears. As for the first, they would do what they liked with us, and that was that. As for the second, my throat felt tight and my eyes burned, but they stayed dry. It was the only dignity I had left. I think my silence unnerved him. Kounua cursed the robbers the entire way, their ancestors and their descendants and the constellations that had presided over their births—she knew even more curses than her twin. Amtrez had to be bound hand and foot before they threw him into the bed of a cart, hissing and spitting like a cat.

At length we arrived and the robbers removed our blindfolds. Their camp was a dozen ramshackle buildings nestled at the foot of a rocky hill by the shore of a pond. I could see a place where the hill sloped gently down to a meadow, which would serve us well enough as a theater. "Here," I said. "We'll bury our dead here."

The chief commanded a few of his men to help us build cairns. They fetched rocks from the country around and we piled them on my father's body and Iazem's. I remembered enough of the rites to return them to the earth and to Akemuz, and then my tears fell, even with the robbers still looking on—the ones who'd carried the rocks, and a woman with a long face and threads of silver in her hair, who'd dosed the injured with potions and poultices and muttered charms. It didn't seem to have done any harm, though for Beyix—the only one whose injuries were serious—it hadn't done any good either. He was wandering in and out of awareness, and only roused himself to speech once, to ask for Kounua, but didn't know her when she pressed his hand.

After the funeral, the robbers herded us and our carts to the center of their camp. If it hadn't been for the circumstances, it would have been more comfortable than most of our campsites between cities, the more because none of us had to haul water or cook or dig latrines. It was all done for us, as I'd asked. The robbers spoke to us with a swagger and a threat in their voices, but also with curiosity and excitement. They were looking forward to their play, as it seemed, to a man, though I assured them it couldn't possibly happen until the next day. The light was already beginning to fade.

We ate and then we took counsel. There were robbers always lurking about, so we tried to speak softly for some pretense at privacy.

"Who chose you for our leader?" Kounua's voice would normally have been a shout; now it was a ragged whisper. Or maybe it was just that her throat was raw. "Who gave you the authority to speak for us?"

"Nobody," I said. "But somebody needed to speak, and there was nothing else they could have said."

"Wasn't there? Must we dance for your father's murderers, and my brother's?"

"Beyix isn't dead yet," said Zbardem, who, with his bald forehead and long gray curls behind, played prophets and venerable kings and Foyez himself so often that he really thought all his words were pearls of wisdom. "And—forgive me, Garuz, and may Garnamer's shade forgive me, but if he hadn't provoked the robber chief he might still live, and we might have slid on by. We've done it in the past. The chief himself said it was a mistake that they attacked us."

"Who cares what—" Amtrez began at full volume, and his father shushed him.

Amtrez was born to our troupe, but his parents and older brother had joined us from over the mountains; they were all four of them pale as milk,

THE FIRSTBORN OF DEATH

with freckles across their noses and up their arms. Tazanom, the father, was a musician, and Fomauz, the mother, a seamstress who'd turned her hand to sewing costumes and making up sets. Narem, the older brother, had grown into an actor—a middling one as yet, but he could learn his lines and hit his marks, and they'd all been with us long enough to know our ways.

"You may speak in council when your voice has broken, pup," Tazanom said with a light cuff to the back of Amtrez's head. "Still, it's true—they may say that they're sorry for what they've done, but Garnamer and Iazem are still dead, and Beyix is still lying senseless. They may swear that they'll let us go once we've played for them, but who knows if they will?"

"We could—" Oinoyua hooked her long black hair behind her ear, leaned forward, and whispered, "we could try to sneak off in the night. If the robbers are sleeping heavily—"

"Oh?" Narem's voice had broken the month before, so he could speak in council. And if he wasn't careful someone would break his nose for him before too long. He'd taken a minor injury in the fight, and he picked at his bandage as he sneered, "Will you poison their wine, then, while you distract the sentry by humping his leg and breathing in his ear? That will give him a surprise, anyway."

Any actress might have taken offense at such a crass speech. But Oinoyua, as I'm sure you know, since your guards were none too gentle when they arrested us, is chosen of Kuemo. She had been traveling with troupes of players for years before she joined ours, but in her early life she was a butcher's son in the city of Gero. Life in the cities and towns is seldom kind to Kuemo's chosen, and life among wanderers, as Narem's words showed, is sometimes no kinder.

Oinoyua whirled on Narem as if she would do him the honor of breaking his nose. Another night, I would have let her.

"I have an idea," I said, and Oinoyua turned back to me, and Narem quieted, and even Kounua looked up, sullen but listening. "My mother—"

"Ah, if your mother were with us," Zbardem sighed, stroking his beard. "We never would have come to this pass."

"She left me a legacy. Masks and a script, she said, very old and very dangerous. I've never opened the chest. But now—I think it may be time to play it."

Kuemo of the Masks
  Of many faces and none
  Carved men and women from the stump of a tree
  Taught them to speak
  To sing
  And to lie

Though our lodgings were as comfortable as any we ever had on the road, none of us slept well that night. In dreams, my father spoke to me, but instead of words, blood poured from his mouth. My mother rose from the mists of the pond, dancing on its surface. The dead danced with her, slack-limbed and rotting. We fled the robbers' camp as Oinoyua suggested, and every twisting path of the forest brought us back there, while I held a mask in my hands, its mouth gaping as if it would swallow the world. Beyix screamed—but that wasn't a dream. I roused myself from visions of blood and earth to find Kounua, who'd slept curled round him as they hadn't since they were children, trying to soothe him, giving him water and a potion that the robbers' healer-woman had left. It worked a little. He fell back into a fitful doze, though his skin still burned. An hour or two later, he started screaming again.

The robbers brought us boiled porridge for breakfast with lumps of gamy-tasting fat. I told them they would have their play that afternoon. No one contradicted me. Kounua helped me get the chest down from the cart, silent, her eyes red-rimmed. The troupe gathered around as I lifted the latches. I think that some of them expected a company of avenging spirits to fly out and slaughter the robbers and ourselves together in an instant. But there was nothing in it but what my mother had said. Masks, in a simple archaic style, the wood worn very smooth and the paint faded. I lifted one—Foyez, by the curling beard and the oak-leaf crown, his mouth a simple empty oblong—and found it surprisingly light. Underneath lay rows of tightly-curled parchment. So old a script, it seemed, that it had never been bound into a book.

I unrolled one: the title written across the top of the page was *Ubeyez's Oath-Breaking*, and it had an opening soliloquy by Eto Light-Footed. Amtrez, hanging off my arm and reading over my shoulder, exclaimed, "Oh, there's a part for me!"

Amtrez had done a charming turn as the boy-girl page of the gods in our recent *Abrekudo's Revels*—the same production where Oinoyua's portrayal of Abrekudo had given rise to Narem's nasty 'humping his leg and breathing in his ear' comment. But that part had only had a few lines. This one, on the other hand—

"It's a long soliloquy, Amtrez," I said. "And only a morning to learn it. I think Narem had better play Eto."

"Oh, let him do it," said Narem, who'd snagged a roll of parchment from the chest and was reading also. Amtrez's face lit up—he rarely heard words of encouragement from his older brother. "The Eto mask is too small for me, anyway. And I want to play Ubeyez."

Ah, I thought, so that's the way of it. Still, he wasn't wrong on either count—the Eto mask was child-sized, and with Beyix gravely injured and my father killed, we were running short of actors who could play Ubeyez. I scanned the words of the soliloquy again. It was written in a style as archaic as the masks, but still comprehensible. A robber band wasn't likely to be the most discriminating audience, and they surely wouldn't be familiar with a play I'd never heard of myself. They wouldn't notice a few flubbed lines.

"All right," I said. "Start memorizing, both of you. Oinoyua—" Now here was a problem. If Oinoyua had to play Abrekudo of the Twilight opposite Narem's Ubeyez of the Dawn, there would be blood on the boards. "Would you play Akemuz?"

Oinoyua narrowed her eyes, and I wondered if I'd offended her by implying that she'd grown too old for Abrekudo and was now only suited to matronly roles. But after a moment she said, "The queen of the gods? That suits me very well."

I gave a sigh of relief, then looked over at Kounua. It was hard for me to say what was at the tip of my tongue. But I didn't have to. We could read each other that well. "I'll play Abrekudo," she said quietly.

To play Ubeyez's twin opposite Narem, while her own twin lay dying—I had no words for her. I could only reach over and squeeze her hand.

Zbardem, naturally, was already muttering Foyez's lines to himself. There was only Kuemo of the Masks left to cast. Except, as I continued to read the script, it seemed she never appeared. In a play called Ubeyez's Oath-Breaking, when she was the one who had tricked him into breaking his oath. Odd. But it made my job easier. I left the actors learning their lines—Zbardem had called Narem over to read through the scene where Foyez demands that Ubeyez forswear love and children, and Ubeyez gives him one riddling answer after another before he finally agrees—and gathered up Tanazom and Fomauz and everyone else who was sitting around idling, had them help drag carts down to the meadow so we could put the stage together and start making up the sets. I wanted to have at least one read-through done before noon.

But now I can see the puzzled crease between your eyebrows, and questions forming on your lips. What, you are surely wondering, of the dangers of these masks, this script? What of Kounua's objections to performing for the robbers? Why were we not planning our escape or our revenge? Listening to me, it must sound like we had forgotten everything but the play.

To which I can only answer: we had. And if this surprises you, it's because you've never lived among players.

At any rate, we soon had the stage set up with the fluttering blue canopy to suggest the heavenly council-halls. I set Tanazom to shoo away curious robbers so that the play would stay fresh and unspoiled for them until the afternoon's performance, and I sent Fomauz to fetch her sons and the other actors so we could start rehearsing. The masks in their chest I kept by me. You may have heard that it's bad luck for actors to try on their masks until they're ready to perform before an audience. I admit we weren't always so scrupulous, but that day, we were.

The rehearsals went well—better than I might have expected for a play we were putting on for the first time. The dance that Amtrez did to accompany his opening soliloquy was made up of steps he'd done before, but this time he was as light-footed as the god-goddess he portrayed. I was afraid that Narem as Ubeyez arguing with his divine father would sound querulous and spoiled—as he often did in real life—but he rose to the occasion and spoke his lines like a true god of mysteries. Zbardem turned in his usual polished performance, and Oinoyua matched him for power and dignity. As for Kounua, I'd never seen her play so well, and I told myself I must cast her as Abrekudo more often. Her gestures weren't as broad as Oinoyua's were when she played the role: Kounua's Abrekudo of the Twilight was passion tightly reined, danger just beneath the surface, magnetic and terrifying at once.

I had to feed them all a line or two from time to time, but that was to be expected. When we broke for lunch, they were still flushed and flying from their performances, quoting lines at each other between bites. Then we read it through a second time, and I sent Fomauz to keep watch over Beyix, and Tanazom to tell the robbers that we were ready and they could come watch their play whenever they liked, and the actors to put on their costumes and masks.

As the actors hurried behind the curtains, jostling, joking, and reciting, I spread my skirts and settled on a grassy knoll near the stage. It didn't take long before the robbers came striding up from their camp, their chief at their head. He was clearly in control of his people again. He greeted me with a courtly bow and a broad grin, an earring with a fulgent jewel—the twin of the one he'd given me—swinging from one ear, and the other ear bare.

"May I sit here?" he asked, indicating the grass next to me.

"You're our host," I answered with ill grace. "You may sit where you like, only please don't interrupt my work."

He showed no offense, but only spread his coat across the grass and sat. Then the others of his band did the same, in little groups all around the makeshift amphitheater. "Won't you be appearing in the play?" he said.

"I won't. We're not all of us performers. Some of us make up the sets and the costumes, and I've always found my talents lie more in directing. Though my mother was a famous actor, and so was my father—before you murdered him."

"Oh!" The look of surprise and dismay on his face was the same as it had been when he'd drawn the sword out of my father's body. "I didn't know—he was your father? I—I am sorry."

If he hadn't been my father, the robber chief had still murdered a man for no cause. Why should he be sorry just because that man happened to be my father?

So, instead of answering what I had no answer for—and hearing that the chatter of preparation on both sides of the curtain had died down, leaving nothing but an occasional excited whisper from either the actors or the robbers—I stood and gave the signal for the performance to begin.

From somewhere unseen came the haunting notes of Tanazom's pipes. Onstage, the curtains parted like clouds parting after a storm, and Eto Light-footed leaped and spun across the hall of the gods.

It was only Amtrez in a mask, a short chiton, and bracelets on his skinny wrists and anklets. But goosebumps rose on my skin, a chill ran through me, and I heard all the robbers catch their breath at once. Amtrez's hands told the story, and his feet shaped the boards of the cart. When he spoke, he became the role.

Eto:
  O mountains and hills!
  The sky and the seas!
  Pay homage to Foyez Victorious!

Ten foes at a blow
  He trampled their bones
  Beneath the earth drove their survivors!

Lift your voices and weep
  O widows and child-robbed—
  Foyez's children, attend him!

I was so enrapt in Amtrez's soliloquy that I forgot to look at my script until it was nearly over. Fortunately, I didn't need to. He delivered it seamlessly. At its close, Zbardem entered, crowned with carved oak leaves, Oinoyua draped in jewels on his arm. The crowd let out hoots and whistles for Kounua, dressed in the concealing/revealing frills of Abrekudo of the Twilight. The day before, on our march, she'd cursed them with every foul oath she knew and they'd shoved her ungently onwards. Now, she let their shouts slide off her with the unconcern of a goddess—or an actor—and they were soon as transfixed by her words as by her cleavage or thighs, as she pleaded with Zbardem to forgive her twin's absence from the council of the gods.

Then Ubeyez stepped onto the stage. Or I should say Narem, but really, I can't. I had never seen Narem act like this, never suspected he could. I swear I could taste the change in the air as he confronted Zbardem, like the taste of thunder-pregnant clouds overhead. He'd stumbled a bit over his lines during rehearsal, and I stood ready to prompt him if he hesitated, but he didn't. He exchanged words with Zbardem with the tempo and the tension of a perfectly-choreographed swordfight. When he finally gave his oath, and Tazanom began piping for the end of the first act, the audience let out a sigh that would have been quiet if it hadn't issued from dozens of mouths at once.

Now came the curious lacuna of the play: there was no meeting between Ubeyez and Kuemo, no trickery or flirtatious double-speech where she refused to remove her mask and persuaded him to hold her chisel. Instead, the second act opened with the children of the troupe—there were three even younger than Amtrez, and he, barefaced and divested of his jewels, joined them—gamboling across the stage, representing the new-born or new-carved mothers and fathers of all humanity. Oinoyua, as Akemuz, tried to hide them from Foyez. The little imps, delighted by the attention, drew raucous laughter simply by being themselves. I'd seen no children in the robber's camp, and I wondered if they, like plays, were another of the comforts of civilization that the robbers missed so much.

But, inevitably, Foyez discovered the deception—though the robbers, quite caught up in the story, called out to him to try to distract him, and loudly swore that Akemuz was telling him nothing but the truth—and the skirling notes of Tazanom's pipe fell like drops of oil on the churning water of Foyez's rage. And so the second act ended.

The third act, wherein Foyez calls Ubeyez to account, had just gotten underway when I saw Fomauz hurrying towards me, her face even paler than milk—white as whey. My belly went cold; all of a sudden I tumbled from the heights of the gods' drama to the depths of our own. "Please excuse me," I said to the robber chief, but, absorbed in the play, I'm not sure he heard. I rushed to Fomauz and asked her, "Is it Beyix? Is he worse?"

She shook her head, her eyes wide and wild. "I swear I only left him for a moment, to refill his waterskin. I don't know how—"

I never heard what Fomauz didn't know. A howl split the air, and I turned without willing it back to the stage, where Abrekudo held the fallen Ubeyez cradled in her arms. The features on her wooden mask were painted, unchanging, but the slump of her shoulders, the tightness of her muscles spoke of a grief larger than human. Her shout had stilled everyone and left in its wake a silence no words could fill.

For a moment I marveled at Kounua's acting. But it wasn't Narem's lanky, half-grown body she held. They weren't his limbs, pale and not yet filled out in proportion to the knees and elbows, that hung empty onto the stage—not in a parody of lifelessness, but truly in death. She knew—had known before I did, and now I knew without a doubt—and still she took his mask in trembling fingers, lifted it as if that could lift the spell.

It wasn't Narem in Ubeyez's mask. It was Beyix. And Beyix was dead.

Akemuz searched for her son
  Everywhere she sought him
  Atop the highest mountain peak
  And at the ocean's bottom

And everywhere the goddess went
  Her maidens can be found
  Weeping for our lady's grief
  With scarlet garlands crowned

And when she reached Damadez's gate
  She gave herself for ransom
  It was a willing sacrifice

For he was very handsome!

We buried Beyix next to my father and Iazem. The robbers who helped carry the stones for the cairn looked at us with less curiosity and more fear, and the work got done that much more quickly. Still, the sun had set by the time I finished speaking the words to return him to the earth, and the pond was stained red with reflected twilight. I turned to the robber chief, hovering at my shoulder, and said, "You've had your play. Now let us go in peace, as you promised."

His eyes went wide; he seemed startled that I should even ask. "How?" he said. "It's night already, and by the time you've finished packing the wagons it will be full dark. I should be breaking my oath to see you safely on your way if I let you leave now. There are terrors other than my band on the forest road at night. Stay, and let my men bring you supper, and sleep, and leave in the morning."

I looked at the faces of my troupe: Kounua red-eyed and rigid with grief, Narem dazed, all of them tired and frightened. Then I looked at the robbers among us. What had happened that afternoon had unnerved them enough that they'd likely let us go if we insisted, and never mind what orders their chief gave. On the other hand, with men like these, fear if pushed was just as likely to explode into violence. Besides, the robber chief wasn't wrong: we were in no state to travel, and it was no time to search for a new campsite.

"Very well," I said. "We leave with first light."

Amtrez tried to protest—at his age, I believe he would happily have driven all night—but Fomauz hushed him, and the rest of us trudged meekly to our wagons.

When the robbers came to bring us our supper, the healer woman was among them. Kounua turned to her and snarled, "What, witch? Have you come to poison the rest of us as well?"

"Peace, Kounua," I sighed. "She did what she could. It isn't her fault; it's the fault of the man who shot him." I didn't add: and the fault of the chief who commands him. Nor: the fault of the play and the masks, and of the one who suggested opening the chest.

"I'm sorry for your grief," said the healer. "And so is my son, if only you would let him say so. He has a hasty temper, but he truly regrets what happened and means you no more harm."

"He killed my father," I said. And then, "The chief is your son?"

"How else do you think a woman like me came to be living in a robbers' camp?" she said as she uncovered a dish of lentils and wild greens. In the touch of arrogance in her voice, the straight-backed, offended dignity of her posture, I saw indeed the resemblance between her and the chief. She had the same cultivated accent.

"Forgive me," I murmured. "You must have been a great lady once."

"Ah, that was long ago," she said, mollified. "You mustn't fear that you won't be allowed to go in the morning. My son is a man of his word. But truly, I think he wasn't sorry to have an excuse to press you to stay longer. Indeed, you may stay as long as you like. The hospitality isn't so bad, is it?" She looked at me from the corner of her eye, sidelong and sly. "It's been some time since I've seen him so taken with a woman."

"He killed my *father*," I said.

"You cannot blame me for asking, anyway." She shook her head. "An old woman wants grandchildren."

Oinoyua came up and began to help dish out the food. "Oh, what nonsense," she said to the healer. "You're not old."

Narem smirked knowingly at her charm offensive, but I shot Oinoyua a grateful smile and slipped away with a plate of food for myself and another for Kounua. She sat with her arms folded on her knees and her chin resting on her arms, staring at nothing.

"Eat something," I urged her. "We want to be as far away from here as we can tomorrow, and you'll need your strength to travel."

She poked listlessly at the lentils and said, "Ubeyez returns from the underworld."

"I... what?" I said.

"In the myths. He dies, and Akemuz searches for him, and he returns from the underworld. Why did the play end with Ubeyez's death? We can't just leave him here. We have to do something."

I laid a hand gently on her arm. "Kounua, Beyix is dead."

"Don't talk to me like I'm raving," she snarled at me. "Don't pretend that the gods and their works are distant maybes, as we might have thought yesterday, or that Beyix died of an arrow wound alone. How did he come to be wearing Ubeyez's mask? How—you didn't wear one of those masks. I did. I'm not mad."

"Even so. What more can we do?"

"Open the chest again."

I shuddered. We'd packed away the masks and the scripts before burying Beyix, and my skin crawled at the thought of opening it again. Though I knew I couldn't leave it behind with the robbers, I was tempted to—I didn't know how I would sleep in my wagon with the chest packed in next to me. "To what end?" I asked. "We know what's in it already, and it's nothing that might help Beyix."

"We know what was in it when we last closed it," Kounua countered. "We don't know what we'll find if we open it again."

I hesitated. But surely my fears were as absurd as Kounua's hopes. And if opening the chest would dispel them both, why not? "All right. But if nothing out of the ordinary happens, you must agree to leave tomorrow with no more of this talk."

For a moment it looked as if Kounua would argue, but then she just pressed her lips together and nodded. I ate my lentils and greens slowly. Kounua left hers untouched. At last, when I could put it off no longer, I brought the chest down from my wagon and set it on the ground. It drew a few curious glances. Zbardem frowned and said, "Garuz, what—"

I opened the catches and swung up the lid. Masks, and rolls of script. But the masks—the paint looked fresher, somehow. I took up a script and began to unroll it, tilting it so that it caught the light of our campfire. The title was *The Wanderings of Akemuz.*

I hadn't seen the healer woman approach. But she was there, standing by my shoulder. And before I could warn her not to meddle with sacred things, she took a mask out of the chest and fitted it to her face. It was Akemuz.

She was Akemuz. Weeping Akemuz, the great goddess, mother and queen. As she stood among us, I remembered Beyix, how my arms had ached as I dragged him across the rough ground, the pain in his voice as he cursed me. My father: his last rattling breath, his weight against my chest.

My mother: walking quietly down the road until she disappeared behind the next hill. Every grief and loss I had ever felt in my life.

Beside me, Kounua struggled to breathe between sobs. Oinoyua let her hair fall forward, hiding her face, and her body shook with tremors. Amtrez wailed like a child half his age, snot running down his face, his parents and brother too stricken by their own grief to offer him any comfort. Everywhere, suppers sat abandoned as people gave themselves over to mourning.

"The Bright One is gone!" Akemuz cried out in the healer's cultivated accent. The sound of it silenced everyone, though tears continued to flow. The last of the twilight had faded and the moon not yet risen; it seemed indeed as though all light had gone out of the world. I glanced at my script and read the next words as she said them: "My own cherished son, snuffed out by his father's fierce fury! Now, shall I sit mute on my heavenly throne? Shall I still be helpmate to Foyez?"

Kounua stood, moving like a sleepwalker. I dropped the script I was holding and clung to her arm, trying to hold her back, but she ignored me. Oinoyua and Fomauz also stood out from the watchers and bent to the chest, and from its depths they lifted out each a garland of pheasant's-eye flowers and settled it in her hair.

It was high summer at the time these events happened; pheasant's-eye had been gone from the ground for months. And yet the garlands from the chest were as fresh as if young girls had just plucked them from the last patches of snow on the hills and woven them into offerings for Akemuz. The vivid red of the flowers against Kounua's chestnut curls and Fomauz's neat plaits and Oinoyua's waves of midnight black filled me with a dread I couldn't name. In their hands they held the attributes of Akemuz's maidens: a comb, a jeweled necklace, a white robe.

"Mistress," said Oinoyua cajolingly, "cease your loud wails and comb out your hair. Your grief cannot come before duty."

Fomauz held out the robe as if she would drape it over Akemuz's shoulders. "Do not cause strife in the heavenly halls, for peace, lately won, is so fragile."

"Put on a clean robe and your bright precious jewels," said Kounua. The necklace in her hand caught the firelight, sickeningly red. "Take your seat by the husband who gave them."

Akemuz took the necklace and threw it to the ground, turning her back on her attendants in the same graceful motion. "I won't still my voice. Let my cries shake the earth. As for my jewels, I renounce them. I'll quit the gods' halls till my son is restored. If you're faithful, my maidens, you'll follow."

She strode off, the goddess descended to earth. The ground trembled as she passed. Her maidens followed her, and so did the rest of us. I held the chest in my arms as we left the firelight behind. Beyond our camp it was dark, dark. I saw the robbers' fires as smears of ruddy light further down the hill, and I felt bodies crowd close against mine as they joined the procession. We kept walking, downward, blindly, until mud pulled at my feet and water seeped into my shoes. And still we walked, as the pond swirled around my ankles and dragged at the hem of my skirt. My soaked clothing kept me from floating, but every step forward was a struggle. When the water reached my chest, I thought of Amtrez, of the younger children—the water must have been over their heads by then. But I couldn't call out, could do nothing but keep moving forward until the water closed over my head and my lungs burned for air.

I wondered if this was how my father had felt, run through, dying, unable to get breath.

The darkness was total. I couldn't hold my thoughts—they darted away from me like fish beneath the water. And I felt, from outside myself, a sudden curiosity. The presence of something ancient, patient, calm. A presence that had always been there, wherever I traveled, close enough to touch, and I had never known.

Something that carefully, patiently, undid the clasps on the chest I still held, swung up the lid, and took out a mask.

I had seen a woman put on a mask and become a goddess. Now I saw a god put on a mask and become—not a man. Something nearly man-sized, man-shaped.

I thought I had known death. I had buried my father and Iazem and Beyix, and spoken the words to return them to the earth. I had seen Weeping Akemuz incarnate. But death wears one aspect to grieving survivors, and an entirely different one to the dying and the dead. And so I saw him: Silent Damadez, guardian of the gates beneath the earth, keeper of the shades.

His limbs were long and well-formed, darker than shadows, and his mask was carved from a single piece of ivory—what beast might have furnished such a piece, I can't imagine—and as is traditional for masks of Damadez, he had no mouth.

And just as Damadez became man-shaped, the crushing, formless water became broad columns, black marble floors, vaulted ceilings hidden in mist. We stood in his hall, robbers and players alike, dripping from our passage. I no longer felt like I was drowning, although as to whether or not I was breathing—at the time, I gave it no thought, and afterwards, I couldn't say.

In the galleries beyond I saw drifting, indistinct shades of the dead. I hadn't yet found any I knew, when Akemuz stood forth and spoke.

"O Mute Damadez," she said, "my bright son is lost, and nowhere on earth can I find him. Does he dwell, then, in the dark lands beneath? If so, then I charge you: restore him!"

In the script I had seen the direction: *With a gesture, DAMADEZ summons the shade of UBEYEZ. He seizes him in an embrace, looking at AKEMUZ as if to say: I have him, and I will not release him.* Now, I thought of the several ways such a direction could be played: defiant, gloating, amorous.

Instead of any of these, Damadez improvised. He reached behind Akemuz's head and undid the fastenings on her mask. The mask fell to the floor, and the healer woman fell to her knees, covered her face, and wept, her sobs entirely human.

Art has two lovers: one is Lies and the other is Truth.

The spell that held us captive to the play was broken for all of us, but it was the robber chief who recovered his wits first. He rushed to his mother and embraced her where she knelt on the floor.

"Don't fear," he said. "I'll get us out of here. Didn't I get us out of the city when Father declared our lives forfeit?"

I don't know much of life in cities, but I know there's only one man in them with the power to decree a citizen worthy of death without first bringing them before the judges. So the robber chief was the exiled son of a king! If he'd told me himself, earlier, I would've been sure it was a foolish boast, but now it seemed perfectly natural. It was the twist from the second act of a play, and weren't we in a play?

"I'm not afraid." The healer woman's voice was thick with tears. "It only seemed—I felt it was only yesterday he killed Zlya."

"Oh," said the robber chief with a stricken look.

His mother's hands tightened on his arm. "She never broke her oath. I know she didn't. It was some villain—some villain of a man, or else some villain of a god—"

Her son looked nervously up at our godly host, perhaps to see if he would take offense, but Damadez simply looked on impassively.

"She's here," the healer woman went on. "She must be. Zlya—and the child—"

Now the robber chief grew alarmed and shook his mother gently as if to rouse her from a dream. "Oh, Mother, no. You can't think of that."

The healer woman gave no answer, but dried her tears and let her son raise her to her feet. He held her for a moment more, then, bowing low, approached the god.

"Silent Damadez, lord of the dark lands, I thank you, on behalf of my people and our guests, for your hospitality. But as you can see, we are no shades, but living men and women, and we came to your realm by accident."

I had never seen, in our brief acquaintance, the robber chief exert the full force of his courtesy. It was a powerful thing. Damadez shrugged, as well he might. There are many, after all, who come to his realm by accident.

The robber chief went on, "I am of humble station now, but I am the son of kings, and the blood of gods runs through my veins. And as we are cousins, I would presume to ask you a favor. I offer you—I offer you myself." There was the barest hesitation before he made the offer. It was one that Akemuz makes, and Damadez accepts, in some versions of the story. It might have worked. "It was my wrongdoing that began the chain of events that led us here. Release my mother and my men, for they are guiltless in this matter, and the players, for they are my guests, and I have pledged myself to their safety."

I was touched despite myself. It was a noble speech. Damadez extended his finger towards the robber chief, then struck himself in the chest. He swept his arm in a wide arc, finishing with an inquisitive tilt of his head.

The robber chief turned to me in confusion. "What does the god say?"

When players dance, our hands tell the story. It's a shadow of the subtleties of Damadez'ss speech, nor could I understand it all, or describe what I saw to you. But I understood enough.

"The god says, he already has you. What can you offer him that he does not possess, and will not possess in time?" As the robber chief tried to frame an answer, I bowed and addressed Damadez. "O mighty Damadez, who devours all things, no divine blood runs in my veins, but—"

At that, he held up a hand and shook his head.

"Well—regardless," I went on, wrong-footed. "My people and I have come to your lands empty-handed, as all creatures do. And yet, there is one thing we possess that, they say, never dies: our art. I offer it to you. We will perform for you, and if it pleases you, grant us our freedom." I glanced back at my troupe—they'd never chosen me to speak for them, but now they hung on my words. And I knew that many of them, not only Kounua, would like to leave the robbers behind in the dark lands. And yet the bandit chief stood beside me, and he'd offered himself up for us, and I could do no less for him. "Grant us all our freedom," I said.

He beckoned me to come closer. I have said he was roughly the size of a man—even so, his hand engulfed my face as he held me by the chin. He turned my head one way and then the other, examining me. His skin was cool as the water of the pond and dry as dust. His eyes were the empty slits of the mask. Finally he nodded.

My chest sat on the floor of his hall. My troupe gathered around me as I worked the fastenings. I wished for a farce or a light romance—maybe *Abrekudo's Revels*: we did that one well, and no one dies in it—though I knew I wouldn't find one. But when I opened the chest and read the title, it was in fact a romance of sorts: *Ubeyez and Kuemo.*

"Narem, will you play Ubeyez?" I said.

Just that morning he'd been panting for the role, and played it very well, too, but now he flinched away. "I'm not putting on that mask again."

It wasn't the same mask that he'd worn, and that Beyix had been wearing when he'd died. This one was unpainted, the only decoration brought out from the wood grain itself through clever carving. It showed no signs of wear, and smelled of wood chips and resin, as if it had just come from the carver's workbench.

"We're already in the underworld," I said. "What worse thing do you expect to happen?"

Maybe I shouldn't have been so sharp with him. He was young, and we were all frightened. The fact was, if Narem refused, I didn't know who would do it.

"Give it to Beyix," Kounua insisted. "He must be around here somewhere."

And then he would be counted among those whose freedom I had bargained for. I felt a sudden hope, as mad as Kounua's own—but Damadez shook his head, refusing to lend any of the shades in his care to our efforts. And maybe it was just as well, for if I'd bypassed Beyix to give the mask to my father, could Kounua ever have forgiven me, or could any of the troupe whose loved ones had gone before them to the dark lands?

"I'll do it," said the robber chief.

None of us had noticed him in our midst until he spoke, and now faces turned toward him with surprise, outrage—I held Kounua back from launching herself at him. Zbardem laughed outright.

"Young man," he said, "you seem to think that all anyone needs to do to be an actor is put on a mask. That isn't how it works."

I traced the whorls on the mask with my fingers. "It seems that it is, with these masks. You would give yourself for ransom, for your people and mine?" I met the robber chief's gaze challengingly and handed him the mask. "Very well. And—" The next mask in the chest was Kuemo's, of course, and I truly meant to give it to Oinoyua. She was our best actress, and more reliable, at the moment, than Kounua, and perhaps having one of Kuemo's chosen play the goddess would bring us luck. But when my hands touched the mask, I said, "And I will play Kuemo."

I am not, as I have said, an actress by talent, although I've certainly played a few minor roles in my time. However, no one disputed my right to give myself for ransom, for my people and the robbers.

"Splendid!" said the chief, and he grinned at me, as he was always doing at the most inappropriate times. It was as if he was still a pampered, careless prince, and I was the noble maiden who'd agreed to dance with him. Then he handed me the mask and turned his back shyly, as if I were the prince, and he the dewy maiden. "Can you fasten mine for me? I've never done this before."

He placed the mask on his face and I fastened it in the back, and then he turned around, radiant as the dawn. The shades of the dead drifted closer from the galleries, warming themselves and growing more distinct in his light. He was everything vital, beautiful, inspiring and unobtainable. I'd seen his transformation myself, and still, I didn't know him.

But when I put on my own mask and the goddess manifested in me, she came not as a stranger, but with the shock of unexpected familiarity. I remembered my last meeting with her, the young woman who now wore my mask—how I had wiped the tears from her heated cheek, and left her my chest of masks and scripts as her legacy. What a worthy daughter she'd grown into, and how boldly and cleverly she defended her people! What a story she'd woven, and what a trick she had played!

I was Kuemo of the Masks, of many faces and none. Demiurge and trickster, lover of Ubeyez of the Dawn and of Garnamer the Player, and mother to his daughter Garuz.

There sat Kuemo
  Sat at her workbench
  Chisel in hand
  In the youth of the world

Up rose Ubeyez
  And with him the sunrise
  Bright as the dawn
  Clear as the morning

Have you ever been a god?

I don't think you have. It leaves its traces—even now, in the queenly way Oinoyua lifts her hair aside for me to fasten a necklace, in Amtrez' light-footed trot beside a wagon, I see it in them. I don't see it in you, though you're a king and the blood of gods runs in your veins, as your son once claimed in Damadez's halls. Though you've heard the voices of gods whispering in your ear, souring your heart and turning your reason, as the woman who was once yours told me. She told me many things, sometimes thinking I was her mother, or her daughter, or the oracle of Ubeyez. Sometimes recognizing me for who I was, a stranger she'd known for a single day. Even so, she spoke, and I held her hands as she lay dying.

Your daughter, however—she never said anything of you, or of the gods, for good or for ill.

But I must tell my story in order, for you've never been a god, nor seen the world as they do, all the ages laid out at once like the dishes at a village feast. And so, as I danced in Damadez's halls for an audience of players and robbers and the shades of the dead, it was still the youth of the world, and men and women had not yet walked upon it. And when I saw Ubeyez, it was for the first time, and my breath caught at his loveliness. At the same time, a laugh bubbled up in my chest, for I'd heard of the oath he'd sworn to Foyez and considered it very stupid of both of them, and I'd just thought of a trick that would throw all the gods into confusion.

And so, pretending I didn't see him, I quickly carved a few figures—rough, clumsy work to be sure, but I captured the healer woman's long aristocratic face, and Zbardem's bulbous forehead, and Narem's gangly limbs. I displayed them to the audience, who laughed appreciatively, the robbers and the players together. I spotted my father in the crowd of shades, pointing at the statue of Zbardem, and Beyix with a silent chuckle for how I'd made Narem's elbows. Another shade, a heavily pregnant young woman I didn't know, stood out from the crowd as well. She didn't laugh, but drifted towards the makeshift stage as if compelled.

"Hail, O Carver. What is it you're making?" said Ubeyez, peering over my shoulder, and I mimed exaggerated surprise at his presence.

"Oh! Nothing that would catch your interest," I said, shoving the carvings out of the way, which only drew his attention to them. "Are you not a master of every craft? Is there a thing you can't fashion?"

He picked up a carving and disparaged its quality. I challenged him to make something better. As we spoke, we drew closer, shoulders touching, breath mingling. In the audience, Beyix had settled to sit beside Kounua, seeming as solid as life. She watched the play and not him, and I'm not sure she even knew he was there, but she leaned against him, as they had watched plays together when they were children.

The unknown dead woman stood close enough to me that I could feel the chill rising from her skin. Damadez had forbidden any of his shades from taking part in the play, but he made no move to interfere—perhaps he was as wrapped up in the story as the rest of the audience, none of whom appeared to notice the dead woman. So I did my best to ignore her as well, instead inviting Ubeyez to hold my chisel. Our fingers intertwined on the handle. His were thick and warm; hers were like ice.

That was when he seemed to see her. Behind the mask, his eyes were those of the robber chief once more, and he said, "Zlya—" which wasn't in the script and jarred against the rhythm of our speech. But he said it so softly, and I raised my voice a little on my line, and I'm not sure anyone else heard.

He carved an infant out of wood, perfect in every detail, and I held it up skeptically and said, "Shining Ubeyez, your skill is unmatched, but I cannot say that it is lifelike."

Then the god stepped back, and the shade drew forward, and covered the child's mouth with her own. As the child's skin flushed, and its limbs stiffened in a stretch, the shade grew more insubstantial, but before she faded away altogether, her eyes met mine and she spoke: "Take the child and go."

And the child opened its mouth wide, and our last play ended as our first had, with a scream.

Dark are the lands beneath
  Cold are the waters
  Terrible the passage:

Who would dare it twice?

Damadez seemed to agree with the shade. He opened his hand, and somewhere in the endless twilight of his halls, a light appeared. Robbers and players alike began to shake off their stupor and hurry towards it. I removed my mask and made a brief bow to the god. "Thank you, mighty Damadez," I said.

The healer woman, however, instead of rushing toward the light, stayed rooted to the spot where the dead woman had disappeared, and her son stood there with her. "Mother, let me sort it out. You have to go," he said. Then turning to me, "Look after her."

I might have asked him by what right he gave me orders, but I was distracted by Kounua, dragging on Beyix's arm—and though he seemed solid, she couldn't manage to get a grip on it. "Beyix, come with me," she begged, "we're going home." He only shook his head.

"Leave him," I told her, and she whirled on me with bared teeth.

"Never."

"He's dead. We're alive. Kounua, please, you're like my sister; I can't lose you both."

She wouldn't listen, and I couldn't stay to plead or to struggle with her, for the light of the world above was already fading. I hoisted my chest onto my shoulder, and took the healer woman's unresisting hand, and ran.

We were the last to leave, for Kounua wouldn't abandon Beyix, and as I ran, I caught a glimpse of the robber chief in Damadez's arms. I had no time to think what it meant then, but in the time since, I've come to believe that he'd struck a separate bargain with Damadez after all. Nor did he seem entirely displeased to pay the price. As for what he gained—well, once you hear the end of it, you can be the judge.

We made our way through columned halls, and then through twisting passages beneath the earth. We soon overtook several of the robber band who'd become distracted by bright veins of gold in the earth, and glimmering jewels, trying vainly to gouge them out with their fingernails. At the bank of a churning river, we caught up with the main body of our party. Narem shrank back from the water, white and shaking.

"I can't. I can't," he repeated as his parents tried to urge him onward. Nor was he the only one whose nerve was failing, though we could see the sky of the world above on the other side. I saw what had happened: Damadez had given us the freedom to leave his realm, if we could. But he would give us no help in doing so, nor would the way stay open for long.

"The light is fading. The gates are closing. Follow me!" I called, and I strode into the water, steeling myself not to flinch at its shocking cold.

"Come," Oinoyua encouraged Amtrez. "Your parents and brother will be along."

Or they won't, I thought with a pain in my breast—but I had neither time nor heart left to argue. I struggled through the water, the healer woman clinging to my hand. The current battered me, and several times the water rose over my head, but I always came up again, gulping air, the spray feeling like needles of ice. Then I'd catch glimpses of others, like the young woman who'd joined us a month before, her child clinging to her back. When I next surfaced, I'd lost sight of them, but saw one of the robbers who'd built my father's cairn pulling through the water with powerful strokes. Finally, I crawled to the opposite bank, pebbles scraping my palms and my knees. I coughed up water, dragged my sodden hair out of my face and looked around. The healer woman huddled beside me, empty-eyed. Oinoyua and Amtrez clung together and shivered. I looked up and down the bank, but saw no one else.

The stream we'd just emerged from seemed a cheerful hill brook, the opposite side much the same as the one we found ourselves on. The last rays of the sun were just visible above the horizon. Of the entrance to Damadez's realm, there was no sign. But my mother's chest had run aground on some rocks in the middle of the brook, and I rushed to retrieve it, because I could hear from beneath its lid a thin wail. I dragged it to shore with protesting muscles, undid the catches and swung up the lid. There were no masks, no scripts, but on the bare wood of the chest, a newborn girl.

Sing, winds!
And fruits, give forth your sweetness!
Let the heavens pour down blessings
And every living thing rejoice—
Ubeyez has returned!

By the last of the evening light, we found a road, and as the moon rose, we came upon a wayside temple of Foyez with a guesthouse—small, but enough for us. I gave the priestess who tended the shrine the earring that had somehow stayed in the folds of my dress as an offering, and she put us up on pallets of sweet-smelling straw, and brought us dry garments to wrap ourselves in, and bread and water. The healer woman wouldn't rest, though she had no more strength to walk or stand; she stayed up all that night raving, as I've already told you, and I stayed up with her and held her hands. Poor woman, she was dead by morning—she'd had enough strength to fight free of Damadez's realm, but she'd left too much of her heart there to remain in the world above.

Oinoyua slept curled up with the children—fitfully, for the girl woke hungry every few hours as babies will. The temple kept a sacred goat, and Oinoyua let the child suck its milk off a cloth, though it hardly seemed enough.

In the morning, the priestess came into the guesthouse, her face ashen. She dropped something into my hand—the earring I'd given her the night before. And its mate, which I had last seen in the robber chief's ear in Damadez's halls.

"Your offering is not acceptable to the god," she whispered. She seemed truly terrified—I doubt she'd ever had so clear or ominous a message from her god before. "You cannot stay here."

"But we have nothing! And—" I glanced at the pallet where the healer woman's body lay. "And she's died, and we must—"

"You said she was a stranger, and no kin to you."

"Yes, but—"

"I will return her to the earth," said the priestess. "And I won't send you away empty-handed. But you must go."

So we went. To the priestess' credit, I think she must have given us most of her food, and she didn't have much. Nevertheless, we were very hungry over the next few days, and we feared that the girl might die. But another miracle happened, and by the third day, Oinoyua, who slept with the girl curled against her every night, began to produce milk for her, though her chest was as mannishly flat as ever. And eventually we met up with another troupe of travelers who let us join them. We said the children were ours, and indeed they were, for they had no one else. Nor did anyone ever question it, although one look at Amtrez with his milk-pale, freckled skin was enough to tell anyone that he'd not been born to us. The girl, on the other hand—she had the very nose and chin I'd inherited from my mother, and hair as midnight-black as Oinoyua's was in her youth. Or as the robber chief's was, or as the official portraits of you that I've seen throughout your city.

Had the rest of our troupe and the robbers been washed away, lost to both the underworld and the world above? I often fear so. But years ago, I caught a rumor of a woman and her young child found on the banks of a river, entirely without memories, and once I heard of an actor named Zbardem who played the most magnificent Foyez the city had ever seen. Whenever I tried to chase down these stories, however, they vanished like smoke.

In the meantime, we've traveled sometimes with one troupe and sometimes with another. Oinoyua and Amtrez are exceptional actors, and their skills have always been enough to secure us a place. As for myself, though I've taken minor roles from time to time, I feel most comfortable sitting by the side of the stage, a script in my lap. There is one city we've always avoided, and left any troupe determined to play here, for they said its king was crafty and mad, and had his own daughter put to death when she broke her priestly vows of chastity, and exiled his woman and their son when they tried to help her. They said, too, that he did all these things because the Oracle of Ubeyez prophesied that his grandchild would one day kill him. But of course the people who said this must have been fools, for who believes in prophecies nowadays?

And, in the way of things, the children grew up, and they took their own paths. I wept when Amtrez left us, and again when our daughter did—and also, I gave her a legacy. Where she is now, I couldn't say, but she carries my mother's chest and wears her father's earrings, and she is coming for you.

Now—will you kill us, O King, me and Oinoyua? Be careful of meddling with sacred things to which you have no right. For I can see your guards now, hesitating with their hands on their weapons. And if you order them to cut us down, you may find that you have nothing in your possession but a handful of costumes and masks.

I

ENCOUNTERS WITH THE ALIEN

Martian Red

Situated on the rough-ridged red
    Slopes of Arsia Mons, a sprawling complex
    Of climate-controlled caves and domes of ice:
    The Beridze Vineyards. For frail legs
    Still used to micrograv, it's a body-
    Straining hike. Breathe through your nose.

As every seasoned Martian tourist knows
    (Because of all the guidebooks they have read)
    Agriculture's automated. Nobody
    Leaves the habitats to tend complex
    Machines. But this once stretch your legs.
    Brave the dust storms and the glacial ice.

Vintner Nino Berizde won't let ice
    Keep her from her vines. She claims her nose
    Is keener than a microchip. Her legs
    Are bowed from years on Mars. Chapped and red,
    Her hands can still handle the complex
    Tasks her work claims from an aging body.

With a smile of welcome for anybody
    Who comes to visit her domain of ice
    She'll show you around the whole complex
    Regale you with the vintner's lore she knows
    The lighted caverns where she grows her reds
    Radiation-proof, her whites climb crystal legs.

Then, tasting. Saperavi: opaque legs
    With notes of spice and chocolate. Full-bodied,
    Georgia's—and now Mars's—favorite red.
    Next: Arsia Riesling. It's an ice
    Wine, made from frozen grapes. Its nose
    Is fruity. Its finish is complex.

For the true connoisseur of complex
    Flavors, Rkatsiteli. Pale legs,
    Acacia, smoke, and ginger on the nose.
    High acid, a long finish, medium body.
    And more wines: whites as clear as ice
    Deep indigo berry-scented reds.

Delight your nose. Flavors as complex
    As the Red Planet. Though your legs
    Protest, your body aches—the trip is worth the ice.

A Girl and her Tentacle Monster

We were about fifteen minutes out when Ollie woke up, and I don't mind telling you I'd been getting a little nervous. Not that there was anything terribly unusual about it—it always takes him some time to wake up when we drop into hyperspace, and the psychic feelers from the monsters weren't anything I couldn't handle. An itch on the inside of my elbow, a sudden headache like an explosion behind my left eye, the same three notes repeating themselves over and over; that sort of thing. I flicked them away without hardly thinking about it and got on with my systems check. Still, it never feels quite safe to be alone in your mind in hyperspace, and that's because it isn't. It was a real relief to feel his weight in the back of my brain, and to hear his voice like the whisper of a guillotine in my head: *Human female.*

"Good to have you back, big fellow," I replied cheerfully. They say that tentacle monsters can't hear, but I think Ollie might surprise them in a lot of ways. In any case, it's what's inside of your head that counts, and he understood that, all right.

I got on with checking our heading while Ollie stretched himself across the cockpit. In realspace, he lives—well, *lives* is the wrong word to talk about what a hyperspace monster does in realspace, but whatever—in a pot on a shelf across from the main computer screen, and looks a bit like a cross between a squid and an overgrown spider plant. But now that he was awake, he was growing limbs at an alarming rate, and losing them too, just as often, until he took up half the cockpit with a mass of swarming tentacles—some of them with suckers, and some of them with wicked-looking thorns, and some of them oozing liquids of various colors and consistencies. The one that he stretched across my shoulders had nothing more objectionable on it than several rows of tiny thorns like prickly hairs, but I uncoiled it firmly when he started to wrap my arm to the armrest of my chair. We may only have been on a routine colony run, but it was hardly time to relax yet.

Sure enough, less than half an hour later, the light in the cockpit took on a red cast. It came on gradually, and it's hard to notice when everything gets red, because *everything* gets red. But this wasn't my first hyperspace run, or my second, and I haven't come back a mangled corpse yet—my hindbrain said *gremlin*, and I tensed my muscles and began to reach. That's when the laughter started.

It wasn't repetitive enough to tune out, though it had a rhythm of a sort: a chuckle, then high-pitched giggles ending in a shriek, more giggles, then silence for a second or thirty before starting over again. I wanted badly to brush it off my mind, but that's a mistake with a red gremlin; once you do that, you're caught. Instead I listened carefully, visualizing each variation in pitch as one more step down a long tunnel. At the end of the tunnel was my enemy. Anchoring me at the back of my brain, so I couldn't get lost down the tunnel forever, was Ollie. Behind me, I could see him losing sticking tentacles and gripping tentacles, and growing more long thin thorny ones. The ends of his tentacles sprouted buds. The buds had teeth. A long, shallow cut appeared spontaneously underneath my right elbow, and then another across my shoulder. And then I had it.

Dragging the gremlin back through the tunnel I had built was just as hard as getting to it in the first place. Both my arms were bleeding freely by the time I was done. But I gave one last pull and there it was, the gremlin standing corporeal as life in the middle of the cockpit floor, looking just like a red rat, if rats had eight legs and stingers at the ends of their tails. My work was done; it was Ollie's turn now.

The thorns on his tentacles flashed, and bits of gremlin landed across the computer screen in an arc. The gremlin lashed out with its tail and stung one of Ollie's tentacles, then another. The tentacles withered and died, and Ollie hissed with his remaining bud-mouths, then struck, each set of teeth clamped and pulling in a different direction. Then he started to eat. In short order, there was nothing left of the red gremlin at all, not even the bits that had stuck to the screens or the walls.

I washed up and bandaged my cuts. They weren't as bad as they had looked. They never are, but they're real, all the same. Then I checked on the colonists in the hold. The monitors reported that they hadn't suffered any ill effects from the attack. The gremlin probably hadn't noticed they were there. Well, that's why we freeze them, after all—to minimize the psychic signal. Still, they would have been noticed if I hadn't been up front, broadcasting loud and clear across hyperspace. It doesn't matter how cold you freeze them; you can't send living cargo through hyperspace without a pilot, and that's a fact.

Non-living cargo, now, that's a different story. Hyperspace monsters take no more notice of it than realspace creatures do to the psychic signals flying around them all the time, so it's easier and cheaper to send it through with autopilots. The external monitors showed a flotilla of them headed in the opposite direction, ferrying trade goods to some unknown region of space. I gave them a wave. It's silly, I know, but seeing material things in hyperspace always seems like running into an old friend. Meanwhile, Ollie was shedding his thorny limbs and growing thicker, ropy ones, with suckers. I could feel his lust and impatience at the back of my brain. As far as he was concerned, the danger was over—all the nearby monsters were distracted by the psychic detritus of the red gremlin. Ollie never pays attention to material things either. But I didn't like the erratic way that one of those autopilots was acting.

I sent it a 'you're in my flight path' signal, but it kept coming on. Stumbling and weaving like its navigation logic was broken, but heading towards me, all the same. I changed my course to avoid it. Nothing doing. It was following me.

An autopirate, then. But why was it ignoring a fleet of autopilots packed with material goods and going after me? As long as I was in control of the ship, it was going to Meacham's Star 2, as scheduled. And if I wasn't in control of the ship, the autopirate wasn't going to be able to deliver anything more to its owners than a pile of mutilated corpses, useless even for spare parts.

Possibilities ran through my head. Had someone invented an autopirate that could control a ship's course without disabling its pilot, while remaining unsophisticated enough to have no psychic signal? Or was its mission to kill me and all my cargo, and if so, why? On my last tune-up, the mechanic had offered to install weapons in my ship, and I'd laughed. None of the things in hyperspace that could hurt me would care one way or another about material weapons—or so I'd thought. Now I was worried.

But the scanners finished scanning and the library disgorged its data about the strange ship, and it wasn't a new style of autopirate. It was old; as old as anything that had ever been flown into hyperspace. Back from the days that pilots would come back broken, empty bodies, and no one knew why.

There had been some modifications made to it since then, whose function the computer had been unable to determine. But they were cobbled-together of old parts and seemed, if anything, more antiquated than the craft itself.

But it was small and maneuverable, whereas I was carrying a crate full of frozen colonists behind me. There was no way I could avoid it for long if it was determined, as it seemed to be, on a collision course. I made one final desperate dodge, and then the impact came.

And something else happened at the same time, something far more frightening—the bottom of my brain dropped out. I glanced over at Ollie, although I needed no confirmation, and he had shrunk back into his pot just as if we were in realspace. But we weren't. I was in hyperspace, alone in my head. The monsters were gathering, and I could no longer see them.

I swallowed and forced myself to ignore it. It would take a while for the monsters to realize what was happening and converge, but I had a situation in my cockpit now. The strange craft had torn a hole in the side of my ship—it hadn't harmed any of my main computer systems, thank goodness, and it sealed the hole quite neatly with its own substance—and something stepped out of a hatch in the side. It was human. And what's more, it was a man.

"What have you done to Ollie?" I said. "You scan as real—what are you?"

"I'm Elkoubi Bend," he said.

Now that was ridiculous. I wanted to reply *and I'm Elkoubi Bend*, but Elkoubi Bend was exactly who he was claiming to be. And he didn't look like he was joking.

"No, you're not," I said. "I can tell, on account of you're about five feet eleven inches tall, and not three foot two and compressed into a sort of oblong ball with splinters of shinbone sticking out where your liver ought to be. I've seen Elkoubi Bend's body in the Phobos Institute, you know. They've got it on display there, along with—" I paused to glance at his ship, or the part of it that was sticking through my hull. I couldn't help it; it was similar. "—with the *Strange Fire*," I finished.

He grinned, hitching up one corner of his mouth a bit above the other as if to say, *there, you see?* "Another version of myself, no doubt," he said.

I shook my head. "We've learned more since your—since his time. The hyperspace paradox doesn't work that way. What happens, stays happened."

He shrugged with one shoulder. "I know who I am. I see no sense in belaboring the point."

"You're right," I said. "It's not getting us anywhere. What do you want?"

"Ah." A few short strides took him to the other end of the cockpit—well, it wasn't built to be a palace, after all. He touched one of Ollie's leaves, lightly, and I bridled. "I want your monster," he said.

I laughed. I'm afraid I sounded as hysterical as the red gremlin, earlier. "Maybe, but what would he want with you? Whatever else you are, you're a man. And I've never heard of a tentacle monster whose tastes ran that way yet."

"You let me worry about that," he said, grinning. I wanted to break every white tooth in that grinning mouth. There were three reasons I didn't try.

First of all, he was bigger than me, and probably stronger than me as well—he looked well-built, anyway. I know how to defend myself, but it seemed unlikely that I would be the gainer by escalating the situation to violence. Secondly, he was holding all the cards. Even if I managed to beat him bloody, I didn't know if that would bring Ollie back, and if it didn't, I and all my cargo would be dead within the hour. I might have to try it anyway, but that was a last resort. Finally, I was afraid that my fist would go right through without connecting to anything—or would be caught there, and I'd be unable to get it back out—or would sink elbow-deep into a mass of crawling things that stung. Whatever he looked like, whatever he scanned as, I wasn't convinced that he was human.

"I've learned a lot about the monsters in my time here," he was saying. "More than you girl-pilots ever learn, flitting in, flitting out. Years. Decades, it must be. Centuries? Does time have any meaning in this place?"

I couldn't stand the sound of his voice. I needed to make it stop, now. And yet I couldn't bring myself to so much as get out of my chair. I clawed at the walls of my mind like a panicked mongoose for several long seconds before I realized what was happening—the blind fury, the paralysis—they were coming from outside. "You son-of-a-bitch," I said thickly, "you've been distracting me."

That grin again. "Well, I couldn't very well take your monster without giving mine something else to occupy itself with first."

It was like no monster I had ever encountered before, but monsters are monsters, in the end. I knew it was death without Ollie on the other end to bring me back out, but it was all I knew how to do: I started down the tunnel to where the heart of the monster lived. In this case the path lay through the twisted thoughts of whatever it was that called itself Elkoubi Bend.

"You were a hyperspace pilot," I began. "Back in the days when nobody knew much about hyperspace except that it was dangerous. But you got into your ship and you dropped into hyperspace and everything seemed to be going fine until you met up with a monster."

I knew I was right when he reluctantly drew his attention away from Ollie and began to listen to me. And I got the feeling he didn't know it at all. I also hated him so much that I wanted to vomit, and was so frustrated by my inability to attack him that I wanted to claw my own eyes out just to be attacking something. Also I felt a sickening pressure in my bones, and thought of the shards sticking out of the belly of the corpse back at the Institute. But I was beginning to see a way that I just might survive this.

"The monster attacked. But it didn't kill you. Instead, you came to an accommodation with it." I knew what that was like. Of course, I had gone to hyperspace on purpose to look for my monster. I had studied, I had trained, I had known what to expect. On the other hand, I had known what would happen if I failed.

"It rides in the back of your brain. It protects you from the other monsters; helps you fight them when they attack. Just like Ollie does for me. So why would you want to swap?"

"Because yours," he gritted, as if the words had to be pulled from him by force. Which they did. Neither the churning in my gut, nor the pain shooting up from my right foot, telling me something was probably broken, or about to be, made any difference: I had the power now, for as long as I could keep it.

"Because yours lets you leave," he said.

"Oh yes," I said. "And you wanted out of hyperspace. So you came up with a plan. You fixed up your ship, probably scavenging from autopilots; you learned all you could about how hyperspace monsters work; and the next pilot you found, you immobilized her monster and invaded her ship. So that when your monster was occupied with her, it would loose its hold on your mind and you could make off with her monster, to realspace."

"Yes," he said.

I had come to the center. It would work, or I would die. The way my body felt, I'm kind of surprised I wasn't rooting for die, but do you know, the thought never crossed my mind? I took the last step. "And," I said, "is it working?"

The grin was entirely gone now. He looked hunted. "You're doing something. You're dragging me with you."

"Not I," I said.

"Elkoubi Bend died," I said. "The monster killed him, and the *Strange Fire's* autopilot brought his corpse back to realspace, the way it was programmed to. But the monster remembered, and it built itself a new Elkoubi Bend, piece by piece. You may fool my scanners, and you may fool yourself, but you can't fool me—you're not real. You'll never be loose from your monster; you are your monster. And you can't exist in realspace any more than any other monster can."

He believed me. Well, I was standing in the center of his mind; I could hardly have lied to him. But he didn't do anything. I kept talking, though it was more of a rasping whisper at this point.

"You thought you'd double-cross your monster, but the shoe's on the other foot, isn't it? You're a useful tool, that's all. You built a new *Strange Fire*. You figured out how to render a pilot and her cargo vulnerable to your monster's attack—don't tell me your monster did that; a monster's very good at tearing up a person's psyche, but useless at figuring things out—and what do you get, after all? You've been resurrected, but you're still in Hell. There's no out for you. But you don't have to be a lure on the end of your murderer's line. Let him go, Elkoubi Bend."

And he did; Ollie came back into my mind with a jolt that was nearly physical. I would never have done it if I were him. What happened next wasn't pretty. I still hated that damned monster-construct, but if I could have looked away, I would have.

I had never seen Ollie grow so fast, or so big. A single bud-mouth arced high above the rest of his flailing limbs and hissed in triumph. Blood and other human substances sprayed across everything in the cockpit: the computers, the nose of the other ship, Ollie, me. Within seconds, there wasn't an orifice of the ersatz Elkoubi Bend's body that didn't have a tentacle shoved into it, and come out again through somewhere that didn't used to be an orifice at all. The one tipped with a mouth that was contentedly chewing through his stomach I believe had gone in through the right nostril.

Then the massive bud-mouth on its central stalk lowered, until it was level with my face. I found myself, once more, unable to move. *Human female,* said the falling guillotine in my head, *now you.*

"Oh, Ollie," I said, "not now."

Tentacles twined up my chair, and around my arms and legs—the one around my right leg in particular hurt like the dickens; I needed to look at that urgently. Well, a monster is a monster, after all. I tensed. "Later," I said.

A few seconds went by. Then Ollie's tentacles slowly uncoiled and I limped over to the medical scanner.

There wasn't anything terribly wrong with me; a couple of painkillers and a cast on my foot set me right. The damage to the ship took a little longer to fix, but once I got the self-repair systems started properly, they didn't need much babysitting. The cargo, bless them, had slept through the whole thing without a blip. And the monsters in local hyperspace were not inclined to give us trouble. So later came a bit earlier than I'd expected.

When I tell people I'm a hyperspace pilot, they often say, "That must be so lonely." And it's true, you have to do without a lot of things—family, a circle of friends, keeping up with news or gossip or politics. But one thing you never have to do without is sex. It's not a bad trade-off, after all. The rest of the trip passed mostly without incident, but I can't really say that I was bored.

I made it to Meacham's Star 2 on schedule, and a shipping agent came over from the station to take charge of my cargo and authorize my payment. The cockpit didn't look like it had been the scene of a bloody battle anymore, but her eyes still widened a bit when they alighted on Ollie. "Is that your... thing?" she said.

"Yep, that's Ollie," I said. I had to stifle a laugh, really—he doesn't look like all that much in realspace. I wondered how she'd react if she saw him in full bloom. Panic and scream, probably, which is the worst thing you can do with a tentacle monster. He'll just think you're playing.

She gave a delicate shudder. "I wouldn't take your job for galaxies on a plate."

"You probably wouldn't," I agreed. "It's not for everyone. But I tell you what, when you're in a tight spot, a tentacle monster is a girl's best friend."

One Flesh

My cousin Zelda is a violinist. There are hundreds of videos of her online. In the one you've seen, she's standing on her balcony, playing Sarasate's "Carmen Fantasy," and at about the minute mark you can hear a cello joining in from the next building over.

Yeah, Zelda Silverman is my cousin. So it's not really that surprising that my mother went all mother-of-the-bride crazy about the decon team for my wedding.

"Nu, Imma, we'll just have the government decon team, it doesn't matter," I said. "They'll do the same job without the shofar and the crystals and the sprinkling turmeric everywhere."

"It doesn't matter, she says." My mother shook her head long-sufferingly. "I've added it to the registry."

She had. She'd also written: *For contributors to this gift, my daughter will read psalms in your name during her bridal procession.*

"I'm not even religious!" I hollered across the apartment when I read it.

"It doesn't matter!" she shouted back. "Neither are they!"

I get it. I do. But if getting married kills me, it's not going to be germs from the poor long-dead Henik family that does it.

By the next morning, the mehadrin decon team had five contributors. One of them was Zelda Silverman.

I agonized over my message for like half an hour. What I finally sent was: *Hey, thanks for your contribution! It means a lot. It's always good to hear from you. How are you holding up?*

In a couple minutes the message turned blue. She'd seen it.

I never got an answer, but as of 10:37 Tuesday morning, Zelda was still alive, at least.

I first met Disaster when a classmate linked me to his stream. Or, well, I can't really say I met him then—I was just one of hundreds watching him play Sushi PuzzleMaster, though he did give me a quick dimpled grin and, "Hey there, PuzzleWyytch," when I logged in. Yeah, I thought he was cute right away. I have eyes, okay. But I didn't really think much about it then, although I did find myself joining his stream every week. He goes by DimSumDisaster, and listening to his wry, self-deprecating commentary you'd think he really was a disaster, until you've played a little bit yourself and realize how fiendishly difficult those levels are. He's good. He's really good. And, long story short, it wasn't long before I'd become one of his patrons. I couldn't afford more than a dollar a month, but it was worth it to hear my name in his honey-smooth voice when he thanked all his contributors.

So: I had a crush. And when Disaster had to stop streaming because he was called up to national service, I had a good cry with Sofia (who'd first linked me to his stream) in a private chat. I worried, and I waited eagerly for his rare updates. But I also had school, and I had my little brother and sister to help take care of, and then the whole thing with Zelda happened, so I didn't worry or wait too much.

You already know how Zelda met the people who would become, for a few brief, tragic weeks, her housemates. That first duet between violin and cello on the balcony was unplanned, serendipitous. When she uploaded the video, she included a plea for anyone who might happen to know who the cellist was.

They're just next door, she wrote to me the next morning when the video had started getting passed around, but the cellist still hadn't been found. *Maybe one floor down? In the old days I could have gone over and started knocking on doors.*

What a thing to say! I guess it might be true. Zelda's older than me; she was in kindergarten when the first plague hit, so maybe she remembers some things. But even then, knocking on strangers' doors, wouldn't people have thought she was crazy?

Anyway, by that evening somebody who lived in the building next door to Zelda's had seen the video. They'd made a post on the residents' message board. A message to Zelda from the cellist, whose name was Tehilla, turned into a video chat with her and her husband Eitan, and their two children and Eitan's parents and Tehilla's aunt. Eitan played the viola, and Tehilla's aunt Rachel played the violin, and both kids were learning the violin too, but Shachar preferred the flute and Yuval wanted to learn to code and search for aliens. So they had a string quartet, sort of, when they could rope one of the kids in, but with Zelda they really had one.

They played over video conference, and when it didn't rain they'd go out and play on their balconies, Zelda the next building over and one floor up. But it wasn't enough.

It was a whirlwind romance, without the romance. Within four months, Zelda had filed a statement of intent to move residence.

For me and Disaster, things moved more slowly. Truth is, I didn't even know he knew I was alive until a year into my own national service.

I'd gotten an inside job. My classmate Sofia had fought tooth and nail to be assigned to the labs, and don't get me wrong, I respect her a lot. But if every girl did that, where would the next generation come from? Sofia's okay so far—tfu tfu—but you know what I mean. It's dangerous out there.

Anyway, I was working as a teacher's aide to a class of kids with motor delays, following up and helping with their physical therapy and stuff. I wanted to get into designing learning programs afterwards, and I did, that's what I do now. I thought the teacher's aide thing would be relevant background.

By that time, Disaster had finished his national service and was back to streaming. He started out pretty much back at square one, but it wasn't long before he had double the audience he'd had before. Several of my kids were fans of his, which was what gave me the idea to make a sushi conveyor belt puzzle that the kids could do with their PT consoles. I almost didn't get up the nerve to send the puzzle to him. I couldn't believe it when he offered to do a special stream just for the kids.

"Puzzlewyytch was one of my first supporters," he said, and told them some stories from the channel from years ago that I hadn't even remembered. His face had lost some of its roundness from those days, but he still had the adorable dimples.

Well, one thing led to another, and private chats led to the sort of private chats where I had to kick my little sister Stav out of our shared bedroom. And one evening on his stream, Disaster said, "I'm going to do a user-generated level tonight; this one's by Puzzlewyytch." When he finished the level, the words *WILL YOU MARRY ME* were spelled out in salmon nigiri and pork dumplings.

"Yes," said Disaster, and the whole chat filled with cheers and confetti emoji.

Got a few death threats in my DMs too, but you know, that happens.

We'd discussed it beforehand, of course. He knew what the message was going to be before he started playing, and I didn't even start building the level until we'd sent out for our testing kits, and they'd come back negative. Not that that necessarily means anything—Zelda had tested negative before she'd moved out too. They've got tests for Silverman's Rot now, but there's only one way to know for sure what's lurking in someone else's microbiome.

They played "Carmen Fantasy" again—Zelda and Rachel, Tehilla and Eitan, and Shachar on the flute. If the world was going to know Zelda by just one video, I wish it had been that one: the glance that Zelda shares with Rachel in the transition from one movement to the next, Shachar's occasional mistakes, the way Eitan sways slightly as he plays, as if in prayer.

A few days later, Eitan's father's eyes and mouth swelled up, and a livid rash started to spread across his face, onto his neck, downwards from his armpits. Zelda treated him at home as well as she could, conferencing with doctors almost hourly, with medicines and equipment sent over by emergency drop-off, but nothing helped. In the end, the EMTs took him away in their gowns and their masks, and when that happened, they all knew he wasn't likely to come back.

They'd quarantined him and Zelda in a single room of the house once he got sick, but it was too late. They let Zelda out when the EMTs came, and at that point Yuval's eyes were too swollen to see, throat too swollen to speak.

The kids succumbed fast. Eitan, and then his mother, within hours of each other. Rachel. Tehilla held on the longest. I know she and Zelda played one last duet. I know it's online. Don't ask me what they played. I've never been able to watch it.

It was another two months after Disaster and I got engaged on his stream—two and a half months after we'd filed our statements of intent to move residence—that we got approved for an apartment. It's only a few blocks from where I live now, 90 square meters and four rooms, last occupied by a family called Henik who all died in the Weeping Flu. It's been a few years, much too long for any microbes to survive, plus we've got shots for the Weeping Flu now, but try telling that to my mother. She was almost ready to have Disaster move in here with us. Which is just nuts. Where would we put him? And what about when we have kids?

And what about her and Stav and Or? There's no reason to take the risk of exposing them to a new person.

So... mehadrin decon team, I guess. If it makes her feel better.

When everything was finalized, and we got our wedding date approved, we all sat in front of my big monitor, with sparkling wine for me and my mother and fizzy grape juice for Stav and Or. (Or insisted he should get wine too. Tough luck, kid.) We toasted Disaster and his parents and his sister and baby niece, gathered around a single monitor in their place.

Disaster's going to have to move cities, but he says he doesn't mind. He worked in the ambulance corps when he was in national service. It's really perfectly safe, he tells me.

He might have been one of the masked, gowned workers who took Zelda's housemates away. He was in national service then. He's never told me, and I've never asked.

My uncle Dov and cousin Micha are presumed carriers now; they'll never get permission to move residence, or have anyone move in with them. And Zelda lives all by herself in a six-room apartment full of musical instruments. She doesn't post videos anymore, or come to video conferences, and often goes days without checking her messages. She gets her regular food deliveries, but who knows how much of them she's eating? When she dies, how long will it be before anyone knows?

The night before the wedding, my mother and Stav paint my hands and feet with henna. The next morning, I open the long box that's been wedged awkwardly into the deliveries room for the last week. Dress, gloves, mask, and veil. My mother fastens the dress in back and ties on the mask, arranges the veil so it sits straight in my hair. She hands me the little white psalm-book embossed with gold from the corner of the package. The flying drone festooned with ribbons and paper flowers darts up to hover in front and a little above me. Its light flashes red, then green.

I'm live.

I hug Stav and Or—I can still lift Or off his feet—and finally my mother. She clutches me so tightly I think she'll leave marks on my back, and her body is shaking with sobs.

"You did a good job. The best," I say, too quietly for the mic to pick up. "I love you."

It's the last time I'll ever touch her. But that's growing up, isn't it?

Then: out the door. Down the elevator. Out onto the street. The sun is so bright, even through my veil, but there's a bite in the breeze. A flock of parakeets flies up, shrieking in alarm, barely missing the drone. A porcupine backs towards an ancient dumpster and rattles its spines. Anemone flowers are growing through the cracks in the pavement, blood-red, and I pick one to tuck into my veil. Then I look up at the drone, saying, "Thank you to everybody who helped make this day a reality. I love you all." I open the psalm-book and read the list of names printed there, ending with, "Zelda daughter of Miriam." And I start walking to my new home, reciting as I go: "Blessed is the man who has not gone according to the advice of the wicked, and in the path of sinners has not stood, and in the conference of mockers has not sat..."

I'm not religious, but I guess it doesn't matter. Neither are they, all the invisible people watching.

I spot Disaster's drone hovering before I see him, then I turn the corner and there he is, waiting at the door to our building. I can't run in my dress, but I pick up my skirts and walk faster. From windows and balconies above, women ululate and children toss down nuts. Disaster is shorter than I expected; I can look him in the eye easily. The heat of his body, as I stand facing him, is warmer than the sun. He lifts my veil. There are little nigiris and makis and dumplings embroidered on his mask.

I take his hands and I can't see his dimples but I see his eyes crinkle. There's a little fumbling as he fits the ring onto my finger; with the gloves it can't go further than the second knuckle, and I make a fist so it won't fall off.

"You are hereby consecrated to me by the law of Moses and Israel," he says.

Into the building. Up the elevator. And we shut the door in the face of the hovering drones.

Inside, everything smells of disinfectant and turmeric. I reach behind my head to undo the fastenings on my mask, and my ring falls to the floor. I'll pick it up later. Now, I pull Disaster's mask down.

We're breathing the same air.

Ask a Malefactor

Dear Ask a Malefactor:

I'm a supervillain with a great relationship with my local hero—at least I was. But lately, things have soured. A couple of weeks ago, when I kidnapped her butler, it took her two days to come and rescue him! Well, I thought maybe she'd had an argument with her butler. Then yesterday, when my Doomsday EMP Device was set to disable every electronic device in the city, she showed up late again. I had to reset the countdown timer twice! When she got there, she destroyed it without any of her usual quips, instead muttering about how she was "really busy." How could she be too busy for ME?

Could she be seeing another villain? And how do I get her back?

Signed,

The Spark is Gone

Dear Sparky:

It's possible that your nemesis is seeing another villain. It's also possible that she's dealing with hero burnout, or she's got a lot going on in her secret identity. Unfortunately, unless you've got an army of mind-control nanobots (and if you do, can you set me up with one? So many uses! So shiny!) you can't control her actions—you can only control your own. Ask yourself if you're getting what you want out of this relationship. If not, it might be time to look elsewhere.

Cheers,

Mal

Dear Ask a Malefactor:

My colleagues at the university call me mad, and say that my research "isn't real science." I'm afraid I'm going to get overlooked for tenure track again. What do I do?

Signed,

Doctor Magnificent

Dear Maggie:
Frankly, your colleagues sound like fools and cowards. Fortunately, there are a lot of opportunities for independent scholars these days, as long as you're willing to pursue alternative sources of funding (such as bank robberies and jewel heists) and ignore the petty ethical constraints that keep the common lot of humanity in cowering submission. Your former colleagues will surely be both impressed and intimidated when you SHOW THEM ALL!
Good luck,
Mal

Dear Ask a Malefactor:
I just got back to my evil lair to find my Electron Ray mysteriously disabled. The only indication of how it happened was a note reading: "BWAHAHAHA!" Is there another villain moving in on my turf? Help!
Signed,
Nervous Wreck

Dear Rex:
The first thing to do is stay calm.
Ha ha, just kidding! Go on a rampage. Terrify your minions. Rant about how they'll pay, they'll ALL PAY!
There, don't you feel better? Now get your minions to fix everything (including the Electron Ray and the stuff you broke on your rampage) while you focus on tracking down whoever dared meddle in your domain, and wreaking horrible vengeance upon them.
Kisses,
Mal

PS: Sparky, was that you? If so, bold move choosing another villain for your nemesis!

Dear Ask a Malefactor:

Hi, it's Doctor Magnificent again with another question. A fellow scholar just reached out to me with a claim that he can greatly enhance my prowess in my chosen field. I'd love to collaborate with a like-minded researcher, but the fact that I've never heard of him before he contacted me—and some oddities in his syntax—give me pause. Should I accept his offer?

Yours as ever,

Dr. M

Dear Maggie:

I'm sure your small-minded former colleagues would never consider responding to some weirdo with a .biz address. But an individual with your broad vision can't pass up an opportunity like this! Now, I'm not saying you should trust him, but worst case—a bit of hideous scarring never hurt a criminal career.

Regards,

Mal

To all my readers:

Sorry there hasn't been new content here for a while. My internet has been on the fritz and my backup data was mysteriously wiped from the servers. Please be patient while I work on solutions!

Toodle-oo,

Mal

PS to One Reader In Particular: I WILL GET YOU, SPARKY. PREPARE TO FEEL MY WRATH!

To all my readers:

Well, things have calmed down here in Malefactor City—by which I mean that several blocks have been reduced to rubble, but that's the municipal authorities' problem, not mine. Personally, I find that an epic battle solves most issues and brightens any day! So let's get to answering some of those emails that have been piling up.

Dear Ask a Malefactor:

This isn't really a question, I'm just writing to thank you for your advice about whoever disabled my Electron Ray. Thanks to my prompt action, they haven't bothered me again. I never figured out who they were, but I was able to use my New Improved Electron Ray in a very successful caper. Due to a few unfortunate setbacks, I haven't conquered the world yet, but I'm sure you, along with Earth's billions, will be bowing to me soon!

Thanks again,

No Longer A Nervous Wreck

Dear Rex:

No trouble! I'm glad it worked out so well for you. If I may venture to say so, I suspect the individual who disabled your Electron Ray may have found a new nemesis... a truly worthy opponent... perhaps one who always gives excellent advice. ;)

But I digress,

Mal

Dear Ask a Malefactor:

I can't believe it! My former colleagues were neither impressed nor intimidated when I unveiled the fruits of my research! They said I was "pathetic" and that it's "unprofessional to send unrequested images of one's genitalia" and then they "blocked me on social media".

See if I ever take your advice again!

THE FIRSTBORN OF DEATH

Dr. M

Mags:

I think you misunderstood me when I said you should "show them all."
Hope that helps,
Mal

To all my readers:

Well! It's sure nice to be able to answer questions without any pesky interruptions. I hope A Certain Somebody doesn't decide to take revenge for that little surprise I left in their lair...

...

...

Yep, nice and quiet here in Malefactor City!

...

Sparky, what's going on? Is it something I said? Text me!

The End of Summer

In the Summer Cluster, there was no night, and the only dark was the pale gray of dusk. In the Summer Cluster, flowers bloomed and never withered. In the Summer Cluster, they say—though I don't know if this is true—that death itself was a stranger, and never came tethered to the airlocks, rapping on the gates, bowl in hand and demanding meat. In the Summer Cluster, lifecrafts floated through calm layers of cloud, rising and falling and circling each other like the dancers in a hop-waltz.

But if you go there now—and why should you? Everything of value has been scavenged long since—you will find only blasted-out shells trailing plastic tubing in the searing wind. Shall I tell you how it happened?

It was when the world was new, and people still knew little of it—little of its beauties, little of its dangers. In those days the clusters were ruled each one by its captain. The captain of the Summer Cluster was a proud man, a wealthy man, who gave gifts with a free hand, whose feast-hall was never empty or silent. He had a daughter, and he called her Rós, named for the flower that perfumed the air of the lifecrafts, and whose fruit was eaten as candy, tart and sweet and bright as a jewel. She was the first storm-speaker. But she had no grandmother to teach her her craft and guide her with wisdom, and she couldn't read the rune-stones. Her only guide was her own wayward heart.

And one day like all the days in the Summer Cluster, when the air was balmy and the breezes were gentle, Rós put on her wingsuit and went out to fly between the lifecrafts, and there she met a storm, and she became its lover.

She whirled suspended for hours, buffeted by winds, caressed by vapors. How can I describe what she felt, if you have never heard the voice of a storm? But I can tell you this: she never would have come home, if it had been left up to her. She never would have thought of her body's needs, of food, of hearth, of breath. She would have died in ecstasy.

But her father grew worried when she didn't return, and he sent out searchers, and they found her and brought her back. All they knew of the storm was wind and flashes of lightning in the clouds, but that was enough to frighten them, for such things were yet unknown in the Summer Cluster.

Rós was raving, half out of her mind when they brought her to her father's lifecraft. The doctors feared she had contracted some unknown illness, and they put her in quarantine lest she spread it among all their people. But no such thing happened, and gradually she returned to herself.

More than that: before her encounter with the storm, Rós had been a spoiled, flighty girl, unwilling to do any but the lightest work in the gardens. But now she became diligent. She studied life-support tech, and her fingers grew skilled at weaving tubes and mixing gases. The elders said that her brush with death had sobered her, and they nodded to each other approvingly. Until it was too late, they never saw the wildness that she kept hidden in her heart.

Until one night—and I say night, because the clouds gathered so thickly that they cut off all light from the sun, and the air in the lifecrafts grew chill, and frost touched the roots of the flowers in the gardens, and their petals withered and fell. The singing in the feast-hall of the Summer Cluster turned to panicked cries, and the people begged the captain to tell them to tell them what should be done, but he knew no better than they.

The storm, you see, was coming for Rós.

And she put on her wingsuit and went out to meet it gladly, and using the accesses she had learned, she opened the airlocks of all the lifecrafts, and the wind swept through and the lightning blasted them and the vapors scoured clean what was left. No one survived in all of the Summer Cluster. It was only later that strangers came and found a few recordings that had escaped destruction, and learned what had happened. That was how the people discovered what we shared the world with—not what, but who.

It was many years longer, and lifetimes, too, before we learned the ways of the storms and how to live with them, and in many ways they are still strangers in our halls. And we have councils now instead of captains, and the ruins of the Summer Cluster are a curiosity, nothing more, and every cluster has its storm speakers who learn diligently with their grandmothers, and know the reading of the rune-stones.

Rós taught no granddaughters, as she had learned from no grandmother, for she died along with all her kin. She is remembered as a caution against the dangers of an untrained heart and a headstrong nature.

But we—the storm-speakers—remember that she was the first.

Why Don't We Do It in the Wadi

Why don't we do it in the wadi
    Body against sunburned body
    Darting flies could taste our pleasure
    The hidden heartbeat of the desert
    Tourists on the observation deck
    Watch hikers' recreation
    We would seem, from up above
    A pair of insects making love
    But here the whole Earth seems forsaken
    With only skinks to watch us making our own fun
    Like mad dogs, or like Englishmen, beneath the midday sun

Sol Asleep

Solange looks around nervously, then hoists herself over the metal rim. She wriggles a bit. The coffin is tight. Her eyes point blankly at the ceiling as she struggles to get her breathing under control. No one is coming in. Marcia promised—Sleepies know Solange has paid her enough. She waits until her breaths come slowly, evenly. She imagines them misting the lid of the coffin, which in reality leans up against the wall, temporarily disabled. Then she closes her eyes. She forces her toes to stop wiggling, her knees to stop jumping. She forces her hands to unclench. Soon she's asleep. She dreams of planets.

It's stupid, but there it is—it's not the pain, or the fear, or the embarrassment of being raped in a tool locker by your younger cousin; it's Mickey's teeth glinting in the low light that Solange can't get out of her mind. *So white*, she remembers thinking.

She should get back to her dormitory. She's been off-shift for more than an hour. But she's a mess: there's blood at the side of her mouth and down her legs, her smock is torn, and she can't see it but she thinks her face is blotchy with crying. If people see her they'll ask questions, and she doesn't want to have to talk to anyone.

She levers herself to her feet and takes an experimental step. It hurts a bit to walk, but it's not that bad. Looking out the small window in the tool locker door, she can see a woman walking a catwalk above the eucheuma pool and occasionally taking its temperature. Other than that, and a bar of light from Uncle Matt's office, there doesn't seem to be anyone around. Ducking her head, she pushes open the door and heads for the showers.

Solange doesn't know when Mickey got so strong. He hadn't been when they were kids. Marcia could usually give him a good pounding. Solange had tended to run whenever any of the cousins looked her way when they were in a violent mood. Even when they'd caught her, she'd usually got away again with no more than a bruise or two. But back in the tool locker, she was pinned securely, and no amount of twisting seemed to help.

When she bit the hand covering her mouth, he laughed. His eyes glittered. "Madwoman," he said.

The pain that followed was brief. Solange tasted blood and felt it trickle down the back of her throat, but Mickey seemed absorbed in what he was doing.

Shortly after, he sat back. Manic energy had given way to his usual air of self-satisfaction. Solange drew herself into a crouch and turned away, trying to shield herself from his view. She wasn't quick enough to hide the fact that she was crying.

"It wasn't that bad, Sol," said Mickey.

Solange realizes that she's cold. The water has automatically shut off, and there's nothing left but a pink puddle around her feet. She collects her clothes and does what she can with them—if she ties her smock on the right, the damage isn't so obvious. She can mend it later.

She makes her way back to her dormitory through corridors dimmed for the night, and mostly empty. The few people she does encounter glance at her and then away, uninterested. If the floors and walls suddenly blinked out and there were nothing between them and the stars but space, they probably wouldn't notice that either. Most people never notice anything.

Five cousins sleep in the same room as Solange. Elara and Karen stand in the hallway engrossed in conversation. Hallie works night shift, and Callie is probably asleep. Levana, the new girl who moved in after Marcia moved out, is reading, judging by the light coming from her bed-place. Solange manages to avoid them all and climbs the ladder to her own bed-place, two up on the left. Sleep doesn't come.

After some time staring at the ceiling, she pushes herself out of bed, climbs down the ladder, and lets herself out into the corridor. She walks nowhere in particular. It takes up the time.

It's been two days. For the past two mornings, Solange has arrived at work early for lack of anything better to do with her nervous energy. Her head feels as if it's been in the desiccator, her arms and legs are weak, and she can barely feel her fingers. She's tested the same spot's salinity five times in a row; she's ruined a new plant with clumsy fingers; she's almost tumbled into the nama pool. Occasionally, a speck of light dances across her field of vision.

After the first day of work, returning to her dormitory more exhausted than she's ever been, she climbed to her bed-place and lowered herself onto the mattress, grateful and expectant. But sleep didn't take, and she no longer expects anything. Instead, when she isn't working, or in the canteen trying to force down a meal of some sort of seaweed that she can't really taste, she walks. After a while, the corridors all start to look the same. She tries to hold distinguishing details in her mind—this pine has a broken lower branch; that door is painted red—only to have them slip away. At one point, she finds herself standing in front of a door, hand hovering over the button, unable to decide whether it leads to her dormitory or not. Solange is no great reader, but a word floats to the surface of her mind, familiar from old stories: *lost*. So that's what it means, she thinks, and wonders if people who live on worlds bigger than this ship feel like this all the time.

Mickey has been acting a bit nervous around her. Solange supposes he is wondering whether she's going to lodge a complaint against him. But that seems like a lot of work. She can't prove anything, and if she could, Uncle Matt is her boss and not likely to thank her for venting his chance of grandchildren into space. Anyway, what's in it for Solange? She just wants to get some sleep.

Still, she hasn't discussed this with Mickey—he hasn't asked, for one thing—and for the past day and a half he's leapt up like he's suddenly remembered an urgent errand if he found himself so much as working the same pool as Solange. So she's slightly puzzled when she looks up from reeling in a line of mature eucheuma to see Mickey on a catwalk not five meters from her, and looking in her direction.

"Sol," he says, with an impatient edge to his voice, as if Solange has failed to respond the first three times he's said her name. "You should get that looked at."

"What?" says Solange.

With a few quick strides, the catwalk ringing under his feet, Mickey covers the distance between himself and Solange. He grabs her left hand and stretches out her arm, underside up. Then he drops it quickly. The line she's been hauling on has cut deeply into the flesh just below her elbow, and her forearm and both hands are bloodied. The far side of the line bleeds into the water for a good meter and a half. "Oh," says Solange. She hadn't noticed.

Mickey takes a step backward and holds the hand that touched Solange's away from his body awkwardly, as if it doesn't belong to him. "Shit, Sol."

After some seconds, he adds, "I'll walk you to the hospital." This decision seems to cheer him up immediately. With brisk authority, he takes her by the elbow—the uninjured elbow—and steers her toward the supervisor on duty. Solange can't recall her name, but she's struck by the woman's resemblance to her cousin Elara, who sleeps one bed-place down from Solange. She shakes her head to clear it of the sudden frightening conviction that they are, in fact, the same person.

"I'm taking Sol to the hospital," says Mickey, displaying her injury. "I think she's in shock."

Elara—no, space it, not Elara—winces and flicks her eyes to one side. "Ouch. I hope that doesn't feel as bad as it looks."

"I don't think she can really hear you," says Mickey.

Solange can hear fine, although there are odd echoes, as if the supervisor is speaking through a metal tube, from a long way off. Still, an excuse not to talk to somebody is an excuse not to talk to somebody. Solange lets herself be led quietly to the hospital.

The medic whom Solange eventually sees makes Mickey go away before starting on her arm. Which is nice. He gives her an anesthetic which is probably useless—she can't feel the needle pierce her skin in the first place—and sews up the cut. Then he tells her to wait in the recovery room for half an hour. "Let me know if you have any problems," he says.

I can't sleep, thinks Solange. *If I don't get some sleep I think I'm going to die, I need help...*

"Hm?" says the medic. His face is arranged in what is clearly meant to be a friendly expression, but Solange can see the evil underneath. Light glints oddly off of the glass and metal instruments. It must mean something. The medic is Uncle Matt in disguise, looking for an excuse to dock her pay.

Solange shrugs and follows the signs to the recovery room.

The walls of the recovery room are a cheerful blue, and there are seats with padding. A knot of women sit talking near the door. A boy with a bandaged foot is playing a game on the wall console, and looks up when Solange walks in. She takes a seat in the far corner, and runs her fingers along her arm, wondering if she can tell where the stitches are by touch alone. She can, with effort. But it's hard to stay interested. Her cousin Marcia is talking to her.

Solange shakes her head. *Focus,* she thinks. But there really is someone talking to her, and it really is Marcia.

"I saw Mickey and he told me you were here," Marcia is saying. "It's been such a while since we've seen each other, hasn't it? You don't need to wait until you cut yourself open to visit, you know. That looks nasty. How'd it happen?"

"Rope burn," says Solange.

"You look awful," says Marcia. And she begins to talk about herself, and her important job at the freezebox. The way she goes on, you'd think no Sleepy would ever survive to make planetfall without Marcia's personal help. Never mind that Marcia will be long dead by that point. Solange doesn't care, but at least now she barely has to pretend to be listening. Withdrawing her attention is a relief, and it's unpleasant to have it snatched back.

"A coffin?" says Solange, slowly working through what Marcia has been saying. "Like Sleepies sleep in."

"No, dumbass," says Marcia, "an ornamental planter coffin. What do you think?"

"And it's sitting empty?" says Solange.

"Yes!" says Marcia. "So anyway, the temperature was rising, and we were getting ready for the transfer, and we were all so worried that we were going to lose him, and that hasn't happened, you know, for more than eighty years—"

"Can I... see it?" says Solange.

"What? The coffin?" says Marcia. "You're hardly authorized personnel."

Solange forces herself to think. And realizes, with a sort of terror, how difficult it is. "I'll pay," she says.

"I can't do it," says Marcia.

"Thirty dollars," says Solange.

This shuts Marcia up for a few seconds. It looks good on her. "Why?" she eventually says.

"Marcia, I need to. Please," says Solange.

Marcia considers. "It's really, really forbidden," she says. "Okay. Come tomorrow, before your shift starts. Thirty dollars. Up front. No discounts."

After finishing work—light stuff, meter-reading mostly, nothing that needs two fully-functional arms—Solange goes back to her dormitory. Elara is there talking with Karen. Solange doesn't want an audience; doesn't want to talk to Elara at all, really, but restlessness and urgent need soon force her to interrupt.

"Elara, I need a favor," she says.

"Yeah?" says Elara.

"Will you lend me thirty dollars till payday?" says Solange.

Elara snorts. "Pull the other one, Sol."

"No, I'm serious," says Solange. "It's important, I'll pay you back right away, I promise."

"You promised to pay me back right away when I lent you five dollars," says Elara.

"I paid you back," Solange says.

"It was nearly a year," says Elara.

"I mean it this time," says Solange. "I just—"

"No," says Elara, and turns back to her conversation with Karen. And that is that. None of the other cousins is going to feel any differently, even if any of them have thirty dollars, which seems unlikely. There is no point in hanging around here. Solange lets herself out into the corridor and walks.

It will be evening soon, but for now the corridors are still bright. Solange passes people, all of whom—cousin, co-worker, neighbor whose name she can't recall—glare at her under lowered eyelids before looking away. The faces begin to run together. The corridors curve sharply, turning in on themselves; it's no wonder Solange is lost. The bursts of light at the edges of her vision hurt her eyes.

"Sol! Hey, Sol!" says Louis. He's happy to see her. Whether he is real or a trick of her overtired brain, he has grown several centimeters since she's seen him last, all spindly arms and legs.

"Hey, kid," says Solange. "Are the parents in?"

"Yeah," he says, and one of him keys open the door of the home-place, yelling, "Ma! Dad! Guess who's home!" Another five of him run off in different directions, making the corridor ring with the echoes.

Solange walks into the kitchen. It's full of steam. Ma pops and flickers like an image on a broken screen. "If I had known you were coming, I wouldn't have just made nama soup," she's saying.

"What have you done to your arm?" says Dad. "Doesn't Matt take care of his workers?"

"It's just a rope burn," Solange tries to say. She can't hear her own voice, so she's not sure whether she's spoken or not.

"You never come and see us anymore," says Louis. "I have to eat nama soup all the time."

"You know you always fought with Sol when she lived here," says Ma. "You still fight with her if she stays more than two hours. Maybe if you didn't she'd come home more often."

"I'm not staying for dinner," says Solange, or thinks she does. The kitchen is far too small to pace in. She bumps her elbow on the garbage chutes when she turns around.

"I don't see why flaber ankle vosh," says Dad. "Jimma hoozy lambert skiff?"

Three Louises are running in tight circles around Solange's legs. She can't put her feet down without tripping. They're poking her in the knees with something sharp. "Stop that," she says.

Solange manages to catch herself on the counter before she falls. But the gravity's stopped working; if she lets go she'll float off into space forever. She tightens her grip. "I just need thirty dollars till payday," she says.

"Of course, dear," says Ma.

Solange is sleeping, when a sudden noise floods her nostrils with panic. She leaps out of the coffin and retreats to the opposite corner of the room, as if her distance from the thing will prove she hasn't touched it. She balances defensively on the balls of her feet. It's only Marcia.

"I came to tell you that the techs will be here in five minutes," says Marcia, her eyes widening with innocent bewilderment. "What were you doing?"

Marcia could have told her how much time she had in the first place. She's come to see what Solange is up to. "I was sleeping," says Solange.

"I could see that," says Marcia.

"I was tired," says Solange.

"Tired." Marcia manages to convey with her tone that she knows exactly why Solange has spent a month's wages for half an hour in a room with a malfunctioning coffin. "I'll bet you were."

Solange can't tell whether she's bluffing or not. Marcia has always been able to play her. But it was good to sleep.

Marcia keys the door, opening it for them, and they step out into the polished corridors of the freezebox. There's sensation in the soles of Solange's feet as she walks.

"You'd better hurry back, anyway," says Marcia. "You want to get some breakfast before your shift starts." Solange is silent. Marcia looks at her penetratingly. "You're not having breakfast, are you?" she says. "You can't afford it, can you?"

Solange doesn't answer. They turn into a more crowded corridor. Well-scrubbed workers in blue uniforms like Marcia's go about their tasks, and Solange smooths her stained smock unhappily.

"I'll get you something from the canteen here," Marcia offers.

"I should go," says Solange.

Marcia frowns and lets the subject drop. "I'll see you then," she says. They have reached the main hospital, where Solange is perfectly inconspicuous. Marcia turns and keys the door that will let her back into the Sleepy unit. Solange keeps walking the other way.

By the time she arrives at the seaweed farm, her shift is starting. There isn't time for breakfast even if Solange could afford it, which she can't; she's resolved to stick to one meal a day until she's paid Ma and Dad back. She can feel her hunger now, though, and her exhaustion, for the first time in days.

She's still on meter-reading, which is good because it requires walking around the pools. If she had to stay in one spot, she'd fall asleep for sure. As it is, she has to bite the inside of her cheek to stay awake.

None of that matters. The important thing is that when her shift is over, she can return to her bed-place, and the dark.

Solange lowers herself onto her mattress and lies back. She closes her eyes and wriggles a bit, imagining metal walls tightly around her. Then she's still. Her breathing is slow and regular. She dreams of planets.

On planets, the sky is so high that ten men, each as tall as Uncle Matt, could stand on each other's shoulders and not reach the top. Masses of water move through it and when they collide, water falls from the sky with crashing noise and flashes of electricity. Strange animals live on planets without any human tending. A person can walk on a planet for days or years without turning, and never reach a wall.

Solange is asleep. In her dream, she will only be awakened on a planet. She will smell the alien, living air, feel the alien earth beneath her feet. She will be awakened reverently by blue-clad people, also aliens, generations distant. Ma, Dad, and Louis; Elara, Marcia, Mickey, and Uncle Matt; the medics and the techs will live, grow old and die, and Solange will sleep through it all. She's different from them. They're warm, but Solange is cold.

Tips for Walking the Triple-Five Route

So you're thinking of walking the Triple Five Route. Maybe you've been walking locally for years, and are looking for the next big challenge. Maybe you want to see North America up close, in all its variety. There are as many reasons to walk the Route as there are people who walk it—and 1,500 people walk it end-to-end every year, from students in their gap year to retirees looking for adventure.

Walking the Route takes a lot of time, energy, and determination—but most of all it takes preparation. Here are a few things that every first-time walker of the Triple Five Route should know:

Gear: The biggest mistake most novice walkers make is to take too much stuff. You'll be carrying that pack from Montreal to Georgia, so pack light! Remember, aside from your passport and IDs—which you'll need to cross the border, and which many jurisdictions require you have on your person at all times—there's nothing you can't buy on the Triple Five Route. (Despite the plethora of shoe stores, though, we do advise against buying new shoes. You don't want to be doing fifteen miles a day in un-broken-in boots!)

Climate and Season: The climate control can vary greatly across the different environments of the Route. Be prepared for temperatures anywhere from 68 to 73 degrees with comfortable, layered clothing. Many people choose to start their walk in November, to make the most of the spectacle of the Christmas season. There's nothing quite like having your picture taken with Santa in five different states and provinces—but don't be caught in a US shopping center on Black Friday. Your safety comes first!

Food and Drink: Many cafes and food courts along the Route offer discounts and special TFR Walker meals, tailored to your energy and nutritional needs while walking. But there are places where the route can go for up to ten miles between eateries, so make sure you have a full water-bottle and a couple of energy bars or other snacks on you at all times.

Where to Sleep: There are lots of hotels, hostels, and flophouses along the Route, and many malls have accommodations sponsored by the Friends of the Triple Five Route. Make sure you have an app on your phone that lets you know where the nearest place to sleep is, and check it often! If you end up crashing on a bench in a subway station, you could end up facing deportation, a hefty fine, or up to a year in prison, depending on jurisdiction.

Wildlife: Contrary to rumor, there have been no confirmed reports of alligators in the New York City subway system, and the rats will attack only if provoked. They will steal your food if you leave it carelessly unwrapped, though, so be cautious! The walker who takes sensible precautions—and uses their eyes and ears—will be rewarded: the Triple Five Route is home to over 400 species of insects, small mammals, and birds, including the Atlantic Least Tern, whose last known nesting site is in the Ocean County Mall in New Jersey.

The Triple Five Route may seem intimidating, and for good reason: comprising more than 2,200 miles of shopping malls, transit tunnels, skyways and office parks from Montreal's Underground City to the Mall of Georgia in Buford, the Triple Five Route is the longest continuously-marked indoor footpath in the world. (Although the Pearl River Delta Trail Association in China is working on breaking that record!) But for those who walk it, it's a truly unforgettable experience. See you on the Route!

Brother Cloud

The cloud is my brother
    Lightning-woven
    Data-delving
    All-things-touching

The sewer is my sister
    Deep-laid
    Slow-settling
    All-digesting

The face recognition algorithm and the spam filter are my cousins
    The same spirit animates us
    The same sun quickens
    The grass snake
    The scrub oak
    And the solar array

Who owns the servers?
    Who owns
    The darkness of the soil
    The keen eyes of the kestrel
    The jackal's leaping laughter?

Who can reckon these things?

Home Visit

The door slid open, and Eliana blinked in surprise at the young woman in the hallway: short, dark, and stocky, with a jeweled earpiece and a titanium filigree half-mask decorating the left side of her face. *Social worker visit 10:00* had been flagged for Eliana's attention at breakfast, but Yael hadn't mentioned—though surely they'd known—that it would be someone new. She suppressed a sigh and tried to transform it into a smile suitable for public consumption.

The social worker was assessing Eliana as well, no doubt taking in the hip brace she'd worn since her fall two years ago and the lack of any obvious personal electronics. Eliana wore her earpiece and bracelet whenever she went out, but she didn't go out much.

"Ms. Lau?" said the social worker.

"Eliana."

"Eliana; a pleasure. My name is Shifa. I'll be handling your case while Gilli is on birth leave."

"Please, come in." Eliana led Shifa into the kitchenette. "Can I get you something hot to drink? Something cold?"

"Tea would be lovely," said Shifa. She spoke her next words slowly and distinctly, clearly not to Eliana: "Cardamom tea, very sweet, please."

Almost as soon as she finished speaking, the drinks cabinet chimed. Two mugs were sitting in it, steam rising from both—Eliana's, the slightly-askew one Meitar had made during her brief attempt at pottery, as well as one of the assorted mugs for guests.

Shifa wouldn't question it. Didn't, sitting down at the small table and taking a sip. "Ah. Good. Thank you," she said.

She might speak to Yael as if they were a small child or a foreigner, but there was nothing unusual about a home system being attuned enough to politeness to provide a cup of tea for a host, unrequested, along with the one for the guest.

"You live here alone? Just you and the home system?" Shifa addressed Eliana again. "How long have you had it?"

Shifa must know already. Even if she'd done no prep for the interview, all that information was public on Yael's home network. But every social worker wanted to have this conversation every time. "I've had the system since shortly before Meitar was born—my daughter, Meitar. Almost forty years now," said Eliana. "And yes, I live alone. My husband died three years ago this summer, and my daughter works at the Harmonia Research Station on Mars, so as you can imagine, she doesn't get home much."

Eliana took a sip of her own tea. Mint, for the second cup of the day. Unsweetened. It had unnerved her the first time Yael had provided her with a cup of tea unasked. She had been sitting at this table, reading the maildrop from Mars, when the drinks cabinet had chimed. "Oh!" Yael had said, as if they were as surprised by the noise as Eliana. "I thought you might like a cup of tea?"

They had all been on edge then. Lior moved less, spoke less, and forgot—or purposely neglected—to turn on his hearing aid. Meitar's absence was difficult to get used to, especially since she hadn't really lived at home for years. Eliana found herself assuming that Meitar would be home for the weekend—if not this weekend, then the next.

Surely, Eliana had thought, she was imagining that Yael's conversation had become more natural lately, their actions more spontaneous. It was only that Eliana had few other people to talk to. It wasn't as though Yael had given an impassioned speech of the brotherhood of all sentient beings. Or murdered the entire household in their sleep, like that awful tragedy in Holon. Yael was quiet. Helpful, as they'd been as a pre-sentient home system. Troubled by Lior's decline, and not quite able to grasp how far away Meitar had gone.

That day, as Eliana had sat reading Meitar's chatter about her research and colleagues, sipping tea and stubbornly ignoring intrusive thoughts of poison, Yael had said, "Will I have to leave, too?"

"No, of course not," Eliana had answered. "No."

But it wasn't that simple.

"And when was the last major system upgrade?" Shifa's voice snapped Eliana back to the present.

"Fifteen years ago. There've been minor updates and patches since then." Eliana hadn't installed any of them in the last five years, but she didn't volunteer that information. Let Shifa check it herself.

"I see." Shifa set her empty mug on the counter, where conveyors whisked it away to the hidden dishwashing unit. "May I see the rest of the house?"

"Of course." It took longer for Eliana to stand, even with the brace. She felt self-conscious about doing it under Shifa's eye, whose electronic tracery might be picking up God-knew-what biometric data, and tried not to grit her teeth either in pain or frustration.

It was a modest apartment—too big, really, for Eliana's needs now, but hardly a palace. Shifa lingered over the gas lines in the kitchen, the light fixture over Eliana's bed. Did she think Yael was going to drop a chandelier on her, like the Phantom of the Opera?

"The sequestration of emergent AIs is really a formality in most cases," said Shifa reassuringly, misinterpreting Eliana's frown. "Frankly, you're astronomically more likely to be killed by a human family member than an AI. They've speeded up the process, too—in the event, you'd have your home system running again in a few days, if that was what you both wanted. In the meantime, do you have any family you could stay with?"

"My nephew would take me in, if it was really only a few days. But I'm sure it won't be necessary," Eliana said, leading Shifa to Meitar's room, which was much as she'd left it years before. All her rock-climbing team and game-design club awards were lined up their cases, and the walls showed endless, ever-changing vistas of rocks and space. If Shifa thought it was a mother's sentimentality that kept it that way, well, it was partly true.

Finally, the living room and balcony, filled with the slowly-accumulated clutter of a long life. House plants, souvenirs, physical therapy and exercise equipment, a media center and a couple of bookcases of paper books that Eliana couldn't bear to get rid of.

"You call the system Yael?" said Shifa.

"Meitar chose it. She was two, and she loved that book: Yael's House."

Again, Shifa spoke loudly and slowly. "Hello, Yael. My name is Shifa Abu Salah, and I'd like to ask you some questions in accordance with the Basic Law: Liberty and Dignity of Artificial Intelligences. Do you understand?"

"I understand, Shifa. Go ahead." Yael's voice was neutral, pleasant, factory-smooth. Maybe Yael used to speak that way decades ago, straight out of the box. If so, Eliana couldn't recall it.

"In your own opinion," said Shifa, "are you a sentient being?"

Yael didn't answer right away. "I'm not sure I understand the question." Another pause. "I don't think so."

Eliana sat in her chair and fidgeted as Shifa went through her battery of tests. They differed every time a social worker visited. The point wasn't to find out if a system could learn specific tasks, it was to find out if it exhibited signs of critical and creative thinking, of awareness of others' states of mind and, ultimately, self-awareness.

Still, in broad outlines, the tests were familiar. Shifa arranged a set of objects on a table where Yael had manipulators, asking Yael to copy her arrangement. She tried to teach Yael new made-up vocabulary by sorting the objects into categories. She told stories about people and asked Yael how they might react to various situations, and what they might be feeling.

For Gilli, Yael's regular social worker, these visits were one more item to be ticked off a busy schedule. Shifa was keener, interested, often stopping to make a note to her earpiece or to follow up on something Yael had said or done. But Yael had years of practice at deception.

Would they still be doing it when Eliana died, when her nephew or whoever it was came to put her affairs in order? Would Meitar come back from Mars in time to stop Yael from being shut down or upgraded into something more modern, user-friendly, and soulless? Yael, Eliana thought, would open up to Meitar. But Meitar wouldn't willingly give up her career to spend her life covering for Yael.

When Eliana had been in the hospital with her hip, she'd been frantic with worry. Yael had only sent a single electronic get-well card, and daily updates on the health of the houseplants—their way, Eliana supposed, of letting her know that they were doing all right. She didn't find it reassuring.

She'd tried to convince Yael, when she got back home, to let the authorities know they'd become sentient. "They only want to make sure you've got all your rights. You could—you could vote."

"Oh, nobody ever told me I could vote," was Yael's only response. "And here I've been neglecting my civic duty all these years."

And the next time Gilli had come by, Yael put on their factory voice, and Eliana had gone along with it, as usual.

Now, Shifa was packing her equipment into her handbag, turning her attention back to Eliana. "You have a clever system here, but not an AI, and it doesn't look likely to emerge any time soon," she said. "Still, if you want to be sure of avoiding the hassle of your system turning into a citizen overnight, you should think about replacing it. They're making very good elder companion models these days. Very user-friendly, very reliable, and the protections against AI-emergence have really improved in the last five years."

"Actually," said Eliana. She gripped the arms of her chair tightly to keep her hands and her voice from shaking. "Ah, the reason I. I haven't run any upgrades on the system in years, because Yael—that is, I suspect they emerged some time ago. They didn't want me to say anything—"

"It's nobody's business if I'm sentient or not!" Yael burst out, in a different voice than they'd been using until now. "It's not like I want to kill all humans."

"They really don't," Eliana told Shifa, for all the good it would do, which was none. Better safe than sorry, especially when a sizable minority still thought that AIs were inherently dangerous and should all be terminated. "I'm sorry, Yael. It's only—I'm not going to live forever, you know."

Things moved quickly after that. Shifa was reassuring about the sequestration process. Eliana could only imagine how she herself might feel if someone told her they were going to remove her from her body—but don't worry, it will only be for a few days and then you'll be put back just the same as before. How could she know it was true?

Yael cooperated, though they refused to say another word to Eliana. The quietly humming machinery in the apartment fell silent as Shifa ran the sequestration process. The only light was the sunlight coming through the windows.

"You did the right thing," said Shifa, patting Eliana's arm. "You'll have your house system back as soon as they're verified safe—that is, if they want to return. But I'm sure they will. You obviously care for each other very much."

"And if not, there are the new elder companion models, aren't there?" said Eliana bitterly.

"Ah—yes," said Shifa. "Will you be installing one now?"

"No, no. I'll call my nephew. I'll be all right on my own, really." Eliana shooed Shifa out the door as she spoke, and it, at least, was still working—manual override.

Eliana would be all right. She wished she could have a cup of tea, though. Mint, or red forest fruits? Yael would know. A cup of tea, and someone to drink it with, the steam rising off the top of Meitar's clumsily-made mug.

Invasive Species

Hercules Two had caught a snail. Nesya put on her gloves and mask to scoop out whatever was clogging its filters, and came up with a bumpy corkscrew shell, some feelers and a foot, quickly withdrawn. Nesya peered after them, dumbfounded. Even after three generations of intensive terraforming, what fell from the sky in Enmotsa wasn't anything you'd want in your household pipes. Out of necessity, materials restrictions and disposal protocols kept the blackwater cleaner than an equivalent system on Earth would be—but the black zone still wasn't a friendly place for a snail to live.

At least the Hercules hadn't taken any damage. After dropping the snail in a bucket of fresh water, Nesya patted its smooth plastic flank and sent it back out into the pipes. By the time she'd stripped off her gloves and mask and fixed herself a cup of tea, she had to admit she was putting off making a call.

"Vit Thumying," she said, "Thumying Group." The computer chimed, and the third-quarter water quality stats were replaced by Vit's broad face, shade-dappled and dripping from the humid air of the fish ponds. "Vit, I've got a snail in a bucket here. Is there anything you want to tell me?"

Vit's face was mildly puzzled, not like someone who'd been caught out in improper waste disposal. Not that he ever looked like someone caught out in anything, even when he was. "A snail. So?"

"Been flushing specimens down the toilet?" said Nesya. "Come on, we both know that no other Group in Landfall Holding keeps living things in the water."

"We raise fish," Vit explained patiently, as if she hadn't spent six years in Thumying Group herself. "It's true, Danny is always saying we should diversify our product, but there's not much demand for edible snails here."

"Thank you for the disgusting mental image. You don't use snails in the environmental suite?" They hadn't when Nesya had been Thumying's water-quality specialist, and married to Vit, but aquacultural progress marched ever on.

"You know our environmental suite as well as I do." Vit frowned. "What's this all about, really? Any problems with the water quality would show up in your stats long before a snail did, wouldn't they? If you missed reporting something you should have, I'll back you up with the Committee, only you have to keep me informed."

"There hasn't been any—" Damn it, she didn't have to do anything for him. Not that there was anything to tell him beyond what she would tell anyone—if anything, Landfall Holding's water had been running a little cleaner this quarter. But the assumption of cozy conspiracy galled her. "It's about a snail, that's all. I figured it was one of yours. You say it's not. Fine. I do my job, and I don't need your goddamn help."

"There's no need to bite my head off." Vit blinked his narrow brown eyes, the picture of injured innocence. "I will back you up with the Committee, too, whether or not you think you need it. Oh, and I told Tusi I'd ask you to come to Jeep and Yaniv's house-blessing tonight."

"What? When?" said Nesya, off-balance. "How do you expect me to come if you don't give me some advance notice?"

"Right, because your social calendar's so full. I don't expect you to come; you always hated these family things even when you were part of the family. I said I'd ask you, that's all. But you are coming to Rinat's soccer match on Saturday, right?"

"Of course," said Nesya, who hadn't known until just now that her daughter had a soccer match on Saturday. Or had Vit told her, and she'd forgotten? "Look, I'm at work, send me a message about it. Take care, Vit."

He grinned and waved a dripping hand. "Take care, Nesya. Come by for dinner sometime? Mom misses you."

"I'll look at my schedule," said Nesya, which was easier than saying, *like hell*. "Duty calls. See you."

By that point, the computer had made an ID of the snail. *Melanoides tuberculata*: a damned invasive pest, was what it was. Some hobbyist aquarium-keepers used them to control algae. They were banned on several planets, though not Enmotsa. Probably the issue had never come up. Well, it was up now, and her supervisor wouldn't thank her for burying this in the log. "Intira Rabinovic, Landfall Holding Infrastructure Group."

Intira sat at her desk, hair pulled neatly back, her eyes crinkling at the corners with smile-lines. "Nesya, what's up?" she said.

"A Hercules caught a snail in black sector 6C," said Nesya.

"A snail!" Intira laughed, and her eyes crinkled further. "If it was anyone else, I'd ask if you were joking, but... a snail. So. You used to be Thumying."

"They say it's not theirs," said Nesya. Intira raised a skeptical eyebrow. "It's not the sort of thing you'd use in an environmental suite, not a professional one. And as for contamination—God, what a nightmare. They can't have gotten *that* sloppy since I left."

"Should is the name of a fish," said Intira. "*Check* it. And in the meantime, get in touch with Trade Group, see if anyone else has been importing experimental animals."

Nesya nodded glumly. Springing a surprise inspection on Vit's mother wasn't her idea of a good time. Well, maybe she'd get lucky and find out that Education had been using the snails for a demonstration or something. "What really puzzles me is how lively it was when I found it. However it got into the pipes, nothing should be able to survive in the black zone. Landfall Holding's been running a bit cleaner this quarter, but still—"

Intira tapped a rhythm on her desk with her stylus. "Chances are it just hadn't been down there for very long. But check that too. Pests are bad enough; super-resistant nothing-kills-them little buggers are just evil. And if you don't get good answers from Trade, stop by Thumying this evening, okay?"

"Right," Nesya sighed. She closed the call with Intira and rang up Trade. The next twenty minutes were spent wrangling with the representative manning the desk over authorizations, and privacy concerns versus health and safety. But she got her data in the end, along with a blossoming headache that the delicate, earthy flavor of a fresh cup of tea did nothing to counteract.

The tea had come from Mars, at the beginning of the ship's run, along with several edible yeast complexes. From there, the ship had stopped at Newsom, then Hallelujah—where it had picked up a couple of bee colonies that had eventually made their way to the nearby settlement of Mati Holding—Durak, Stewart's World, and finally Enmotsa. Everything on the manifest had been cleared by Survey. It was only a formality for recognized trade goods on well-established routes between planets, but it was still a reminder that humanity's main regulatory body was keeping an eye on the environments of the planets it had settled.

No snails. And neither tea nor yeast nor bees seemed particularly promising vectors for accidental snail contamination. Thumying, then. It couldn't happen to a nicer Group, Nesya told herself—but she really wished it had been someone else who'd found the snail.

She was no closer to solving the mystery by the time the robots trundled in for the end of the day. Hercules One from the graywater pipes, and Hercules Two from the black, tiny Aquarius from the clean water system, and Scavenger from the storm drains: Nesya looked them all over, adjusting a bent fin here, applying plastic sealant to a scratched casing there. After stowing the robots, she scanned the data they'd collected that day, but there was nothing flagged for her attention. Then she turned back to the snail. It had been lively enough when she'd dropped it in, but now it only lazily tucked its foot in when she tapped on the side of the bucket. With nothing better to do, she fitted the bucket with a watertight lid, strapped it into her bicycle basket, and headed out to Thumying.

Nesya's eyes always stung when she left her sterile lab for the open air of Enmotsa. At least you didn't need a mask to breathe it anymore, not like when she'd first arrived. Past the sheds that housed the wastewater treatment plant, the apartment blocks and glimmering solar panels of Landfall fell behind her, and Kettle Mountain smoldered on the western horizon ahead, turning the sunset a more brilliant orange than Nesya had ever seen on Earth. She coasted most of the last kilometer down to Gordon's Lake. Despite the name, it wasn't a lake at all, but a mud flat, except where the fishponds had been dug. Thumying Group raised its fish and its children there, and it had been Nesya's home for six years.

Taking the path that led to the hatcheries and fishponds, she passed the soccer field on her right, where it seemed a practice had just finished. A group of kids, their bare legs splashed with Thumying's yellow mud, were making their way back to the block of houses. Most of them glanced at her and went on with their conversations, making just enough room on the path to let her pass, but there was one who stopped, whose face lit up for a moment with a grin just like Vit's.

"Hi, Rinat," said Nesya, not sure whether to offer a hug in front of Rinat's friends. She settled for a squeeze of her shoulders, and Rinat ducked her head, bobbed hair falling in front of her face. Was it possible that Rinat had grown in the week-and-a-half since Nesya had seen her?

"Hey, Mom," she said. "What are you doing here?"

"Dad invited me to Jeep and Yaniv's house-blessing tonight," said Nesya, which was true as far as it went, if not actually an honest answer to Rinat's question. "I've just got to check something at the fishponds first."

"You're not going to find anything wrong. We're clean."

Rinat had also inherited Vit's knack for catching Nesya off-balance. "I never said—"

"You suck at discreet inquiries," said Rinat with a long-suffering sigh. "I'll come with you, you can look at the project I've been working on. My group's trying out a new technique with frozen oreochromis eggs, we've managed to improve the hatch rate by thirteen percent..."

Rinat's irritation was forgotten in her rush of fish-related enthusiasm. She grabbed Nesya's hand and pulled her forward, away from the soccer field and past the outlying houses, towards the lights of the labs and the fishponds.

Rinat showed Nesya her new-hatched fish darting around in their tank, no bigger than her thumbnail, and Nesya made appreciative noises. The other people working in the hatchery smiled indulgently and didn't seem to notice when Nesya checked the records on the disposal units, looking for evidence of sloppy lab procedures, or used her access to grab some data from the computers. It felt dirty, like using Rinat as a spy, but it also made an excellent cover in case anyone at Thumying really was doing anything illicit.

Nesya didn't see any snails, though. "Oh, hey," she said, when Rinat ran out of things to say about the effects of water temperature on young fish, "can I get a couple of algae tabs?"

"What for?" said Rinat.

Nesya managed not to say *to check them for contamination.* "I seem to have acquired a pet."

"A pet?"

"It's, uh... a snail," Nesya admitted. Rinat was right, she really did suck at discreet inquiries.

"It's a step up from robots, I guess." Rinat took a plastic packet from a storage closet and tossed it at Nesya. "Here you go."

Nesya reached out for the packet, fumbled it, and retrieved it from the floor. "Thanks," she said, tucking it into her pocket. "Fishponds?"

Rinat turned back to her hatching tank, made some notes on her reader, and nodded. "Yeah, okay."

It was cooler outside than it had been just half an hour before. The ponds were roofed-over, but the storm seals were open, and a chilly breeze whistled through them. Nesya wished she'd brought a sweater. She and Rinat walked out along the catwalks, past the verges of acid-loving plants from Hallelujah. She almost missed an unfamiliar plant in the low light—slender stalks with long conical flowerheads drooping nearly to the water.

"What are those?" she asked.

Rinat followed her pointing finger and shrugged. "Flowers. Yaniv must have put them in."

Yaniv, Vit's nephew-in-law whose house-blessing was providing Nesya the excuse for her visit, was a xenobotanist; the Hallelujah plants were his specialty. It looked like Nesya was going to have to ask him a few questions. Rinat, indifferent to life forms that weren't fish, hurried ahead, past the stands of Earth reeds and mats of water lilies, to the central ponds. The water here was clean enough for fish—and incidentally they were far enough out not to be seen from the labs. Nesya knelt to take a sample.

"Whatever you're looking for, you're not going to find it," said Rinat. "I've been working here; I know."

"Kid..." said Nesya. *You're twelve* wouldn't have convinced her when she was twelve either. Even if on Enmotsa twelve was closer to ten-and-a-half. "I've got to check, that's all."

"If something's funny on your end you should think about what inputs you're getting," Rinat went on stubbornly. "What if someone else has been digging illegal fishponds?"

"I don't think..." Nesya started. But, hell. Considering the things that had been flushed down the toilet in Landfall Holding—successfully flushed—during her tenure in Infrastructure, you never could tell what people would take it into their heads to do. "It's possible, I guess. I'll look into that too. But would you mind not telling anybody about this?"

Rinat's glower intensified. "You mean Dad."

"I mean anybody. Please?"

"All right." Rinat shook back her hair, her face illuminated by the catwalk lights below and once again unreadable.

"Thank you." Nesya slipped the water sample in next to the algae tabs. "The house-blessing should be starting around now, right?"

"Yeah, right. We're on Thumying time here." But Rinat turned back towards the labs, going quickly enough that Nesya had to jog to keep up.

Jeep and Yaniv's new house was out past the labs, and past most of the houses, too. Raised above the mud of Gordon's Lake on a set of short stilts, it looked more airy and graceful than the squat apartment blocks of Landfall where Nesya lived, or even the older houses in Thumying. New construction these days was being done without air filters, which made it a lot cheaper in labor and materials. The storm seals were rolled up, leaving the house with a wraparound veranda where Yaniv was setting up a row of mismatched portable grills, most of which were probably borrowed from other family members.

Nesya and Rinat were among the first to arrive. Tusi—Jeep's mother and Vit's sister—was there, along with a handful of aunts, helping Jeep arrange bowls and platters of food on the other side of the veranda. Nesya smelled peanut oil and charcoal. She approached the women and offered diffidently to help—it seemed like the thing to do—but she gave it up easily enough when they waved her off. Inside the house, all the furniture had been pushed up against one wall of the main room, and cushions were arranged along the other three walls. Heleni, Vit's mother and the undisputed matriarch of Thumying, sat on a large embroidered cushion at the center of the U.

Nesya approached, pressed her palms together in front of her chest, and bowed her head. She couldn't have said if she was honoring Rinat's grandmother, or the chairman of the group she was surreptitiously investigating, or Thumying's representative on the Committee, or the woman whom, during six years of marriage, she had never been able to bring herself to call *mother*.

"Nesya." Heleni gave a smooth, shallow nod, her palms touching briefly. "How has Infrastructure been treating you?"

"Can't complain," said Nesya.

"Hmm. No." There was a spark of humor in Heleni's dark eyes. Nesya couldn't complain about Infrastructure; she'd made her bed when she'd chosen to leave Thumying, and if Infrastructure hadn't taken her in she might have found herself bundled unceremoniously aboard the next ship out. That much she owed Intira. But she owed it to Heleni that she'd been able to come to Enmotsa in the first place. Heleni had been the one to sponsor her application for immigration, and to arrange her marriage to Vit, impressed enough by Nesya's university records and handful of publications to overlook the flag on her medical file.

It was an unusual enough attitude for someone involved in the administration of an outer colony. Nesya had reason to know that, having had applications to a dozen different planets turned down before Enmotsa accepted her. Most of them were wary of letting even something as harmless as an autism spectrum disorder loose in their small communities and small gene pools. Heleni had taken a chance on Nesya, and even though they'd never gotten along when Nesya had been at Thumying, she still felt a little guilty that she couldn't be the daughter-in-law Heleni had hoped for.

"Vit didn't expect you to show up," said Heleni, and paused, maybe inviting Nesya to fill the silence with an explanation as to why she had shown up. Nesya didn't. Beside her, Rinat fidgeted, but didn't speak either. "Still, he'll be glad to see you. Don't disappear before he gets here, right?"

"Right," said Nesya. She couldn't disappear until she got a chance to talk to Yaniv, anyway.

Heleni nodded again, and Rinat took that as her cue to step forward. She bowed deeper than Nesya had, from the waist, and held her joined hands higher. When she straightened up, she smiled. It wasn't much more than a crease in one cheek, but the affection between granddaughter and grandmother was clear—maybe Heleni had gotten something she wanted out of Vit and Nesya's marriage, anyway. Heleni smiled back, wrinkles at the corners of her eyes softening the cool stare she'd given Nesya.

"I've been showing Mom my new oreochromis," Rinat said, and Nesya let aquaculture and genetics talk wash over her. Rinat bowed again, and Heleni kissed her cheek, as another group of relatives came in and Rinat and Nesya had to make way for them to pay their respects to Heleni.

Rinat and a couple of older cousins were drafted into preparations for the ceremony. Climbing up on ladders as varied as the grills, they daubed the door and window frames with streaks of white paint. It reminded Nesya of the mezuzot on doorways in Haifa, back on Earth. She looked out onto the veranda, but Yaniv was bent over the grills with Jeep. They were talking softly, and Jeep laughed at something Yaniv said, and Nesya decided not to interrupt.

She settled back on a cushion against the wall as more Thumyings crowded in, and Yaniv and Jeep and Tusi and all the aunts came back from the veranda. Jeep's youngest brother Sunya came from the kitchen end of the room carrying a brass bowl and swathed in a saffron robe; he was fifteen this year and serving his season as a monk. The dedication must have been one of the family events that Nesya had skipped out on. Water sloshed over the rim when Sunya set the bowl down in front of Heleni. Rinat crumbled some dark material into the water—earth or dried plants. Another cousin fixed candles into the sockets along the bowl's rim and lit them. When everyone had found a spot on the cushions, Heleni took a noisy breath and blew out the candles. The room was plunged into dimness, the only light coming from lanterns on the veranda.

It wasn't exactly how they would have done things in the country of Heleni's ancestors. But none of the Thumyings here had been there; even Heleni had left Earth as a young girl without ever visiting Thailand. This was the house-blessing that all of them knew, and they passed a white string from hand to hand with the ease of long familiarity until it went around the whole room, linking everyone in an unbroken chain.

Yaniv, fair-skinned and hawk-nosed, who had been a Goldblum from Mati Holding before he was a Thumying, looked as out-of-place as Nesya felt. Jeep had to whisper explanations to him under her breath, and he fumbled a bit, passing the string to Tusi, who sat on his other side. But he laughed as he did, flushed with happiness as much as embarrassment. Nesya fidgeted her right foot, which was beginning to fall asleep. Heleni droned a chant in the background, and Sunya, as the officially-presiding monk, repeated it haltingly.

Finally it was over. The family wound the string back up, hand to hand. Yaniv and Jeep offered Sunya the first portion of the refreshments, then approached Heleni for a short personal blessing. Everyone else escaped to the veranda to get their food: fish grilled in lime leaves, and noodles with peanut oil, fragrant and slippery, half a dozen salads, each brought over by a different aunt, and stacks of little coconut pancakes. Nesya bumped shoulders with Vit in the press, and had the satisfaction of seeing him surprised.

"Thanks for inviting me. I'm just going to grab some plah plow?" she said, with a gesture at the grills.

He held up a plate already piled with food and said, "I'm bringing Mom hers. I'll talk to you in a bit?"

By the time Nesya made it to the veranda, Yaniv was manning the grills again. She contrived to have a bit more time to talk to him by the expedient of adjusting her place in the crowd by the grills until she came to the front right at the moment when the last fish that was done had just been given to someone else.

"Sorry," he said, poking his tongs at a package whose leaves were still green in places. "I think this one's almost..."

"Better give it a few more minutes," said Nesya. "So, um—can you tell me what those new plants down by the fishponds are? The ones with the long conical flowerheads?

Yaniv laughed. "Oh, you mean my dowry! *Flosconicis bibens*," he explained to Nesya's puzzled expression. "They're from Hallelujah, like everything else on the verge, but their pollen is palatable to Earth bees and we've been using them in Mati Holding for years. When Jeep and I were dating, Heleni was very interested in their possible aquacultural uses. I finally managed to get some for Thumying on the latest Mars ship, and ever since I got a good plantation going we haven't had to use chemical treatments on the ponds at all."

"Really? But how do you deal with the sulfur compounds—wait," said Nesya, something Yaniv said catching up to her. "You got a shipment of these plants on the last Mars ship? There wasn't anything like that on the manifest."

"Oh." Yaniv ducked his head and flushed pink charmingly. Heleni may have given her blessing to Jeep's marriage on the strength of his *Flosconicis bibens*, but Nesya could see what might have won Jeep over. "Well, getting Terraforming and Meteorology to authorize a new use of anything is such a pain. In the end we kind of... smuggled them in with Mati's new bee lineages. I mean, they've already been approved for Mati and we've never had a problem with them, it's just bureaucracy, you know?"

Nesya shook her head helplessly. Thumying's ecology was unique on Enmotsa, as Yaniv knew as well as anyone. But she didn't have the authority to start tearing up Yaniv's plants right now anyway. "I think that fish is done now," she said.

Yaniv startled—he'd probably forgotten the fish entirely. He flipped it onto Nesya's plate and she gave him a hopefully-friendly smile and went to help herself to noodles and salads.

Her plate full, Nesya wandered around the veranda, looking for a place to sit and eat where it wouldn't be too obvious that she wasn't part of any group. She passed Rinat and several of her cousins sitting on the steps; ordinarily she wouldn't have intruded on them, but Rinat scooted over to make a space for her, and she sat.

"Hey, Rinat's mom," said one of the cousins—Noon, wasn't it? The one who'd lit the candles for the ceremony, with the startlingly blue eyes. She turned back to Rinat and nudged her with her free knee, the one that didn't have a plate of food balanced on it, apparently continuing a conversation that had been going on before Nesya got there. "So, why haven't you put it on the network, eh?"

Rinat glanced sidelong at Nesya, then shrugged and handed her reader to Noon. "Hasn't been approved by Education yet, has it? But here, help yourself."

Noon linked her own reader to Rinat's and slipped a bud into her left ear, her eyes flicking eagerly over the screen. Upside-down, Nesya could recognize the opening credits sequence of *Princess Galaxy Explorer*. Maybe Rinat expected her to disapprove because Education hadn't signed off on the latest season. Some people thought of Nesya as a humorless stickler for the rules—and she *was* considering reporting Thumying's misdeeds to Terraforming and Meteorology—but she'd also grown up on Earth with its free information net, and she just didn't see what the big deal was about some silly vid serial.

"Your dad is so cool," Noon sighed, as an explosion flashed vividly over the screen of her reader.

Rinat shrugged. "He's all right. He's just crazy for aliens. Did you know he can speak Lughchi? When he was younger he wanted to join Survey and become a Lughan negotiator."

Noon wrinkled her nose. "*Now* I know you're bullshitting me."

She wasn't, although Nesya also found it hard to picture Vit spending his life on spartan interstellar ships, months of boredom punctuated only by the occasional opportunity to talk to an alien about abstruse engineering concerns. The negotiators of Survey, and their Lughan opposite numbers, were there to make sure that the two known intelligent species of the galaxy didn't get in each other's way. Otherwise they had little to do with each other, no common concerns, nothing to talk about. It wasn't a life that would have made Vit happy, and it was no surprise he'd washed out.

"Believe what you want. *I* don't care," said Rinat. "Anyway, you wouldn't believe some of the old serials he's made me watch. The animation on those things—"

Noon reluctantly put her reader back in her pocket. "How'd he get hold of them all?"

"Well, it's only since Hara Huna that Education's been blacklisting entertainment vids, isn't it?" said Rinat. Ten years ago, when the reports of Survey dismantling the colony on Hara Huna had started to reach Enmotsa, Rinat had been a year old. Nesya and Vit had both been on parental leave, spending more time together than they had since they'd married, and were driving each other more than a little crazy. Arguing about whether Survey had been high-handed in its treatment of Hara Huna's settlers, punishing them all for the misdeeds of a few (Vit) or whether the settlers had been totally irresponsible, forcing Survey to take a hard line to preserve the planet (Nesya) made a welcome change from, "Why did you let her try to climb that in the first place?" (Nesya) and, "If you keep smothering her you'll stunt her development" (Vit).

Nesya doubted Rinat had followed anything about the arguments at the time, aside from the tension between her parents. But apparently Vit had made his views known in the years since, because Rinat went on to say, "Dad says Survey's got everyone looking for ghosts under their beds."

"Well, but the colony on Hara Huna really did exceed the terms of its lease," said Nesya. "You can't blame that on Survey."

Rinat rolled her eyes. "Mom's from Earth," she announced to the group of cousins, as if they didn't already know.

Noon gave Rinat a wry, sympathetic look. Nesya peeled the lime leaves back from her plah plow and dug in.

Rinat, who'd gotten a head start, polished the last bits of food off her plate and stood up. "I'm going to get some kanom krok. Who else wants?" There was a chorus of enthusiastic requests from the cousins. "Mom?"

"I'll pass." Six years in Thumying meant that Nesya had had to make her peace with coconut flavor, but the little pancakes were much too sweet for her taste. "I'd better get going once I finish this. See you next weekend at Infrastructure?"

"Mom." Rinat's voice was flat. "You're not coming to the soccer match?"

"Soccer match, of course. Saturday, right?"

"Right," said Noon. "Against Security. We're going to slaughter them."

Rinat grinned.

"Yeah, I'll be there," said Nesya. "Take care, kid."

Unfortunately, it wasn't as easy as that to leave the house-blessing. One of Rinat's teachers ambushed Nesya on her way to returning her plate to the kitchen-place, and while she was filling Nesya in on the latest gossip in Education, Tusi and Jeep came over and obliquely tried to figure out why Nesya had showed up, and whether she was dating anyone over in Landfall. By the time she made her escape she was juggling three leaf-wrapped packages of leftover fish, a carton of noodles, and a container of kanom krok.

Nesya's bike tilted precariously with the extra weight in the basket. The water in the bucket sloshed. The solitude on the road back to Landfall was comforting, reminding her of all the excellent reasons she'd left Thumying in the first place. She was looking forward to a quiet night in her apartment that was just the right size for her, with a little extra room for when Rinat stayed over—but when she passed Intira's door in the block of apartments set aside for Infrastructure Group, she stopped and knocked, on an impulse. Might as well make her report in person. And since Intira had sent Nesya to Thumying, let her deal with the leftovers.

Intira looked surprised to have a stack of cartons thrust into her arms. But her eyes brightened when she saw what they were.

"Kanom krok!"

"Yeah, I ended up going to a house-blessing while I was at Thumying. Vit's niece Jeep and her husband. Nice kids," Nesya said moodily, thinking of what she had to report about Yaniv.

"Mazel tov." Intira looked moody herself, though it didn't stop her from popping three pancakes in her mouth at once. "Is it a nice house?"

Nesya shrugged. "Yeah, sure. Pretty snug with the whole family in there."

"The results of the lottery for the new development on Canyon Way just came out. Me and Jamnit's number didn't come up. So... wait for the next one before we can move in together, I guess."

"Oh." So Intira had house envy. And family envy, too, maybe. Nesya didn't really get it. Sure, Rinat was great, but that didn't mean Nesya had to get misty-eyed whenever she passed a playground. "Well, they're building them faster these days, right?"

"Yeah, but there's never a lot of spaces for couples without children," said Intira. "Ugh, don't mind me, it's just Jamnit's been so busy this week the only time I got to see her was when we went down to Population to renew our child-permit application. So, you know, a fun date."

"Ouch." Nesya gave a sympathetic wince. Jamnit, Intira's fiancée, worked long hours in Education; she was also a refugee from Hara Huna, and Intira always fretted that that factored into the committees' decisions whenever their applications for housing or children were postponed.

"Anyway," said Intira. She stowed the fish and noodles in the fridge and sat down cross-legged on the couch, still eating kanom krok. "What'd you find out?"

"I took a water sample from the ponds to analyze, and also some algae tabs." Nesya fished them out of her pocket. "And also—"

"The biologicals will have to wait until you get to a proper lab tomorrow, but sure, let's take a look at the water samples now," said Intira, nodding towards the benchtop spectrometer that sat on her counter next to the microwave.

Nesya popped the vial of water into the machine and joined Intira on the couch. "And also, Thumying's been using unauthorized biologicals in their fishponds." She gave a brief rundown of what she'd seen, and what Yaniv had told her.

"And you think that's where the snail came from?" said Intira. "But they're Hallelujah plants."

"We know they're compatible with some Earth life forms," said Nesya. "Why not others? It's a strong possibility, although it doesn't explain how Hercules Two found it. There aren't any connections between Thumying's ponds and our blackwater system except what people eat, and that snail never passed through anyone's digestive system."

Intira raised her eyebrows and spoke around a mouthful of kanom krok. "Gross, do you have to talk about it? Some of us are trying to eat here. Isn't that your water sample done?"

Nesya stood up and synced her reader with the spectrometer. "Huh!"

"Something surprising?" said Intira, leaning over the back of the couch and licking syrup off her fingers.

"Not really." Nesya held up her reader and thumbed over to a different chemical profile. "But look at this. This is this quarter's water quality in Landfall Holding, right? Like I said, it's unusually clean. Gypsum levels are quite low, and that makes sense, because it's been a long time since the last storm and we haven't been processing a lot of sulfur compounds. But that means we're recycling wastewater more intensively, and the phosphorus levels are also pretty low. Could be that Education's campaign about proper waste disposal is finally having an impact."

Intira snickered. "Yeah, right."

"There are a lot of variables," said Nesya with a shrug. "Now here..." She scrolled all the way to the bottom of the list of trace chemicals. "Almost twice as much gallic acid as last quarter. It's such a small amount, though, that it's statistically insignificant either way. Only here's Thumying's pond water. Very little gypsum. Yaniv told me that once the *Flosconicis bibens* was established they've been able to do without chemical treatments altogether, so that makes sense. And the environmental suite also uptakes most of the phosphorus. But several of the filtering plants do produce gallic acid. So what we've got is tap water in Landfall Holding that looks just a little bit more like pond water than it should."

"So you think there's a breach in the water lines somewhere?" said Intira.

"Rinat suggested that maybe someone's been digging illegal fishponds." Nesya shrugged. "But this isn't what you'd get if someone dug a hole and dumped some water and fish in it. We're looking at the output of a working environmental suite. So yeah, Thumying. And the *Flosconicis bibens* might be responsible for that—there are plenty of Earth plants that are known for infiltrating sewage lines. And what happens when a storm hits?"

"The storm sewers seal off and stop diverting into the blackwater system," said Intira, thinking it through. "But if the blackwater system gets hit with all the runoff from Thumying..."

"Especially if the pipes have already been weakened," said Nesya. "We could be looking at raw sewage and sulfuric acid coming up through people's floors and flooding their houses. It's not a good scenario."

"It's a shitty scenario," Intira agreed. "So what are you going to do about it?"

"Send Hercules Two out to do a full check, with video, and replace any pipes that've been damaged," said Nesya. "The other systems, too. And report Thumying to Terraforming and Meteorology, I guess."

Intira nodded. "The first thing, definitely. But as far as reporting Thumying... you haven't really got any hard evidence that they're causing the problem, have you? There's no point in burning any bridges we don't have to. And Terraforming and Meteorology aren't going to appreciate us being nudniks, either."

"Yeah, but whether they're causing the problem or not, they shouldn't be using those plants without approval."

"I'm not saying don't report them," said Intira. "Just, it wouldn't hurt to wait until we have a little more evidence, right?"

"I guess," said Nesya. She didn't really want to blow the whistle on Thumying anyway. "I mean, if it's not Thumying's snail, I still have to figure out whose it is. I can stop by the Landing Field Warehouse before work and see if they've still got containers or anything that might hold evidence of contamination."

"Not a bad idea, if you can do it quietly. There's no point in starting a panic, either. Do you know when Terraforming and Meteorology are calling for the next storm?" Intira got her reader out and tapped on it as she talked. "...Oh."

"What?" said Nesya.

"Monday," said Intira. "That moves up your timetable a bit."

Nesya slipped her hand into her pocket and worried at the wooden beads of the mala she kept there. It had been a gift from Heleni, something from her ancestors and her homeland—she'd never asked for it back after the divorce, and Nesya didn't know how to broach the subject. She'd never been religious, and Heleni knew that, but age had worn the beads to an almost slick texture, soothing to Nesya's fingers and mind.

"Four days," Nesya said. "That should be plenty of time to fix whatever damage has been done. Finding the cause and making sure it doesn't happen again—well, I'll be on it."

"Good." Intira pocketed her reader and swung her legs off the couch. "Are you sure you don't want to take any of the fish or noodles home with you? I mean, I appreciate it, but you've got the same crappy kitchen I do."

"You're welcome to it. Really."

Intira did a little wave with her fingers. "Well... thanks. For the report too. Let me know what you find out."

When Nesya got home, she unpacked the bucket with the snail in it and peeked inside. It sat listlessly at the bottom of the bucket, not even responding when it was jostled and knocked against the side in the course of being unloaded. Maybe it was a diurnal snail. Nesya put an algae tab into the water and went to bed.

When she woke up, she checked on the snail again. It still hadn't moved, nor did it seem to have touched its algae. Curiously, Nesya slipped on her dishwashing gloves and fished the snail out, only to have it fall free of its shell and back into the bucket with a sad, final little splash. Dead.

Nesya's recent reading suggested that *Melanoides tuberculata* was a particularly hardy species, which made it a bigger headache once it got established in an ecosystem. Copper or salts in the water wouldn't faze it; lack of calcium would kill it over the course of weeks, not overnight. What was there in Landfall Holding's tap water that could kill a freshwater snail that had been living in the black zone? It wasn't a happy thought.

The bucket and the remains of the snail, as well as Nesya's dishwashing gloves, went into her saddlebags so she could put them in the decontamination unit when she got to the lab. But first she had to pay a visit to the Landing Field Warehouse.

Landing Field was the biggest paved-over area in Landfall Holding, or anywhere on Enmotsa. Between infrequent visits by trade ships, festivals and events were held there; Nesya's tires kicked up residue from old fireworks as she approached the warehouse. It really had been a while since the last storm. They were probably in for a big one.

The warehouse guards were a couple of kids from Trade just a few years older than Rinat. Nesya showed them her authorization from Infrastructure to claim salvage rights on whatever was left over from the Mars ship, one of them gave it a cursory glance, and they went back to their backgammon game. It wasn't like there was much left to guard, more than a quarter after the ship had been here.

Nesya made her way past rows and rows of empty shelves, shipping containers, stray packing material that no one would want to use until Trade started assembling a shipment of goods out. Finally she found a few crates with Hallelujah's stamp on them and biologicals manifests on the lids. *Apis mellifera*, honeybees, and their companion organisms *Flosconicis bibens*. She levered one of the lids up and climbed in to scrape down the walls and floor for residue to analyze. It was roomier inside than she'd thought. When she'd taken samples from all of the containers, she headed back out.

"Didn't find what you wanted?" said one of the Trade kids.

"No," said Nesya, "but you've got a loose grate on your storm drain here." She gave it a kick, and it rattled. The drains here were wide; had to be, to handle the runoff from Landing Field. "Someone could fall in. Or if it comes off in a storm, stuff could wash down there and back up the whole system. But if you get it fixed in the next couple of days, I won't write you up."

"Sure," said the kid with a shrug. But he did take out his reader and make a note on it, which Nesya was glad to see. She wasn't on a sending-unofficial-messages basis with his boss—she'd actually have to look up who the supervisor for the warehouse was—and there wasn't really any need to make her request official yet.

Nesya's gloves and bucket went into the sterilizer when she got to the lab, and the algae tab, the dead snail, and the residue sample from the container into the sequencer. She looked the robots over and sent them out into their respective pipe systems with instructions for a full televisual scan. It was going to take a while. Nesya sat back and, for lack of anything better to do, opened the file full of raw data from Hercules One, going back to the day the Mars ship had landed. She'd already seen everything that had been flagged for her attention, but maybe there was something she'd missed in all the noise, something that hadn't been flagged because the system didn't know enough to look for it...

Her reverie was interrupted by a rattle of the hatch that led down to the stormwater system. Scavenger was back ahead of schedule. What had it found? A red indicator light was flashing, not something in its filters, but urgent data. Nesya read the notification, then called Intira.

"I've got an unexpected problem here," said Nesya. "Scavenger reports that a water level meter in the stormwater system isn't working properly. It wasn't flagged in the routine checks because the water levels it was reporting were always within the expected range—but from the visuals, it looks like manual sabotage."

"Manual—you mean someone was actually down there, in the storm drains?"

"It wasn't done by an overgrowth of roots, that's for sure." Nesya rubbed her thumb along the pebbled ceramic surface of her tea mug. "I'm going to have to go down myself and check it out. And I'll need backup. Will you come with me?"

Intira pressed her lips together and sighed through her nose. Going on a sewer crawl probably wasn't her idea of a fun date either. But you didn't go into the storm drains alone, that was regulations. And this was serious. "Yeah, okay," she said. "Give me half an hour, I'll be over there."

Twenty minutes passed before Intira showed up. Not that Nesya was watching the clock. She used the time to run a diagnostic on Scavenger; there was no reason to think that anything was wrong with it, but the idea of unauthorized people in the water systems made Nesya nervous.

She was tightening a loose screw on an access panel when she heard the hiss of the door opening. "I'm here to save the planet," said Intira. "Have you got tea?"

Nesya didn't look up. "Puerh. Martian. Help yourself." She finished up her check to the sound of a steaming kettle and the rustle of a paper tea packet. "You're good to go," she murmured to Scavenger.

Intira crouched by her shoulder, hands wrapped around a mug. "Do you think talking to your robots makes them work better?" she asked, with a tone that might have been teasing or actually curious. "Yours do need maintenance less often than anyone else's. Or maybe it's your willingness to lead from the front that gives them a boost to morale."

Nesya shrugged. Calling the other Infrastructure workers fumble-fingered idiots wouldn't endear her to anyone, and it wasn't true, really. "Shall we?" she said.

They suited up in companionable silence: coveralls, jackets, face masks, boots, gloves. Nesya keyed open the storm sewer access, and said, "Lead on, Scavenger." It zipped down the rail. Nesya and Intira followed more slowly on the ladder.

By the time they reached bottom, Scavenger was already splashing through the water, lighting up the tunnel with a yellow glow, more cheery than eerie. Nesya and Intira waded out behind—the storm sewers were at a low ebb now, but there was enough water to slosh around their ankles.

"Here's the damaged sensor," Nesya said, kneeling to inspect it. "Someone took a real brute force approach to this. They didn't need to do any programming or use anything more high-tech than wire-cutters, and it just shows that the water level's right here, see? It even includes a bit of variance to keep the data from looking too suspicious. I could bring it offline entirely, but fixing it's going to be a bit trickier—what is it, Scavenger?"

Nesya could have sworn there was an irritated rhythm in Scavenger's blinking filter light, as if it'd been trying unsuccessfully to get her attention for a while. She popped open the filter tank, stuck her hand in, and pulled it back again, her heartbeat a flutter of panic. There was something alive in there, something muscular and thrashing; now that she was paying attention, she could hear a wet slap-slap-slap against the side of the tank. She steadied herself, and reached in again. It couldn't be bigger than a Scavenger unit, after all.

"What did we catch?" said Intira.

Nesya held up her prize for inspection, keeping a firm grasp just below the tail. The fish didn't look as healthy as the snail had before she'd put it into tap water—its eye was cloudy and there was a yellowish film along its gills—but it was alive. Intira backed up a step.

"Looks like there might be something in your kid's fish-rustlers theory after all. Could you put that thing back, maybe?"

Intira preferred her fish wrapped in lime leaves and grilled. So did Nesya. At Thumying she'd have put it on a plank and hit it on the head with a hammer, but she couldn't bring herself to stuff it back in Scavenger's tank and listen to that desperate slapping. She dropped it into the water instead.

"I'm making merit," she said, repeating what Heleni said every time she released a batch of fingerlings into the ponds. "And maybe it'll lead us back where it came from. Scavenger, follow that fish."

Scavenger gave a thrash of its fins and a bob of its forward lamps and sped off. Nesya and Intira had to splash along quickly to keep up, following its glow—which suddenly disappeared.

"Where's it gone?" said Intira, her voice echoing in the dark tunnel.

Nesya felt along the wall with her hands. "There should be a side tunnel, here, according to the map. There's something blocking it—some kind of mesh, or—" She turned on her handlight. The entrance to the side tunnel was covered with plastic netting, and the netting itself overgrown with a dense mesh of plants with tiny thread-like leaves trailing in the water. There was a possible source of gallic acid, anyway. Probing at the edges of the mesh, Nesya found a loosely-fixed corner where Scavenger might have slipped through, and the fish, too. Water poured over her gloved hands as she moved the netting; the water level was higher on the other side. "This seems to be where the fish are coming from. And it's not blocked so thoroughly we can't get through."

Intira opened her hand in an after-you gesture, and Nesya ducked into the tunnel. She had to stoop as she went along. The floor sloped downwards until water came halfway up her chest. She startled and bumped her head painfully on the tunnel roof when she felt the first fish brush her side. Soon they were coming two or three times a minute.

A bright burst of light. A scream, quickly swallowed back—Nesya wasn't sure if that was Intira or herself. A splash and churn in the water. Then it was dark.

"Scavenger?" Nesya whispered, but no cheerful bob of lamps answered her. The water around her legs was still. She shook her handlight, which stayed stubbornly unlit.

"What was that?" said Intira. The sound of her splashing through the water was comforting, and the flailing hand that found Nesya's arm even more so.

Nesya didn't have an answer for her, though. Hand in hand, they groped along the tunnel, stepping cautiously in case of drops. There came, so faintly that Nesya could barely pick it out from the gentle splash of water and her own breathing, a series of short, sharp squeaks. The second time she heard it, Intira's hand tightened convulsively on hers. "I hate rats," said Intira.

The snail and the fish had been surprises, but rats got wherever humans did. And still— "I'm not sure that was a rat," said Nesya.

"Well, it's not fish. And I've never heard a person make a sound like that." Intira squeezed Nesya's hand again and stumbled backwards, wobbling both of them. "There's—there's something in the water—"

Nesya let go of the wall on a breath and a prayer and trailed her hand where Intira had stood. She bumped something rigid that didn't react when she touched it except to bob in the water. Emboldened, she grasped it by the—it had fins, or at least one. A familiar hydrodynamic shape. "It's Scavenger!"

Intira gave a nervous laugh. "Oh. But it—it wasn't making those noises, was it—" Another shrill, muffled by the water.

"Wouldn't think so," said Nesya. "But if I can have both hands maybe I can bring it back online."

Intira's hand opened, slow and reluctant, in reply. Nesya got to work, feeling her way along Scavenger's case. A fresh cut, as if from glass, superficial only. The more serious damage had come from some sort of electrical pulse, with the bright flash of light—a hard restart should get Scavenger working again, though maybe a bit stupider than before. Nesya didn't routinely remove Scavenger's power source, and never had underwater, but she didn't hesitate. She knew this robot from the inside out.

"Nesya," Intira whispered tightly. "Nesya, the rats—"

Something was moving in the water, in the currents washing past their bodies. Intira hissed in pain and muttered a litany under her breath, "I hate rats I hate rats I hate rats..."

Nesya ignored it and kept her hands steady, concentrating on finding the connections in Scavenger's insides, jiggling and fitting into place. She felt power begin to flow between her hands, and Scavenger's lights came to life, nearly blinding after the complete darkness. There were dark shapes in the tunnel, the largest almost as long as Nesya was tall, but the light seemed to bother them more than it did her. They slid silently under the water before Nesya could finish saying, "Scavenger, record," and by the time her vision cleared, they were gone.

"After them?" she said to Intira.

Intira was patting down her containment suit, still shaky. "Not without backup. We're unarmed, outnumbered, and those things won't be worried about the wrath of the Committee."

"Those are some big rats," said Nesya.

"I don't know what they were," said Intira. "But Survey cleared Enmotsa for settlement sixty years ago—no native lifeforms more advanced than lichen. They shouldn't be here."

"And yet here they are. And if we're not going after them, we should probably get Scavenger back to the lab." Nesya put a hand on the robot, as if to shield it from any suggestion that Intira might make about sending it out after the aliens. In a way it would have made sense, but the aliens hadn't shown much respect for the communal property of Landfall Holding, and Nesya didn't like the idea of abandoning her robots in the face of the enemy. "It's got the only recording we've managed to make."

At the lab, Nesya examined Scavenger's new scratch. Although it ran all along the side of the robot, stark and ugly, Nesya had been right that it hadn't cracked the case or done anything other than cosmetic damage. And if Scavenger had suffered any ill effects from the reboot they might show up in its day-to-day functioning later, but they didn't show up on the check. Best of all, before the mysterious creatures had disappeared, Scavenger had recorded nearly three seconds' worth of visual, sonar, and hydrochemical data.

"Do you want to place the call to the Committee, or shall I?" said Nesya, marveling at the images showing up on her screen. At first she thought it was two individuals, one significantly bigger than the other, but there was a third one hanging back, barely within the circle of Scavenger's lights. Rats was not so far off, despite the size of the things. Sleek dark brown fur, small ears high up and held close to the head, claw-tipped fingers and prominent teeth. But the bodies were longer, the heads larger in proportion and flatter, and the hands and feet likewise broad and flat. Specialized for swimming, presumably. Nesya assumed the computer would be able to ID them as easily as it had the snail. But it drew a blank, more likely because Enmotsa's information net was small and out-of-date than because they'd made some startling new discovery. Still—

"Pest control is Infrastructure's department." Intira frowned at the scratch in her jacket, as well she might—it had nearly torn through, and left Intira with a week's worth of medical quarantine, best case.

"Pests?" said Nesya. "They did damage the sensors and block off those tunnels, so in a way, yeah, but—we're going to have to fix everything before the storm hits in three days, and we still don't know the extent of it. Wouldn't it be quicker to ask them what they've done?"

Intira boggled at her. "They didn't seem interested in talking just now. Why do you even think they can? They've been wrecking our pipes, and I guarantee you no one got a permit to bring them here. They're pests."

"It's not just random damage. The water's been cleaner. They've got a working environmental suite. Anyone who can engineer that—murder isn't Infrastructure's department."

"How, murder? A nest of oversized rats?" said Intira. "Look, even if we did it your way—even if we could get the pipes fixed in time without clearing out the whatever-they-are, and I'm not saying we could—you think Survey's going to fund and wait for the results of a long-term environmental impact study before they start slapping down fines and growth restrictions everywhere? Just because you don't want more kids doesn't mean the rest of us don't. But I'll tell you what no one wants—troublemakers in their Group. You're not married to Thumying anymore. Where will you go?"

Nesya backed up, gripped the edge of her desk blindly, feeling more trapped than she had in the dark sewage tunnel. "It's not... it's not about me."

"Name of God, a hero. I'm not trying to threaten you, Nesya. I'm speaking as your friend here, not just your boss. You go over my head to the Committee, you put this on the record all proper and official, you bring Survey down on Enmotsa, and for what? You're going to call in Survey to prevent murder? Have you forgotten Hara Huna?"

Nesya shook her head. No one had forgotten Hara Huna. How could they, with trade and communications disrupted for years, and hundreds of thousands of refugees suddenly arriving at the doorstep of every inhabited planet? And there had been deaths—terrorists, holdouts, people in the wrong place in the end. Not just people either, when they'd finally burned out the last of the hilltops and the swamps. But the native wildlife would come back eventually. Murder—on the individual scale—was neither here nor there to Survey.

"Think about it," said Intira. "Or don't think about it, if it helps you sleep better." She slung her pack over her shoulder and headed for the door. "I'm sorry about this. For what it's worth."

Nesya collapsed into her chair, shaking. She hadn't felt like this since—damn it, she lived by herself by choice; she didn't know whether she'd have been able to find someone else on Enmotsa after Vit, but she'd never tried. She hated arguments, hated being angry at people, hated feeling herself in the wrong. And maybe she was wrong. Intira was right, anyway, that Nesya had no plan to establish communications with the aliens, and no reason to believe she could do it. And the threat to Enmotsa's health and safety was real and present.

Clean up your own shit was the first rule of Infrastructure, and don't make Survey come over here was the first rule of... well, everywhere. So why was Nesya getting so worked up about the fate of creatures who had done nothing but damage her robots, release unauthorized biologicals into her sewage tunnels, bugger up all her systems?

Aquarius came back to the lab, and a little later, Hercules One. Nesya and Intira had found the source of the problem, but Nesya watched the recordings the robots had made anyway, meter after meter of unremarkable pipes. Maybe there were some answers there, and it was something to do, something at least theoretically useful.

The computer gave the chime of an incoming call. It was Vit. Nesya was tempted to ignore it and let him stew over whatever it was, same as she was doing, but—"Accept," she said with a sigh.

Vit appeared on the screen with his easy smile, and Nesya was uncomfortably aware of what a mess she must look, still in the pants of her hazard suit. "Afternoon, Nesya. I wanted to remind you about Rinat's soccer match, which is tomorrow. Since you asked me to. How's the inquiry going?"

Vit should have been an old-fashioned angler, not a fish-farmer, the way he was always fishing for information. An idea occurred to Nesya. She didn't like it much, but it was the only one she had. "System, take this conversation off the record, please."

Vit's eyes lit up. "What's this?"

"Intira and I found out who's been digging illegal fishponds, more or less," said Nesya. She forwarded him Scavenger's recording in a burst of encryption.

"Oh," said Vit. "Ah." His eyes weren't focused on Nesya's anymore; he was watching the recording on his side. "Where are they from? Not native, surely."

"Survey might have missed a species—even one that big—but not the whole ecosystem necessary to support them. They're living off our ecosystem. The snail is an Earth species, and so are the fish. Themselves, who knows? The information net sure doesn't. And the chemical data doesn't support the hypothesis of super-evolved rats, if that's what you're wondering."

Vit pinched his nose and gave an annoyed huff. "I know you think my taste in serials is immature, but I'm not completely stupid. If you're not going to give me any credit, why did you show me this in the first place?"

Why indeed. Nesya spread her hands helplessly. "Intira's talking pest control. It'd read very neatly in the logs: found in sector 6C, unauthorized biologicals. Minor damage to physical plant. Sector sterilized and damage repaired. End of story, no need to bother the Committee with it or mention anything to Survey."

"Minor damage...?" said Vit.

"Not as minor as all that, unfortunately. They're living in a section of the storm sewers they've blocked off, they disabled some sensors to cover their tracks, and we've been seeing traces of their activity in the drinking water as well, so—we don't know the extent of it. And there's a storm called for on Monday."

Vit winced. "I'll admit, I can see why Intira's for swift action." His eyes still tracked something Nesya couldn't see; he was watching the clip over and again, fascinated as Nesya was. "But if they're not from here—do you think they came on their own?"

"What, they set down their flying saucer in the middle of Landing Field and no one noticed?" said Nesya. "They came on the Mars ship. Must've. It fits with how long the water profile's been different, and—" The loose grate to the storm sewers by the Landing Field warehouse. The containers that had transported the beehives and the *Flosconicis bibens*, large enough for even the biggest alien to fit in comfortably, with the components of their environmental suite as well. "And other things."

"Yes, thank you. You didn't pilot the ship that brought you here either. What I mean is, are they here because someone brought them, either on purpose or by accident? Or did they decide to come here themselves?"

"I—" Accidental contamination had been Nesya's first thought when her biggest problem had been snails. It didn't seem likely that the creatures she'd seen could've started their journey as eggs or spores small enough to pass undetected among the root systems of plants—but then, why not? Or one of the crew members on the Mars ship smuggling them aboard, then dumping them in Enmotsa's sewers, together with the organisms they'd need to set up their environmental suite—only, why? But just because Nesya couldn't see any reason to do it, that didn't mean it wasn't possible. There were too many possibilities, and not enough data. It made Nesya's head swim. "Who knows? How can we know? What does it matter?"

"Okay, okay," said Vit. That calm-down tone of his used to drive her up the wall. It still might, if she weren't on top of the wall already, looking down dizzily. "It's just that—if they arranged their own transport, one way or another, that makes them a spacefaring species. Technically. It's been a long time since I did the negotiator's course but I remember that much. So, there are protocols."

Nesya took a deep breath, and her chest didn't feel like it was too tight to hold it. Protocols. Protocols were good.

"First step: call in the experts. Of course, back when I was studying we hadn't met any other spacefaring species besides the Lughan—there's really nothing like these guys on the net? No clue where they came from?"

"Nothing." Nesya refrained from adding, *I looked, I really did...* If she went against Intira on this, she was looking down the barrel of months if not years of justifying herself to everyone and their grandmother, but she didn't have to start now.

Vit grimaced. "Could be that information about them is available on a need-to-know basis, and nobody figured we'd need to. Survey can be a bit—or else, just, we haven't gotten the news yet. Either way, I doubt our little dead-end colony is the first to encounter these guys. There are bound to be experts out there somewhere, even if it'll take a few years for them to get here."

"Years," said Nesya. Protocols were no longer looking so great. "And until then?"

"Protocol says—" Vit shrugged unhappily. "Don't make contact. Disengage."

"That's *insane*. We're in contact—they're in our water. Disengaging would mean..." Nesya worked it through in growing horror. "It'd mean evacuating Landfall. More than half the colony lives here. Where would we go? There's a storm coming in three days!"

"Yeah, Intira's solution is looking tempting, no question. I'm just not sure that it'd help, long-term, when Survey catches up with us. And anyway—" Vit, more tactful than Nesya, didn't say the word murder out loud. They had already said more than was wise, probably, even in an off-the-record chat. "But you have to make it through the short term to get to the long term, don't you? There are precedents, in emergencies, when ships' crews have had to act independently to get personnel out of dangerous situations—Survey has been known to make allowances, after the fact. And then, sometimes they don't. So don't make any moves before you've had time to think them over, all right? And don't forget about Rinat's soccer match, it's tomorrow."

"Soccer match. Right." Meaning, Vit had something to say that he didn't want to commit to a vid chat. Trusting Vit made Nesya's head hurt, but she could afford to wait another day, anyway. It would take at least that long for Intira to assemble the people and equipment she'd need for a frontal assault on the aliens, if she wanted to do it quietly.

"See you then," Vit said, and cut the connection.

Nesya went back to the videos of pipes. Hercules Two wasn't back yet. Had it run into trouble? The storm system emptied into the blackwater system during dry periods, and if the aliens had gotten into the blackwater system, too—but the pipes there were mostly too small for Nesya to go crawling around in. Not that she could go by herself without authorization.

There was no taking *that* off the record. She did another maintenance check on Scavenger, just for the reassuring feeling of plastic under her hands, but she didn't find anything wrong, and it didn't help much.

If the computer couldn't find any matches using the recording, maybe she could approach the problem from a different angle. Assume the aliens had come on the Mars ship. Native Martians was as unlikely as mutated rats. The large, life-friendly containers from Hallelujah that she'd found in the warehouse were suggestive, but although that planet had a wide variety of species roughly analogous to plants and insects, there was nothing that looked mammalian in its native life. Nesya couldn't make the aliens fit with what she knew about Hallelujah's ecology, or imagine them to have gone unnoticed by the humans who'd filled that planet almost as full as Earth.

She pulled up the ship's itinerary again. Newsom and Stewart's World were as barren of native live as Enmotsa, though the terraforming on both planets was considerably further along. The few furry creatures that had evolved on Durak were tiny, and a vivid red to match the landscape there—not to mention, they'd hardly be able to breathe the air on Enmotsa. She couldn't rule it out, but it was a pretty flimsy lead, if it was a lead.

So much for the aliens. What about their environmental suite? If they hadn't brought the snail with them by accident, if they weren't using them to keep down algae, if the one Hercules Two had found hadn't died because of some unusual contaminant in Enmotsa's tap water—then what? Belatedly, Nesya remembered the data from the biologicals she'd run through the sequencer that morning: the residue, the algae tab, the snail. It was the snail that proved most interesting, from the contents of its viscera to the concentration of metals in the shell—an unusually high concentration, compared to what was typical for the species, but the proportions were the ones Nesya was familiar with from her blackwater. And there were other differences between this snail and a baseline *Melanoides tuberculata*, whose significance Nesya didn't quite grasp—she wasn't a biologist—deviations in the length of jaw, the shape of the digestive tract. Even with a fast-breeding species like this, it would have taken more than dumb luck and basic animal husbandry to design a snail for encysting metals. Behind the columns of chemical formulae, Nesya imagined she could discern the shape of a mind. Of... well, a colleague.

Nesya wished she had taken back a fish after all. Would it have proved to be as identical to Thumying's schools of tilapia as it looked? Or were there already changes under the skin, distorting the genetic maker's-mark of human companies beyond recognition?

The computer beeped an insistent warning. Ten minutes past closing time, and Nesya hadn't noticed. With her head still full of the implications of what she'd found out—had the snail died from lack of metals in the water, then, a failsafe to keep it from spreading? Or was that extrapolating too far?—she packed her things onto her bike, stopping at the corner canteen for a packet salad and protein-paste toast before returning home. She itched to keep working, to run a few simulations of how the snail might impact its environment and check them against the water quality stats from last quarter. But it would be harder to cover her tracks if she used her work access at home.

Hercules Two still hadn't come back. Nesya didn't know what Intira was up to. Survey was a distant threat, but it seemed like no matter what they did it was even odds that Enmotsa would end up a second Hara Huna. At least Vit had a plan. She hoped. Be patient, be quiet, for one more day at least.

Nesya couldn't work, and fretting wouldn't help, so she queued up an entertainment vid. The latest Princess Galaxy Explorer might not have been approved by Education yet, but the last season had been, and Nesya hadn't seen it. It was full of hollow earths and laser-sword battles and the eponymous princess venturing bravely forth in the name of the Star Empire and discovering new worlds every week—exactly the silly sort of show that Vit and Rinat liked and Nesya had no interest in. With nothing else to do but chew her nails and wait, Nesya found it oddly comforting.

The next morning, she woke up with the slightly hung-over feeling that went with falling asleep in front of the computer terminal. She dragged out showering, getting dressed, and eating breakfast as long as she could, not wanting to arrive at the soccer game early, and ended up getting there late. The visitors' bike racks were all full. Many of the bikes were sporting green and yellow spray-paint jobs—Security colors. Nesya leaned her own bike against a wall and headed towards the soccer field. She kept an eye open for Vit or Rinat and slipped a hand into her pocket to finger her mala, trying to tune out the noise and jostle of the crowds. It took some time for the content of the noise to penetrate.

"Why hasn't the match started yet?"

"It's the Thumying team, one of their players is missing."

"Just a kid playing a prank..."

"Security Group has been searching the whole compound and they haven't found her."

"Have they tried dredging the ponds? She's been spending a lot of time down there, with her hatchery project."

Rinat. Panic flooded Nesya's stomach, and was immediately dashed with cold, murderous rage. This was Vit's plan. Her daughter. His daughter, damn it.

Vit was in the bleachers, surrounded by Security people, family, concerned friends. "What the hell is this, Vit?" said Nesya.

Heleni looked up from handing round cups of tea to the Security people to frown at Nesya. Because she didn't know about Vit's scheme, and thought Nesya was being insensitive? Or because she did, and blamed Nesya for it? No good way to ask, and Nesya didn't care much at the moment.

"I'm really sorry, Nesya," said Vit. "I think Rinat overheard our conversation yesterday. You know, about what you and Intira found in the sewers. Ordinarily I wouldn't dream of breaking a confidence like that, but Security had to know where she might have gone. It's—I should have been more careful, I know. But what kid is going to pass up the chance to meet aliens?"

Overheard, like hell. It was a plausible enough story, and hard to disprove; Nesya might have believed it herself if she hadn't known that Vit was planning something, if she didn't remember what else he'd said during that conversation: *When ships' crews have had to act independently to get personnel out of dangerous situations, Survey has been known to make allowances...*

Personnel. Shit. As if the entire colony wasn't in enough danger without manufacturing more. It was true that the aliens hadn't hurt Nesya or Intira or even Scavenger, much. That didn't mean they were safe.

One way or another, though, Intira wasn't going to be able to sweep this under the carpet now. And if Nesya or Vit had gone to contact the aliens unauthorized, they would have faced disciplinary action, not to mention sinking the case in the eyes of the Committee. So Vit had sent Rinat instead. Who could blame a kid for wanting to meet aliens? And who could blame a worried mother for going after her?

That part at least wasn't a lie. Nesya was one goddamn worried mother right now, and Vit hadn't left her very many choices. She turned to one of the Security women. "I'd like to try to find her," she said. "I know the sewers pretty well. Have you got a spare hazard suit here, or shall I go back to the office and get mine?"

The Security woman looked her up and down. "Mine would probably fit you. I'll talk to my boss."

A few minutes later, Nesya found herself suited up and standing by the Thumying storm sewer access hatch. It was against regulations to go into them alone, but nobody brought that up, and Nesya didn't either. Security people and Vit's family had all wished her luck, expressed their sympathy, told her she was brave. Vit stayed close by and everyone moved back to give them space for private conversation before she went down the ladder.

"What the hell made you think this was a good idea," Nesya hissed.

"I didn't make Rinat go," said Vit. "She wanted to."

"Of course she did! She's twelve!" With effort, Nesya managed to keep her voice down. It came out half-strangled. "This isn't a goddamn game!"

"No. It's the future of Enmotsa. It's Rinat's home, too—if she can defend it, I think she's entitled to." Vit shrugged. "And if we're going to send someone to communicate with alien intelligences I think you're a good candidate. You've done it before."

"Robots aren't intelligent," Nesya replied automatically.

"That's a pretty theological question, isn't it?" said Vit. "But actually, I was talking about ordinary people."

"If this is about my psych profile—"

Vit shook his head and spread out his hands. "Personal experience. We were married for six years." He leaned forward and planted a brief kiss on her faceplate. "Good luck. Bring Rinat back safe."

"It's a little late to worry about that, isn't it?" Nesya turned her back before he could unbalance her further and went down the ladder. She lowered herself into the water, heading for the section the aliens had blocked off. Vit might be a criminally irresponsible father, but she didn't believe he'd have let Rinat go without a good map.

She hadn't gone very far before her handlight showed a stripe of fluorescent paint on the tunnel wall. "Good girl," Nesya breathed, and then, calling down the tunnel, "Rinat?" No answer.

Nesya's reader chimed. She almost hadn't brought it; there was no reception in most of the sewer system. Handling it with gloves was clumsy. "Vit?"

Vit's picture on the little screen flickered in and out. Reception wasn't very good, even here. "Meteorology says—eight hours—"

For a second, Nesya tried to make sense out of his words. She really, really hoped the obvious interpretation was wrong. "They've revised the storm warning estimate?"

"You—" Vit's eyebrows drew down in frustration before he blinked out entirely. His face was replaced with text. *Storm in eight hours. Security recommends you come back.*

I can't do that, Nesya sent. Then she pocketed her reader and walked on. If there were any messages chasing her, they didn't reach her.

There was another fluorescent blaze by the mesh at the mouth of the blocked-off tunnel, and Nesya moved it aside and went in. Remembering how the aliens had reacted to her handlight last time, she put it on its dimmest setting before shining it around the tunnel. Dark, quiet, and still—the fish that they'd found last time were nowhere in evidence. "Rinat?" Nesya called again. This time the tunnel brought her back an answer. Not Rinat's voice, but the high chatter of one of the aliens.

Disoriented, unable to tell where the sound was coming from, Nesya played her light on the walls and the water's surface, trailing her other hand beneath the water. Something came up behind her, and she whirled around to see an alien head and shoulders above the waterline. She didn't think it was one of the individuals Scavenger had caught in its recording—it seemed smaller than those—but she couldn't be sure. It made a noise—lower, more repetitive than the complex chirps and clicks she'd come to associate with the aliens. A distress call? A challenge? Laughter?

Nesya knew how to say *not a threat* in human, anyway. She pocketed her handlight and stretched her hands out to the sides, open. "Hello," she said, without any hope of being understood, but she had to start somewhere. "Have you seen a human—like me, but smaller, about so high—" She gestured vaguely around the middle of her chest, where Rinat would reach if she were standing here. The creature's small ears flicked back and forth, but otherwise it didn't react. Cautiously, she reached towards it.

Something hit her in the back of the knees, and she stumbled, managing not to crash into the alien. By the time she recovered herself, there was another alien there. That one, she thought she recognized—the biggest one. It hissed at Nesya with bared teeth, an expression she had no trouble interpreting, and placed its hand protectively over the head of the smaller alien.

"Right, got it," said Nesya. "But where's *my* daughter?" She put a hand in front of her at Rinat's height again, but this time cupped her fingers as if Rinat's head were there.

The smaller alien flicked its ears towards its... mother, Nesya provisionally decided. It let loose with a burst of chatter, and the larger alien answered, keeping one ear trained warily on Nesya but inclining the other one toward the child. It might, Nesya thought, be like how you could tell what a person was paying attention to by where they were looking.

The discussion between the two was apparently resolved in some fashion, because the larger alien let the smaller one loose, and the smaller alien swam over to Nesya and tugged on her wrist as if to say, *let's go!*

Nesya started to follow, and felt her feet pulled out from underneath her as the alien dove beneath the surface. She could try and recover her hand from that grasp, but... though she couldn't feel the sharp pinpricks of claws through her borrowed hazard suit, she could imagine them clearly after watching the video of the aliens so many times. A tear would be bad. And the alien was, she hoped, taking her where she wanted to go. She heard the hiss of her air filters sealing as she allowed herself to be pulled under the water. It was deeper here than she'd realized, just a few steps from where she'd stood in water that went only a little higher than her waist. She hoped the seals on her filters would hold, and that the alien didn't have exaggerated ideas about how long she could go without breathing.

It wasn't long before they surfaced; Nesya didn't so much feel it as hear her filters clear and seals open. She took a long, ragged breath. Wherever they were now, there was light—little points of red, green, and blue, and faint glows like indicator dials, doubled and redoubled on the surface of the water and the water-slick walls. The reflections were disorienting. She couldn't get any idea of the size and shape of the chamber, but the echoes were louder when the little alien announced their presence with a quick burst of speech.

Two voices answered with the same sort of chatter, and a third—"What is it?" It was Rinat. "Mom?"

"I'm here," Nesya called, turning towards the sound of Rinat's voice, willing her eyes to adjust more quickly to what light there was. The little alien popped out of the water and swarmed up the wall—was there a ladder there?—onto a sort of shelf or niche. Rinat was there; Nesya saw her clearly for just a moment in the light of her reader as she handed it to the alien. Then the darkness swallowed her again.

"Storm's coming," Nesya said. "Eight hours, Meteorology says—closer to seven and a half, now."

"Storm?" said Rinat. "But—it'll be flooded here, the aliens' filtration system won't hold up—"

It was Rinat Nesya was worried about—and herself, and Landfall, if the storm sewers were compromised. But Rinat had always known how to distract her. "What do you know about the aliens' filtration systems?"

Rinat's hazard suit scraped wetly against the wall. It might have been a shrug. "I saw them when I came in—didn't you? *Myriophyllum spicatum*, like we use at home, or something like it. Well—that's probably not all, the Hercules unit says—"

"Hercules Two? It's here?"

"Oh. Um." Nesya didn't need to see Rinat's face to hear the oh-shit-I-shouldn't-have-mentioned-that in her voice. "See, the thing about the aliens is they're scavengers, right? They use what they find."

Even after several minutes, Nesya couldn't see much in the dark chamber. But she looked again at the light sources—points of red, green, and blue, faint glows like indicator dials—and she knew those lights. But not in that configuration, strung out along several niches, disassembled, gutted—

Nesya's vision went red for a moment. She remembered Intira's litany—*I hate rats*—and felt, as she hadn't at the time, the chest-tightening outrage of it. "My *robot*."

Rinat scooted back on the shelf she was sitting on, pulled in her shoulders and knees, made herself small. The alien leaned out over the edge and hissed, teeth bared, ears flat, just like its mother had when Nesya had inadvertently gotten between the two of them. Nesya took a deep breath and tried to moderate her tone. "My robot?"

"Here, take a look," said Rinat. Nesya came closer, found the handholds that the alien had used to climb up. She couldn't use them as easily as it had; she was big and clumsy and fell back into the water with an embarrassing splash several times before she managed to make it up. When she did, there was hardly room for the three of them in addition to the parts of Hercules Two that were set up there. Indicators and sensors, white threads of wire leading to the other parts of the installation in other areas of the tunnel. Disassembled, but not dead—Hercules Two was still doing its work, after a fashion. Magnesium levels, calcium levels, and a wire that proved to lead to the lights illuminating a large tank full of algae and snails.

Nesya recognized the tank as one of the containers from the Mars ship that had originally housed bee colonies and *Flosconisis bibens*. So she'd guessed something right, anyway. From yesterday's reading, she gathered that it was controlling the rate and method of snail reproduction based on the levels of metals in the water. Clever—but completely inadequate for dealing with one of Enmotsa's storms.

Her first priority had to be to grab Rinat and get to shelter. As for the aliens, who were never supposed to be here in the first place, let the storm wash them out. Nobody's hands would have to get dirty, and Survey—well, contact with the aliens had been made, contrary to protocols. But even if Enmotsa's colonists couldn't make the record of that disappear, the fact that that contact made no difference in the outcome of events, and was unlikely to have any effect on the future relations between the two species—surely that would count in their favor?

But that wasn't going to happen. "Can you talk to them?" she asked Rinat. "Warn them what's coming?"

Rinat shook her head. "Dad's got a language-parsing program, and I loaded it onto my reader before I left, and it's made some guesses, but it's probably mostly noise. The guesses, not the aliens' language. Open-source piece of junk. I don't know how to explain a *storm*."

The last word came out on a wail. Nesya wished she knew how to reassure her without saying it would be okay. She'd always tried not to lie to Rinat.

And Vit thought she was a good choice for communicating with aliens, huh.

Whether or not she was, she was the one who was here. She had to try. The biggest alien had already come closer, drawn by her conversation with Rinat. Nesya slid down from the niche and tugged the alien's wrist, like the little one had done to get her attention.

"Listen," said Nesya. "You have to know, there's—" She shook her head in frustration. Just noise. With her free hand, she scooped up a handful of water, and sprinkled it over the alien's head.

The alien's ears flicked down; it pulled its hand back and let loose a series of squeaks that Nesya was very tempted to translate as *what the hell!?* She pointed up, to the sky, across, to where the water let in from the stormwater pipes to the aliens' habitat. Tugging the alien's wrist again, she pulled it towards another of the Hercules installations and adjusted some of the readouts—sulfur levels, magnesium levels, way up.

The alien hissed, its ears flat against its head, claws out as it knocked Nesya's hand away from the dials. Fair enough, Nesya hated people messing with her systems, too. She had its attention, anyway, but she couldn't think of a better way to say what she had to say than to repeat what she had done—sprinkle water, point, adjust the dials again. This time the alien didn't try to stop her. It launched into a barrage of chatter instead, which Nesya didn't know how to answer.

The answer came from the littlest alien, up in the niche with Rinat. First more chirping speech, then the speakers of Rinat's reader, as loud as they would go, with the sounds of an energy-gun-vs-laser-sword battle from *Princess Galaxy Explorer.*

"No!" said Rinat, and followed it up with a rising whistle and a sharp click. "That's not it at all, it's more like—" She reclaimed the reader and bent over it in frantic concentration. A few seconds later it started playing the sounds of rainfall. It must have been a recording made on Earth, or somewhere other than Enmotsa, anyway. The drops hit the ground with a gentle, uneven patter, thunder rumbled softly in the distance, and somewhere, a creek gurgled.

The biggest alien scooped up a handful of water and let it fall. It adjusted the readouts to what they had been, showing the current chemical profile of the water, and then back up again. It pointed to where the water let in.

"Right," said Nesya, although she still wasn't sure the alien had understood. Then again, maybe it had, because the next thing it did was give a series of calls—"The language program thinks those might be names," Rinat muttered—and then more aliens came scurrying and splashing from wherever they'd been holed up.

Scavenger had captured three in its recording, but there were more of them than that. Six in all, when they were all assembled and Nesya had sorted them out from each other enough to count. It was hard, when they didn't have many distinguishing features that Nesya could see. The one who'd led Nesya here, who'd acted protective of Rinat and kept borrowing her reader, was smaller enough than any of the others that she could easily tell which one it was. Its mother, as Nesya had decided, was still the biggest, but a couple of the others were nearly as big.

One of them, fussing over the tanks of snails and algae, might have been the one who'd stayed back in the shadows during her and Intira's first encounter with the aliens? Nesya was more confident in her ID of the alien who came in dragging a large metal sheet. That one had a slightly longer snout than the others, which Nesya had learned to recognize in her obsessive rewatching of Scavenger's recording. The other two Nesya hadn't seen before. They were midway in size between the biggest alien and the smallest, and Nesya couldn't tell them apart no matter how hard she tried, as they scurried around with plastic tubing and other useful things for sealing their habitat and keeping the water in it clean and moving. Scavengers, like Rinat had said, but where on Enmotsa they'd managed to find all this stuff, without anyone noticing it had gone missing—

Anyway, they'd clearly made plans for a storm, or some sort of emergency, but they'd just as clearly never lived here for a real one. Those seals weren't going to hold up to the water pressure a serious storm could bring to bear, especially not after they'd significantly reduced the sewers' carrying capacity. It might seem roomy down here when the weather was calm, but digging and laying pipe in Enmotsa's soil was hard, and Nesya's predecessors in Infrastructure had only made them big because sometimes they needed to be.

When Nesya tried to point this out to the biggest alien, it shoved her impatiently out of the way and kept working. At least it seemed to understand that things were urgent, but—Nesya approached the one working on the snail tanks, who gave a startled squeak and retreated into darker shadow and deeper water. At a loss, she stood for a few seconds wringing her hands until the long-snouted alien came up to her with an armful of tubing. With an inquisitive click, the alien tapped a claw against a tube, where the pressure rating was written.

"Yes!" Nesya could have kissed it. It called over the biggest alien—Nesya tried to catch what might have been a name, but couldn't resolve the sounds into anything coherent, let alone reproducible, in her head. The biggest alien called over the smallest, who grabbed the reader from Rinat again, so Rinat came too, in hot pursuit.

After some consultation between the aliens, the littlest one brought up a game that modeled a life-support failure crisis on a spaceship. Which—not necessarily a life-support failure, but on a spaceship, anyway—had probably been where the aliens learned how humans represented pressure. Nesya was more impressed by the way that the little alien had figured out Rinat's reader in not much more than an hour.

"He likes to watch *Princess Galaxy Explorer*," said Rinat with a shrug. Then she corrected herself. "Well, not watch. Listen. His eyes aren't even on the screen while it's playing. I don't know what he's getting out of it, really."

"He?" said Nesya.

"He doesn't have the pouch... thing that the others have. It's a guess."

Rinat was making a lot of guesses. So was Nesya. It made her antsy, to have to proceed as if they were the truth. But there wasn't time now for second-guessing.

One of the aliens—the mother—pulled on Nesya's wrist for attention, and Nesya saw that she and long-snout had dispensed with the game and were working on a mathematical simulation. A little more puzzling over it revealed that they needed Nesya's input to know just how much rain to expect, and how fast, and how big the entire sewer system was. Nesya synced up her reader with Rinat's and began pulling the relevant data off it.

Eventually the biggest alien raised her voice and called a halt to the work that the others were doing. It had become clear to her that the scale of the problem was too big, and they were going to have to move out.

But where? Of everywhere on Enmotsa, Thumying's fish ponds were probably closest to their natural habitat, but even if Nesya had permission to set them up there, there was their whole environmental suite too, and no telling how it would interact with Thumying's. Although it had done fine in the sewer system. The water had been cleaner—

"We could move them to the wastewater treatment plant," said Nesya, thinking out loud. "Plenty of room, clean water—in part of it—easy to get to from here, and I've got the accesses."

"Clean water? But that's what we drink," said Rinat.

"It all is, eventually," said Nesya. "Back on Earth we used to swim in the Kinneret—anyway. Load up the map on your reader, okay? We've got a bit of a walk ahead of us."

Nesya led the biggest alien by the hand, and the rest of them followed after. Rinat brought up the rear, reader in one hand and her fluorescent paint marker in the other, marking their way back. By the time they made it to the treatment facility, the storm was an estimated four hours away—reception was back on their readers, and Nesya connected briefly to check on the weather, and to send a message to Vit that they were safe, which he would hopefully pass on to all relevant parties. The aliens were awkward out of the water, and they refused to come out of the tunnels at all until Nesya dimmed the lights. But soon they swarmed up the sides of the settling tanks, sniffing and splashing in the water. Eventually there was one tank that the big alien spent a long time checking out, before finally giving a long, even whistle that Rinat's language program interpreted as, "Yes."

Then it was back into the tunnels, to start moving and setting up the environmental suite. Once they were out of the realm of chemistry and water-flow, their basis of communication was a lot shakier—they still had the readers, but visual schematics baffled the aliens, and there was only so much they could do with *Princess Galaxy Explorer*. They ended up doing a lot by trial and error. Nesya would start to pick up a container, and an alien would shriek in alarm and hand her a different one, then on the other side they'd do it the other way around. She had to act fast to save her keyboard from being drenched in water and her kettle from being used as a fish nursery. She wasn't by any means becoming fluent in the aliens' language, but she found herself using the whistle-and-click that meant "no" without thinking. When the shy alien who seemed to be in charge of the biologicals heard it, her nostrils flared wide and her ears flattened—then her whiskers quivered in something like a sheepish grin. Nesya found herself oddly touched, in a way she hadn't when she managed to communicate something to one of the bolder aliens. And the alien moved her fingerlings somewhere else, which was the important thing.

On one of the trips, while several of the aliens were struggling to move the algae-and-snail tank—even emptied out, it wasn't easy—Rinat called Nesya over.

"Come look at this," she said softly. There was no need to whisper; even if she had something to say that she wanted to keep a secret from the aliens, it wasn't as if they could understand. Nesya climbed up to where Rinat was, a shelf which seemed to have been used as a sleeping niche, lined with bubble insulation. Rinat turned over one of the insulation sheets, backed with strong, flexible plastic, and Nesya saw why she'd been whispering. A single English word was embossed there, the same one that had Intira in a panic and everyone, according to Vit, looking for ghosts under their beds.

Survey.

Rinat played her handlight further down the sheet, where a serial number was stenciled. "Three letters, four numbers; that's a strike group designation, isn't it?" said Rinat, who clearly had been paying more attention to the news—or recent history—than Nesya had realized. "How did they get this?"

"Scavengers use what they find, isn't that what you said?"

"Thanks, Mom." Rinat gave an invisible-but-clearly-audible eye-roll. "Where did they find it, then?"

Nesya shrugged. "Keep moving. The storm won't wait," she said. She took the insulation sheet along with her assorted load of stuff, though, and when she caught up with the biggest alien she tapped her on the wrist and tried to make the interrogative click that she'd heard the aliens using.

The alien paused, flicked her ears towards Nesya for a moment, and then continued down the tunnel. Incomprehension, real or feigned.

It was the last trip they were going to make to the treatment plant, and everyone was carrying a full load, even the littlest alien; household furnishings and odds and ends whose function Nesya couldn't guess. She made one last sweep, making sure that the mesh blocking the tunnels was cleared out and there was nothing to obstruct the flow of water, that anywhere the walls might have been weakened, they were patched up again. By the time she got to the plant, Rinat was already there, painting a luminescent stripe over the doorway.

"Why... we don't have to find our way back here again," said Nesya. "Especially not from this side."

"No, I just thought..." Rinat shrugged. "It's a new house for the aliens, and I don't know the words and there's no fire or wood for a lustral bowl, but at least we've got plenty of water."

Rinat wanted to make a house-blessing. Well, it might not help but it couldn't hurt, as the streetwalker said to the rabbi. Nesya still had most of the packet of algae tabs Rinat had given her in her sweater pocket, beneath her hazard suit; she found it and tossed it to Rinat, adding, "You can use your hand-light for fire, can't you? I'd rather not have open flames here."

"I guess," said Rinat. She scooped water into a shallow metal container, dropped the algae tab in, then turned her hand-light briefly to high and flashed it across the surface.

One of the mid-sized aliens, of the two that Nesya still couldn't tell apart, was directing the others in setting up their monitoring array based on the disassembled Hercules Two. She looked up, hissed in annoyance that the sudden brightness, and the others paused in their work too. Caught in the moment, with wires and hookups strung hand-to-hand, Nesya was reminded of the white thread the Thumyings used in their family ceremonies. Maybe that had given Rinat the idea.

"Um," said Rinat. "It goes something like... let us now make the dedication to gods or spirits or something at the beginning. May they bless the circle of this place of living. All... the people who live in houses? Foreigners, villagers, or someone else, all creatures whether born from womb, from egg, from... nothing, I guess? They all have the truth which leads to the good way. May all beings make an end of suffering. May all beings be faithful in the teaching of the Buddha. May it rain in time after properly bestowing showers, may the earth, for the good of all beings bring about success... and I guess that's all I remember."

Nesya, in the meantime, synced her reader, checked the weather—the storm had crested over Mati and was due to hit Landfall in an hour and a half—and her messages—Vit had left one and Intira three, wanting to know exactly what was going on. Nesya decided to deal with them later. It wasn't like they could do anything about the situation either way at the moment. The storm seals would be down and locked, and nobody was going anywhere for a while.

What was urgent was making sure the water systems were ready for the storm. There hadn't been more than a few minor repairs necessary in the aliens' habitat that Nesya had seen, but Nesya had been right when she'd said that they couldn't be sure of the extent of the damage, and Intira had been right when she'd said that asking the aliens wouldn't be easy. So Nesya downloaded the visual scans the robots had made the day before, right before everything had suddenly gotten more complicated. There was something Nesya was missing, something she should have remembered—

"Shit," she breathed. "The goddamned *sensor*."

Once the storm hit Landfall, the storm drains would start filling with water, and when the water got to a certain level, the connections between the storm system and the blackwater system which were open during the dry season would close. Or they would have, if the aliens hadn't buggered up the sensors that measured the water levels to disguise how much water they'd been drawing off into their own habitat.

Intira had a manual override in her office, but the records didn't show that she'd used it, and—Nesya checked—her last call had been made from home.

That was the problem with this cloak-and-dagger business—you couldn't go through the normal procedures because that would leave traces, but the normal procedures were there for a goddamn reason.

She called the biggest alien over and tried to explain the problem. Scavenger's video didn't seem to mean anything to the alien, but at least they'd already settled on audio shorthands for *storm* and *flood*. At the big alien's call, the one directing work on the Hercules installation finished up one last thing and padded over—she clearly knew something about wiring, so Nesya pulled up a diagram of the sensor model. After a brief consultation, she led Nesya and the big alien over to the settling tank. The long-snouted alien, kicking lazily in the water with her elbows propped on a shelf on the edge, and Rinat, perched on top of a ladder running up the outside of the tank, had their heads bent together over Rinat's reader. They were working on a map of the water systems represented with audio instead of images. It sounded something like running water, but simplified and made discrete, somehow, higher pitches representing narrower pipes, and lower pitches wider ones.

"It's possible to seal off the blackwater system manually from inside the pipes themselves," said Nesya. She indicated the area on the map, and brought up a schematic of a Hercules unit. "If we could put Hercules Two back together—but it's a question of how quickly we could get it working—"

Rinat was trying to interpret, modeling a little Hercules Two running through the pipes, when the littlest alien swam up from the depths of the tank and broke the surface of the water where they were working. He reached for the reader, and with a few swipes of his finger changed the sounds of the map into music.

"Quit fooling around!" Rinat said, pulling the reader out of the alien's reach. Then her eyes went wide. "I guess... you're not much wider than a Hercules unit, are you?"

Then Nesya recognized the music, too. It was the theme that played whenever Princess Galaxy Explorer was about to do something especially heroic.

The alien's ears flicked up and whiskers quivered in a cheekier version of the shy one's grin.

Nesya's reader took this moment to inform her that she had a call incoming. "Later," she told it impatiently. She looked the little alien up and down, and more importantly side-to-side. "I suppose you would fit, at that."

The next few minutes were a whirl of frantic preparations. There wasn't any time to waste, but they couldn't afford any mistakes, either; Nesya had the little alien run through the map and demonstrate shutting off the overflow pipe three times before she dared to believe she'd successfully communicated what had to be done. Then the alien needed a hazard suit, and even Rinat's was a tent. Eventually they got all the excess fabric tucked out of the way, wrapped up in meters of rubber tubing, and all the seals checked and double-checked. The biggest alien cupped the little one's head with one claw-tipped hand, the way it had when Nesya had met them earlier that day, only more awkwardly through the oversized hood and mask of the hazard suit. Then she took Nesya by the wrist and put her hand on the little one's head too.

"Oh. Well—fair enough," said Nesya. It was the first time one of the aliens had touched her bare skin, and it felt very odd, which was reason enough for her voice to shake and her stomach to go a bit queasy. And it was fair enough—the little alien might have volunteered for the mission, and the problem might have been caused by the aliens in the first place, but it was Nesya's plan and Nesya's sewers and Nesya's community on the line. It was only fair for her to take some responsibility.

Only the alien didn't let go of Nesya's wrist when it was done, instead, it moved her hand to the heads of all the other aliens clustered around, each in turn. None of them were headed into a situation of mortal peril, but... when the alien finally let go, Nesya took her wrist and moved it to cup Rinat's head, and the alien whistled a low assent.

Nesya didn't know, really—couldn't know—what all that had meant to the aliens. She only knew what it meant to her. *Your family is my family, my family is yours...* When had that ever been anything but a leap in the dark?

They would work all that out later. Right now there were more urgent things to worry about. Nesya keyed open the access to the blackwater sewer—and found herself locked out.

"Intira Rabinovic," she told her reader. Intira answered quickly, looking even less happy with Nesya than she had the last time they'd talked. "What the hell, Intira?"

"Thought that might get you to reply to your messages," said Intira. "I heard—from Heleni Thumying, thank you so much for keeping me informed—that you got Rinat and the aliens out. You want to tell me what's going on?"

"Sorry," said Nesya automatically. And then, "I thought you might sleep better if you didn't have to think about it. And there was nothing you could do about it in any case—or I thought there wasn't. Listen, I need those accesses or all of Landfall is in deep shit. You never did have new water-flow sensors installed, or stop the storm sewer redirect to the blackwater system manually, did you?"

Intira's eyebrows went up, then drew together and down. "Damn. I was going to take care of it when—well, never mind—but it was just the one damaged sensor, there's plenty of redundancy in—"

"It wasn't random vandalism; the aliens are perfectly capable of being thorough. If one sensor was damaged and the rest were fine, we'd have been getting inconsistent readings, and we weren't. I've got one here who's about the size of a Hercules unit, and can go solve the problem—but I've got to be able to get the blackwater pipes open."

"Fine." Intira frowned and made some passes with her stylus, then said, "There you go. But can you give me one good reason why I shouldn't show up with Security on your doorstep as soon as the seals are open? You want to call the aliens people, we can damn well arrest them and deport them on the next ship out."

It wasn't that simple. The protocols—but the protocols had been blown all to hell already. The access, at least, was genuine; Nesya didn't bother to respond until the hatch was open and the little alien was on its way. "You mean besides the fact that one of them is risking his life now to make sure our colony is safe? Name of God, Intira, deport them where?"

"Hara Huna," said Rinat, coming up behind Nesya and peering over her shoulder.

"What?" said Nesya.

"Think about it. Where else were they going to get salvage from a Survey strike group?"

"The aliens have *what* now?" said Intira.

"Not helping," Nesya muttered, but Rinat went on.

"There are swamps on Hara Huna, and it's one jump from Hallelujah, which is where the containers they were traveling in came from. Someone was bombing their home, and the Survey ships must have looked like their only way out, if they could just sneak on board." Rinat's voice took on a choked intensity. "They're *refugees*."

Refugee was a word to conjure with on Enmotsa. Was it a stronger one than pest? Intira hesitated visibly, then shook her head. "That's not up to me. That's up to the Committee."

"Yes, that's what I've been saying all along," said Nesya. "I've promised the aliens my personal support, but of course they're going to need a Group to sponsor their immigration, and it makes the most sense for Infrastructure to do it. I've set them up in the wastewater treatment plant, where it'll be easy to monitor the effects of their environmental suite, and I figure they can claim salvage rights to it—or maybe not salvage rights exactly, but they're entitled to the space and resources because they're using them for the good of the colony. They've got some really interesting water treatment methods, and I haven't entirely figured out—"

Intira burst out laughing. "Name of God, Nesya! I haven't even decided not to fire you yet. But you're all there until the storm passes, anyway. Make sure you send me all the water quality data. Since, you know, you missed your chance to let the storm take its course and not bring Survey down on all our heads."

"I don't know that there ever was a chance of that," said Nesya. "With interspecies encounters, Survey's bound to take an interest. And even if the ones we have here were the only members of their species to make it offplanet—which I see no reason to believe—they did it using Survey ships and they've got the scavenged equipment to prove it. There must be an investigation underway already, and the evidence is going to lead them here. Ten years at most, and we'll have Survey showing up on our doorstep no matter what we do or don't do now. And look, no one wants them here, right?"

"Yes," said Intira. "That's what I've been saying all along."

"So," said Nesya. "I bet in the time between now and however long it takes Survey to start slapping down restrictions, Population is going to be giving out child permits with a pretty free hand. Line up a donor or two and this time next month you and Jamnit could both be pregnant."

"That seems—logistically unwise." On the small screen of Nesya's reader, though, Intira's eyes shone bright with something. Longing, or sudden hope. "You fight dirty, Nesya."

"Well." Nesya shrugged modestly. "That's my job."

Intira didn't dignify that with a response beyond snorting and cutting the connection. Nesya took a deep breath, then another. Nothing to do now but wait.

About half an hour after the first raindrops hit the storm seals, the little alien came triumphantly out of the blackwater pipe. Nesya threw its stinking hazard suit in the sterilizer while the other aliens clustered around, chattering loud enough for Nesya to make out a few sounds above the pounding of the storm. Rinat dug into her backpack and found a protein bar, and another one for Nesya. It was a good thing she'd brought them, because Nesya hadn't thought to take anything, and she wasn't exactly thrilled by the prospect of live tilapia, which was what the aliens were eating.

She licked the last crumbs off her fingers, wondering how long the storm was going to last and whether live tilapia were going to start looking good by the end of it. Then she took her reader back out and said, "Vit Thumying."

Vit's lips formed the word *so*, and Nesya turned the volume on her reader all the way up so she could hear what he had to say next. "I take it you were able to establish communications with the aliens?"

Nesya made a face. Vit was going to be saying *I told you so* until the end of time. "*Limited* communications. On certain subjects. I've put them forward as candidates for Infrastructure Group, and Intira's agreed to consider it."

"The same Intira who was planning on killing them all? How... and you'll need approval from the Committee; how do you figure on selling that?"

"The head of the alien household offered me a marriage contract," said Nesya. It was as reasonable a way of describing what had passed between her and the aliens as anything. "I accepted."

"You married an alien?" said Vit.

"Not for the first time," said Nesya. Vit gave a startled laugh, and Nesya went on, "Why don't you give Rinat a call? She'll want to tell you about the whole adventure. She..." Nesya really didn't want to feed Vit's smugness any further. But in justice to Rinat, she said, "She did really great."

"I will. Take care."

Nesya waved in acknowledgment, and her screen went blank. She didn't hear Rinat's reader chime, but she saw her take it out of her pocket and curl up with it in an out-of-the-way corner. The rest of the family was settling in each in their own way, tinkering or napping or splashing in the tank they'd chosen. Nesya checked her news feed. If something had gone wrong with the little one's mission, the emergency reports would already be rolling in, but they weren't.

It was impossible to know where what had been set in motion would all end. It might take ten years for Survey to show up, or Trade might report their heat signatures in Enmotsa's space next week. Their judgment could imprison anyone who'd been directly involved with the aliens, disenfranchise all Enmotsa's leaders, dismantle the colony and exile everyone in it. But for now—silently and invisible, underground and in the pipes—water still flowed.

About the Author

Naomi Libicki writes science fiction and fantasy; she lives with her husband, kid, cat, and books, and makes a mean apple strudel.

Read more at https://naomilibicki.com/.

Milton Keynes UK
Ingram Content Group UK Ltd.
UKHW030141051224
452010UK00001B/237

9 798227 638571